STAND FAST

DEA FAST SERIES

KAYLEA CROSS

STAND FAST

Copyright © 2017
by Kaylea Cross

* * * * *

Cover Art & Formatting by
<u>Sweet 'N Spicy Designs</u>

* * * * *

ISBN: 978-1548224073

Dedication

For my awesome bestie, Katie Reus. Thanks for always being there for me, for lending a listening ear when I need one, and then busting out the pom-poms to cheer me on. Love you bunches. xo

Author's Note

Dear readers,

Here we are at book #3 of the **FAST Series** already! This one is set over in Afghanistan like my **Bagram Special Ops Series** was, but FAST Bravo has a vastly different mission profile from any of my previous casts of characters.

I hope you enjoy Jaliya and Zaid's story.

Happy reading!

Kaylea Cross

FAST motto: "Contain, Disrupt, Dismantle"

Chapter One

DEA Special Agent Jaliya Rabani rushed down the hallway of one of the many buildings that made up Bagram Airfield in Afghanistan, her insides a flurry of excitement and anticipation.

She'd waited months for this chance, and was chuffed that it was finally happening.

A door opened at the end of the hall and Supervisory Special Agent Jared Taggart, commander of the DEA's Foreign Advisory and Support Team Bravo, emerged. "He's here?" he asked her, his blue-green eyes locked on her as he stepped out of the room. A tall, intimidating man who commanded respect with his presence alone.

"Yes." And about damn time, too. After all the previous trouble with getting her informant to commit, she'd been afraid he would no-show again. "He's waiting in one of the interrogation rooms now. Got in about ten minutes ago."

The overhead lights caught on his dark blond hair and the slightly darker stubble on his face as he nodded. "Okay. Let's do this."

She fell in step with him and together they hurried through the building and outside into the late morning sunshine. An icy blast of late December wind cut through her jacket. She wrapped her arms around herself and tucked the bottom of her hijab into her jacket to keep it from flapping around. Though she'd grown up wearing one, she'd stopped doing so in ninth grade, but over here she always wore it when dealing with locals.

The familiar sounds of the base surrounded her as she walked: aircraft engines and trucks passing by, troops out for their daily PT. Agent Taggart followed her into another building on the other side of the base. Armed guards were posted at the door and there were no windows on its exterior.

He and Jaliya showed their agency IDs. The guards let them in and immediately locked the doors behind them.

"Down here," she said to him, leading the way down the long center hallway past the various cells, the sounds of their footsteps echoing off the cinder block walls.

Even with the bright overhead lights glaring off the white-painted walls, this place had a creepy vibe. Behind each steel door they passed lining the hallway, terrorists were locked away to await their fate at the hands of the U.S. judicial system for crimes committed against American troops and interests.

A member of her team from the Foreign Cooperative Investigations unit was waiting for them outside the second-to-last room at the end of the hall. "I couldn't get an interpreter here in time," her colleague told her as she approached.

"It's fine. I'll do the translating." She was twenty-eight years old with a Master's degree in political science, and had recently gained enough trust from her boss for him to allow her more operational latitude within her investigations. These days he pretty much let her run her own show, and in turn she reported back to him to keep

2

him apprised of what was going on.

"I'll watch from out here," her colleague said. The large window in the wall beside them allowed them to look in while those inside the room couldn't see out.

"That's fine." She mentally squared her shoulders, more than ready for this. *Show time.*

Ignoring how fast her pulse raced in her throat, she opened the door and walked into the room, with Taggart right behind her.

At the rectangular table set in the center of the room sat a young man in his late teens. He wore traditional garb of loose white pants and a tunic topped with a vest. His short dark hair was covered by a *pakol*, and a thin, dark beard obscured the lower half of his face. His deep-set, dark eyes locked on her the moment she crossed the threshold, wary and distrustful.

"Barakat. It's good to meet you in person finally," she said in Dari, taking off her jacket and draping it over the back of the chair opposite him.

His eyes widened for a moment in astonishment, then chilled before he focused on Taggart. Dismissing her.

Annoyance bubbled up inside her. She'd seen that look way too often from local men during her time over here, and it never failed to piss her off. *Nuh-uh. You're here to talk to me, not him.*

"I gather you received the medicine and supplies I arranged for you at the hospital earlier?" she asked, ignoring his attitude as she nodded to the knapsack lying next to him on the floor. The guards and her coworker waiting out in the hall would have already searched it for weapons before putting him in here, so he was no threat to her. And definitely not with a man like Taggart standing behind her.

Barakat's gaze slid back to her, flicking over her with clear distaste.

Jaliya folded her arms across her chest and raised an

eyebrow, prepared to wait him out. "Well?"

"Yes," he finally muttered and looked away again.

Fine with her. She didn't care whether he looked at her or not while they had this conversation. "Good. Well, let's not drag this out and waste any more of my time than necessary. What can you tell me about The Jackal?"

He stiffened at the name, and this time when he looked at her, there was pure contempt on his face. "You have no right to ask me this." His tone was even more contemptuous than his expression.

"Oh, but I do. You already owe me for the supplies you've been given. And if you want the money you've been offered, you'll tell me what I want to know." She and her taskforce had been trying to identify the man known as The Jackal for almost five months now, and all their efforts thus far had proven futile.

No one claimed to know his identity, but he routinely smuggled large shipments of opium and weapons through the Hindu Kush either to southern Afghanistan or over the border into Pakistan. And then on to America with the heavy involvement of the *Veneno* cartel operating out of Mexico.

Barakat's upper lip curled into something close to a sneer and he hunched down in his chair, his body language telegraphing his disrespect and defiance.

"There a problem?" Taggart asked from behind her in English. "My Dari isn't awesome, but I'm getting the sense he's being uncooperative."

"He's just upset because he didn't realize he'd be dealing with a woman," she said without looking over her shoulder. Well, too damn bad for Barakat. She'd been working various informants over here for the better part of three years now, and refused to let misogynistic wankers like this one get to her.

"Barakat," she said, her voice sharp. The kid's jaw clenched beneath his scraggly beard and he reluctantly made eye contact again. "We brought you here for a reason. You need to tell us what you know about The Jackal and any upcoming shipments you've heard about, or there's no deal." To press her point, she pulled the chair back from the table, sat down and leaned forward, deliberately crowding his space. Refusing to give him any wiggle room.

He pushed his chair back as though the very idea of having to sit so close to her was offensive. "I do not negotiate with women."

His hateful expression and tone set her teeth on edge. Too often in this part of the world men treated women like livestock or stray dogs, placing no value on them whatsoever, let alone granting them respect as fellow human beings.

Jaliya didn't stand for it. She didn't care what men around here thought about her—she was working to help stem the endless flow of opium out of this country, and she didn't give a shit whether assholes like Barakat liked it or not.

"Well, you're going to have to today, and for as long as you want money from the DEA. You've seen what The Jackal does. How he prospers off the poison he smuggles out of your country, profiting off the broken backs and broken lives of the people he uses to make himself rich. How he kills or tortures anyone who opposes him." She paused. "Including your grandfather, the man who raised you."

Those dark eyes darted back to hers, now burning with resentment instead of just loathing. He didn't answer.

She pushed. "I can help make him pay for everything he's done. But to do that, I need to find him first. I was told you know something that might be useful to us. Was my source wrong?"

No response, just that defiant stare.

All too aware of Taggart and her colleague impatiently

watching all of this happen, she tamped down her irritation as the back of her neck began to heat up. She'd worked damn hard to build a reputation within the agency for getting things done, and being one of the best intelligence personnel they had. She was proud of that, and wouldn't let anything diminish it.

Including the ignorant little shit before her now.

She held Barakat's gaze, refusing to back down. "Don't waste my time. You've got ten seconds to answer me, or the deal's off."

"Well?" Taggart prompted, still standing behind her.

She was glad he couldn't see her face or tell how fast her pulse was pounding. "He's not cooperating," she gritted out, frustrated and embarrassed.

He sighed. "Let's get a male translator in here then—"

"There aren't any available," she said, continuing the staring contest with her so far useless informant. She'd pulled so many strings to get him here, and he was giving her *nothing*. Dammit. "My colleague just said so."

Taggart exhaled impatiently, his boots shifting on the floor.

Jaliya resented being made to look like a fool. It played on her secret fear that she didn't have what it took to pull off this kind of job, that she might fail and lose her position within the taskforce because of her gender. Her father's words were always there in the back of her mind.

Why would you waste your time in that job? You won't do any good over there. You're a woman. They won't respect or cooperate with you. Stay in the States and do something with your life that will actually make a difference.

No. She'd invested too much time and effort to get where she was. She wouldn't allow this bullshit misogynistic behavior to jeopardize any of it.

Jaliya held Barakat's gaze for another few seconds,

then shoved her chair back and stood up. "Take your medical supplies and go, and don't bother contacting us again," she told him in a cold voice. "Have a nice trip back to your village." She grabbed her coat from the chair and turned to leave.

Taggart stopped her with an upraised hand. "Wait. I'll bring in one of my guys to help."

She stared at him. "What?"

He already had his phone to his ear. "He speaks fluent Dari and he's got the necessary security clearance."

There was no doubt as to who he meant.

An immediate protest formed on her tongue but she bit it back as conflicting arrows of dismay and anticipation shot through her. It wouldn't do any good to argue. And she did need help.

It just chafed that *he* would be the one called in to assist.

****

Deeply engrossed in the Web Griffin book he was currently reading, SA Zaid Khan had just flipped to the next page when someone nudged his shoulder. Pushing up on his bunk, he pulled off his headphones and blinked down at his teammate, Reid Prentiss, who stood beside their stacked bunk beds, his dark brown hair damp from a recent shower.

"What?" Everyone knew better than to interrupt him when he was sucked into a book during his downtime. Or at least, they should know better.

"Your phone was ringing," Prentiss answered in his Mississippi drawl, handing it up to him. "You left it on your duffel."

"Oh. Thanks." He and the others were supposed to have until sixteen-hundred-hours off. But seeing the team commander's name on the display, he called back immediately, on alert. Taggart wouldn't call him just to say hi. "Khan here," Zaid said when his commander answered.

"You busy right now?"

"Nope. What's up?" It was out of the ordinary for Taggart to single him out like this. Normally he only addressed them as a team.

"Need a male translator. This informant's not talking and we're all out of patience. How soon can you get over here?" He told Zaid what building he was in.

"I'll be there in a few minutes." He jumped off his top bunk, his combat boots thudding lightly on the concrete floor, and grabbed his duffel.

"What's goin' on?" Prentiss asked, tugging a clean shirt over his head. On the other side of the tiny room, the other bunk bed was empty, their two roommates probably off to the gym. Or in Maka's case, maybe getting more chow. That guy had an appetite unlike anything Zaid had ever seen before.

Their living quarters were Spartan, the thin walls made up of plywood boards. Not exactly the Hilton, but better than a lot of places he'd bedded down during a deployment, and FAST Bravo usually only stayed at Bagram for a week or so at a time anyhow.

"Taggart needs me to translate." Must be the informant the taskforce had been waiting on to meet about The Jackal. The drug smuggler was slipperier than a greased eel, and the DEA's number one high value target for this deployment.

Zaid pulled on a sweatshirt hoodie over top of his T-shirt and then put his jacket over top for good measure as he hustled out of the squad barracks they shared with some SOF guys who rotated through here. Putting on his shades to protect his eyes from the winter sun's glare, he stepped out into the frigid cold and headed across to the building Hamilton was waiting in.

Dry, crisp air filled his lungs, carrying a tinge of jet fuel and diesel. To the east, the jagged, white-capped peaks of the Hindu Kush range speared upward into the sky.

Zaid was looking forward to helping out with an interrogation, especially if the informant could help give them valuable intel. At the detention facility, he showed the guards his ID and entered into a long, narrow hallway lined with cells.

He spotted Taggart waiting for him at the other end, but his pulse quickened when Agent Rabani stepped out of the interrogation room to stand beside Zaid's team leader. Even with the hijab covering her long, wavy black hair, it highlighted the beauty of her face with her large, dark eyes, full lips and high cheekbones. The fitted black T-shirt she wore clung to the pert outline of her breasts, and the beige cargo pants hugged the curve of her hips, making it hard to tear his gaze away from her.

"Thanks for coming," Taggart said to him once Zaid got close.

"No worries." He turned his attention to Agent Rabani, who was watching him with her arms folded across her chest.

She was somewhere in her late twenties or so. They'd first met at a briefing back at headquarters in Virginia several months ago and their paths had crossed several times since he'd been over here for this deployment, but he'd never seen her outside of work-related meetings. He'd like to change that.

"So, he's not talking?" Zaid asked.

A slight flush burned along her cheekbones as she set her jaw. "No. Not to me, anyway," she said, her clipped voice edged with the trace of a British accent that was a little more pronounced in her annoyance.

Ah. The dick in the interrogation room wouldn't talk to her because she was a woman. Not too surprising, considering where they were. Going by her expression, however, Rabani didn't seem too pleased that Zaid had been brought in for this, even though he was only here to help, not to interfere or steal her thunder. He hoped she realized they were on the same side.

Keeping his expression neutral, he gestured to the door. "Want me to give it a try?"

"I'll need to bring you up to speed first." She gave him a quick rundown of what he needed to know about the situation while Taggart stood listening with his hands on his hips. Their commander wanted The Jackal. Bad. They all did.

Whoever he was, the drug runner was a big player in the opium trade that was now streaming from here into Mexico, courtesy of the *Venenos,* to make fentanyl and other goodies to lace their coke and heroin with. Not only that, the money from selling that shit funded terrorist groups, gangs and other criminal entities that posed a security threat to innocent people all over the world.

That's why Zaid and his teammates were here—to act as the sharp point of the spear in the war to destroy them.

When Agent Rabani finished summing things up, he nodded once. "Got it." He glanced at the closed door, then back to her. "Ready?"

"Yes, but I'll feed you questions in English if I need more. And Agent Taggart and I will be in the room the entire time, and hard cheese if our reluctant informant doesn't like it."

Zaid fought back a smile, loving the hard edge to her voice. Over here, she would have to fight for basic respect from the locals a lot of the time. He admired that she was up for the challenge, but it didn't surprise him. She was affectionately known around here as the British Bulldog while involved with an investigation, relentless in her pursuit of anything that would help them find a high value target. "Understood."

"His name is Barakat. Anything that might be useful would be a big help."

"Roger that."

She studied him for a moment, her dark gaze darting over him in a way that was subtle enough to call curious, yet it heated his blood anyway. She turned to the door. "Let's go."

Zaid followed her into the room with Taggart. Barakat was seated on the opposite side of a table set in the center of the cinder block room, his arms folded in a defiant posture, his expression bored until his gaze landed on Agent Rabani. Then his face hardened.

Zaid felt for her. She and the others on the taskforce had been working overtime to find The Jackal, and woman-hating assholes like Barakat gave her no time or respect whatsoever, making her job even harder.

"Barakat," he said, immediately taking the chair opposite him and pulling up to the table. He leaned back in it, his hands resting on his thighs in a deceptively casual pose. Open body language made for a higher chance of building a fragile thread of trust.

The kid focused on him, but flicked another cold look over at Agent Rabani in the corner.

"I understand you can help us find The Jackal," Zaid said in Dari, wanting to take the kid's attention off her so they could get things moving.

"Why is she still here?" Barakat demanded as he stared at Agent Rabani.

"Because she's in charge of this investigation. So if you have a problem with her being here, that's too bad. Because she's staying."

Barakat's expression turned sullen as he looked back at Zaid, like a child who'd just been scolded. But he didn't argue. Progress.

Zaid cocked his head a little. "So. We doing this, or not?"

The kid stared at Zaid's chest rather than looking at his face. "I don't know who he is."

"So then what *do* you know? Maybe you've heard where he is? Where he's going? Or maybe you know something about a shipment. You have to give me something."

He flicked a fulminating look at Rabani again. "Maybe I know something."

Part of Zaid itched to reach across the table and grab this rude little fuck by the throat. But since he wasn't authorized for that sort of interrogation, he'd have to play it cool and save the choking bit as something to fantasize about while he sat here.

"Look," Zaid said, bringing that black gaze back to him. "You know there's no money unless you give us something we can use. And you wouldn't have come all the way to Bagram, risking someone seeing you enter the base unless you had something to tell us. Something you didn't want to say over the phone."

The kid lowered his gaze. "I did hear something. Last night. But I'm not sure how reliable it is."

Finally they were getting somewhere. Zaid crossed his arms casually over his chest. "Let's hear it."

Barakat hesitated for a long moment before answering. "Supposedly he's getting ready to move a shipment. From Kabul to a village in the foothills to the east." He named it.

Zaid had never heard of it, even after all the time he'd spent deployed over here. Must be small and remote. "Go on."

"I heard it's going to be moved over the border into Pakistan within the next few days."

Well, it was something. And at least the kid didn't appear to be preoccupied by Rabani anymore. "What kind of shipment?"

"Opium."

Of course.

"And weapons. Lots of weapons. I don't know what else."

Money. A shitload of money, likely U.S. greenbacks. "And The Jackal ordered it?"

"Yes. I don't know if he'll be there in person though."

One could only hope. Zaid and his team would love to help capture that son of a bitch before this tour was over. "Who did you hear this from?"

"An elder in my village. I overheard him talking to some of the men at a council meeting last night."

Jaliya crossed to the table and spread a map down in front of Barakat. "Show us where the village he's moving the shipment to is."

Without looking at her, Barakat placed a fingertip on the map, right in the foothills of the central Hindu Kush.

Zaid watched her, taking in the sweep of her thick lashes, the strong lines of her profile as she studied the map for a moment, then stepped back. Even without knowing her well, Zaid could tell that having to hand over the reins to him for this was hard for her. "You need anything else?" he asked her quietly in English.

Those bittersweet chocolate eyes cut to him, sharp and direct. He could almost hear the gears turning in her head, analyzing all the data Barakat had just given them.

"Not right now." She transferred her gaze back to their informant, and spoke to him in Dari. She spoke it perfectly, without so much as a trace of an accent. She must have been raised speaking it since she was a child. "You'll be paid what we agreed on. If what you told us is true, you'll get a bonus. I'll be in touch."

Not bothering to wait for a response, she nodded at Zaid and headed for the door. He pushed out of his chair and followed out behind Taggart, leaving one of Rabani's team members to finish up with Barakat. Probably handing out the dough and maybe arranging a ride for him back to his village.

Outside the room with the door closed, Zaid waited a discreet distance away while Rabani conferred with Hamilton and two others from the taskforce. Taggart offered him a nod, his piercing aqua eyes warming a fraction as he half-smiled. "Thanks for helping out."

"No problem."

His commander clapped him on the shoulder once. "See you at the briefing this afternoon."

"You bet." Zaid stood where he was as Taggart strode down the hallway, hands in his pockets while Agent Rabani finished up with her team members. She glanced over at him, her eyes locking with his.

She stared at him for a heartbeat, then put on a stiff smile. "Thank you for your help."

"My pleasure." Except the real pleasure would be getting to know her better, because she intrigued him. There were so many things he wanted to know about her. Where she was from, why she'd joined the DEA and chosen to be stationed here. Afghanistan wasn't for everyone. He'd wanted to talk with her socially over the past few weeks, but hadn't yet had the opportunity. He'd have to think up an excuse.

"Well. I'll see you later."

He nodded and watched her walk away in her combat boots, her rounded hips swaying with each confident stride she took. Strong, yet feminine. Sexy, but professional. The woman was a mass of contradictions, a puzzle he wanted to figure out. But she was also a fellow special agent, and pursuing her was a big professional no-no.

Damn shame he'd sworn off the whole dating thing, because she was the first woman who'd sparked his interest in a damn long time.

Chapter Two

Outside the office window, sheets of gray clouds obscuring the distant mountain peaks promised more snow as The Jackal finished up a call on his personal, encrypted cell phone.

In mid-conversation, he waved a signed document at his assistant, who was flipping through a stack of folders in the doorway. The younger man took it and hurried from the room as The Jackal grunted a terse reply to the person on the other end of the phone and ended the call.

He set the phone down on the desk to get more work done. Just as he picked up the pen, his phone rang again, showing the number of one of his most trusted sources.

As trusted as a source could be, that is.

"Speak," he said.

"Is your end secure?"

"Of course." He personally swept for electronic devices each morning whenever he came here, and he changed personal phones every few days to keep anyone from tracking him.

Only a handful of people knew his true identity. The

ones who did would keep his secret until their dying breath. That ultimate sort of loyalty was easy enough to buy in this country, where so much of the population lived in abject poverty. Having money made so many things easier.

"What have you got?" he asked his source.

"I've just been told that the DEA has offered a bribe to someone from one of our villages."

He stilled. "Have they," he murmured. He was well versed in the dealings of the DEA. Very little went on pertaining to the opium trade in this country that he didn't know about before it happened. He made it his business to know.

"Yes." His man named a village they had used to smuggle shipments in and out of a few weeks ago.

"Who is it?"

"I haven't found out yet."

He scratched his beard. "They want him as an informant?"

"Yes. He went to Bagram to meet with the Americans about it."

Ah. Interesting. He must be extremely motivated to risk such a thing. Either poverty or revenge. "And did he agree to work for them?" The Americans must consider him important if they'd asked him to meet at Bagram.

"No one knows."

The news didn't alarm him. This sort of thing wasn't an uncommon occurrence, although it was rare that his network wasn't able to find out the informant's identity. "Keep a close eye on it. Find out who he is, and inform me right away." Either The Jackal had a possible ally or an enemy, and both could prove useful under the right circumstances.

"Yes, sir. But…"

"But what? Find out who the informant is, and then we will know how to best deal with him." He hung up before the man could answer. He didn't kill people if he could use them first.

His gaze caught on the framed pictures on his desk. He paused, staring at one in particular of his family. *This* was the reason he was willing to risk so much. Hope. Life. Things that were nearly impossible to have in this war torn country.

All his life, and for generations before him, the only things his family had known were war and suffering. The only way to secure a stable future for the ones he loved was with money. Lots of it—more than he could ever hope to make in ten lifetimes at his public job. Influence was gained through power, and he'd learned that power came through fear.

He'd become an expert at administering fear over the past few months.

Staring at the beloved faces in the frame on his desk, a fresh surge of resolve swept through him. No matter who he had to kill or betray, no matter how high the cost, he would do whatever it took to make things right.

****

She still had a ton of work to do, but since Jaliya was so hungry she couldn't take it anymore, she'd decided to run over to the mess hall for a bite to eat. Holding her full dinner tray in both hands, she glanced around the crowded space, searching for a familiar face.

The large building was packed full of tables lined with benches and chairs, a constant buzz of conversation and the clinking of silverware filling the air. Since it was only a few days before Christmas, someone on base had made the effort to make things look a little festive in here with some garland wrapped around the posts and Santa pictures hung here and there. A few people were even sporting fuzzy Santa hats with their uniforms.

The mood was light considering that everyone was far away from their families at this time of year, and surprising since the security on base had been heightened over the past week. On high alert in case any attackers wanted to make a statement during one of the most important dates in the Christian calendar.

Over in the far left corner, one of her team members spotted her and waved her over. Smiling, she started toward the group of DEA agents seated at the table, but her steps faltered when she realized who else was there with them.

The members of FAST Bravo.

They weren't at Bagram for long stretches of time, usually staying at one FOB or another to be closer to their mission targets out in the countryside. Unless it was a briefing or important meeting of some sort, she didn't see them. And when they *were* here, the FAST guys tended to keep to themselves in the SOF area of the base, so her path rarely crossed with theirs.

Almost against her will, her gaze was drawn to the broad-shouldered, bronze-skinned man sitting in the middle of his teammates with his back to her. She was still a bit embarrassed that he'd had to be brought in to translate this morning, and annoyed that it had been necessary.

As if on cue, Agent Zaid Khan turned his head to look behind him and his hazel gaze zeroed in on her like a heat-seeking missile. The instant it did, a funny fluttery sensation tickled low in her belly and her heart did a weird little skip.

He shot her a friendly smile and turned back to his teammates, and somehow that unfroze her. Refusing to acknowledge the way her endocrine system seemed to swoon at the sight of him, she strode for the table and took the only empty spot, next to one of the FAST guys and across from Khan.

She set her tray down and picked up her fork without looking at him. She'd be lying if she said she wasn't attracted to and curious about him. From what she'd seen and heard over the past several weeks, he was easy-going, with a good sense of humor.

Though he wasn't the leader or senior member of the team, he seemed to be the hub of it. She'd seen him hanging out with various members, not just one or two in particular, and from her observations she got the sense that Khan was sort of like the team big brother, who everyone went to for advice.

He was attractive, likeable, smart, and knowing he could handle himself in the face of danger was definitely sexy. The trouble was, she was suspicious that he might be the same guy she'd met via an online dating site a few months ago. How many Zaids around his age could there be, living in D.C. and working for the U.S. government? The odds of that being a coincidence were slim to none.

They'd clicked immediately. She'd been really into him, and after chatting online every day for a few weeks she'd felt close enough to him, safe enough that she had even agreed to set up a date when she was scheduled to come into D.C. next.

But then something he'd said had changed her mind. Little comments here and there, pretty benign on the surface of things, but they sounded too much like something one of the "good Muslim men" her father used to shove at her would say—the ones who disapproved of her views and wanted her to conform to a more subservient and obedient role in the relationship.

They'd been trying to agree on where to meet for the date. He'd named a place, and when she'd asked why he thought he got to call the shots for their first meeting, he typed the kiss of death: *I'm a take charge kind of guy. And I believe the man should wear the pants in a relationship.*

Yeah, *no* thanks.

She'd received the response while waiting to pick up her luggage at Dulles. The comment had smacked of that same kind of male domineering attitude that made her all ragey. Also, if he talked like that early on when he was supposed to be winning her over, what would he be like later on? She'd backed out of the date the night before it was supposed to happen and cut contact with him, because life was too short to waste time on someone who looked like they might be an asshole.

Jaliya didn't do subservient, and she sure as hell didn't do obedient. Not unless it pertained to following orders from one of her superiors. And even then, not every time. Unlike her two sisters who were happy to be with men their father had picked for them, Jaliya wanted to go her own way, make her own choices without her father interfering. Especially when it came to her career and love life.

"So, big night tonight, huh?" one of her male colleagues said next to her, shoveling a mouthful of mashed potatoes into his mouth.

"Yes, sure is." She forked up a bite of salad—she liked to get that part out of the way so she could enjoy the real food on her tray, which included a slice of chocolate cheesecake she richly deserved—her mind already on the coming op that would happen in a few hours. She'd worked all of her contacts for this one after the meeting with Barakat this morning. If the intel was good, tonight they might finally hit The Jackal and his network where it hurt.

"Love to know what you're thinking about right now."

At the sound of that deep voice shaded by a New Jersey accent, she looked up to find Agent Khan looking at her over the rim of a coffee mug, his hazel gaze so intent it brought back that fluttering sensation in the pit of her stomach. He'd buzzed his almost black hair short, and he had the start of a thick, dark beard now. He was rugged.

Sexy. And he radiated an alert kind of confidence she couldn't help but be drawn to.

Was he the same guy she'd met online? He wouldn't know it was her, because they'd never posted photos of each other and she'd used only her middle name for her profile.

She swallowed her mouthful of chicken before answering. "Mentally getting everything organized for tonight."

"Ah. So, overkill then."

"Sorry?"

"Well, you've always seemed to have things well in hand before, so I doubt you need to review anything."

A compliment? She hadn't expected that, or for him to be this friendly after she'd kept their interactions limited to strictly professional dealings. "It's my job."

"And you do it well."

Jaliya wasn't sure how to respond. It wouldn't do to get too friendly with any of them, for professional reasons. To do her job well, she needed to maintain a certain distance and not let personal feelings muddy the waters when she helped plan an op they participated in, but she could make small talk for a little while, and she appreciated his support. "Thank you," she murmured, and turned her attention back to her dinner.

"We were just talking about the holidays," he added, gesturing to his eight teammates seated around the table, all engaged in animated discussion except for the big man next to him. Agent Maka seemed far more interested in what she and Khan were talking about. "Kai here was telling me how he used to celebrate Christmas back home in Hawaii when he was a kid."

"That's right," Agent Maka said, shifting to lean toward her more, his thick forearms braced on the table, black tribal tattoos snaking up beneath the left sleeve of the T-shirt stretched over his massive chest and shoulders.

He was a giant of a man, at least six-foot-five, and ripped. She wasn't sure what size shirt he wore, but it had to be at least XXL. She couldn't imagine what it took to feed a man his size, but his tray was piled high with a mountain of food she would have thought impossible for one man to eat all by himself.

"You ever been to Hawaii?" he asked her, scooping up a giant forkful of food.

It was way easier to make conversation with him than Khan. "Sadly, no. I've always wanted to, though. Were you born there?"

"Born and raised."

"Which island?"

"Maui." He stuffed a huge mouthful of food into his mouth, chewed fast and swallowed, eyeing her the whole time. "I guess you don't…" He frowned slightly. "Do you celebrate Christmas?"

She smiled and picked up her bottle of water. "No, but I still love the season and its message." Peace on Earth and goodwill to mankind? Yes please. The world could use a whole hell of a lot more of it.

He nodded. "Ah. Well anyway, the guys were interested to know how we celebrated back home. I told them how my extended family would have a big dinner together after church. The day before, the men would all get together to roast a Kalua pig. Do you know what that is?"

"No." The passionate way he talked about it was infectious, and charming.

"It's a whole pig that we roast in a pit in the ground called an *imu*. It's all about having the right temperature and enough moisture. We build a fire and wait for it to burn down to coals, then add rocks and let them heat up before we put in the prepared pig on top of a bed of banana leaves. You cover the pig in soaked burlap, add water, then bury it and cook it for about twelve to fourteen hours."

"That sounds like an awful lot of work."

"Yeah, but it's the traditional way, and nothing else tastes like it." He rolled his eyes heavenward before looking at her again. "Best thing you'll ever put in your mouth. You should—" He stopped dead and shut his mouth, the tops of his cheeks turning a dusky red above the line of his dark beard as he cleared his throat and looked down at his plate. "Course, you and Zaid don't eat pork though," he muttered in a low voice.

She couldn't help a smile. She wasn't all that strict about the way she practiced her religion—at least not as strict as her parents would have liked—but some things were just taboo. "No. But that was really interesting. Do you hang stockings and all that too?"

"Yeah, but from the palm tree out front of my grandma's house, because we don't have a fireplace."

Not much need for one in Hawaii. "That's so neat."

Maka nodded as he gobbled down another bite of his dinner, still looking slightly embarrassed.

Agent Khan seemed to be fighting a laugh as he drained the last of his coffee. She shot him a warning look and he lowered his mug to reach out and grasp Maka's massive shoulder with his left hand. "Don't worry about it, man. She doesn't seem offended."

"Not at all," she assured him with another smile. "I really do love this time of year. When I was growing up in Britain I used to love seeing all the Christmas trees and decorations everywhere, and we had good friends who used to have us over for Christmas dinner. They roasted their turkey in the oven instead of a pit in the ground, but it was still amazing."

Agent Khan's green-and-gold-flecked eyes warmed and the corners of his mouth tilted upward in the midst of his beard in a sexy smile, and damned if her heart didn't speed up. "Where did you grow up over there?"

"Manchester, then London."

"And when did you come to the States?"

"After high school. My dad got hired at a private hospital in Michigan."

"He a doctor?"

"Neurosurgeon."

"Ah. So brains run in the family, then."

Her lips quirked. He was charming, she'd give him that. "Yeah, I guess they do." She loved and admired her father, but they sure didn't see eye-to-eye on a lot of things—like her career.

"Bet that Christmas turkey would have been juicier and tastier if they'd used an *imu*," Maka said with a grin.

"Sadly, I guess I'll never know."

"Kai's a master of resourcing stuff. I bet he could scrounge up a turkey and dig us an *imu* right here on base so you could test it out," Khan said to her.

"Oh, no, that's not nece—"

"Yeah, I bet I could," Maka said, a far-off look in his eyes as though he was already planning it out. Then his gaze flicked to her. "Let me see what I can do. I'll get back to you on it."

Okay, he sounded serious about this. "I...all right."

Khan winked at her and continued eating his dinner.

To avoid looking at him or encouraging further conversation, she went back to eating her meal while the team talked around her. It was impossible not to like Khan, even if he was the same guy she'd met online. Another reason not to let him get too close.

Under different circumstances, she might have been tempted to indulge in a little flirtation and see where it went. But not here, and not with him.

A relief, really. In a few hours his team would go into harm's way to carry out an operation based on her team's intelligence reports and recommendations.

It would be dangerous out there far away from base.

24

They could be hurt. Even killed.

The sobering reality made the food congeal into a hard lump in her stomach.

It wasn't the first time the weight of responsibility had sat heavy on her shoulders. But even with the little time she'd spent with the team tonight, instead of a list of names and faces they were now all individuals with different personalities, and all of them had people who loved them waiting back home.

Jaliya mentally shook her head at herself. She should never have opened that door in the first place. Fraternizing with men who would go into dangerous situations on her recommendation was never a good idea.

Forcing down the bite of suddenly dry chicken stuck in her throat, she washed it down with a few sips of water, then gathered her tray and stood. "I've got some more things to prepare," she said to them both as they looked up at her questioningly. "See you at the debriefing." She left the table and didn't look back, hoping her anxiety about the coming op didn't show.

Chapter Three

———◇◇◇◇◇———

*Z*aid cupped his gloved hands together and blew on them as he crouched in the frigid darkness at the base of a rise with his teammates. Overhead, the thick cloud cover obscured the moon and stars.

The temperature here in the foothills of the Hindu Kush Mountains had dropped well below freezing over the past hour and a light snow had begun to fall. Forecasters expected an accumulation of between six and nine inches by morning, meaning FAST Bravo had to make this quick if they wanted to avoid being stuck here in the bitter cold until the storm passed sometime tomorrow.

Back at the comparative warmth of Bagram hours ago, they'd attended a briefing given by Agent Rabani and her team, based on the interview he'd helped with that morning. The tiny village Barakat had mentioned lay nestled in a small valley three hundred yards up the side of the mountain. Zaid hoped like hell the kid hadn't been lying, because this would be a damn waste of manpower and resources.

An icy blast of wind roared down the mountainside, slicing against his face like the blade of a knife. They were way out in no man's land. The terrain here was too rugged for their helo to set down, so they'd had to fast rope in and hump it to the target on foot.

Above him, Freeman was already halfway up the face of the hillside, in the lead as usual as he set the anchors in the rock. Hamilton was next, and Prentiss was a dozen yards behind him.

Zaid slung his weapon across his back to keep it out of the way as he clipped his harness onto the guide rope and reached for the bit of rock sticking out of the snow-covered earth, using it as a handhold as he pulled himself up. The rest of his teammates all waited below for their turn, maintaining a secure perimeter along with the twelve members of the Afghan National Interdiction Unit they were working with for this op.

The twenty-yard climb was no joke with the swirling snow and wind. By the time he reached the top, he was breathing hard and sweating, and his fingers were numb. The instant he cleared the edge of the cliff and unhooked from the rope, the wind howled around him, blowing dust and the light covering of snow around enough to screw with his visibility.

After adjusting his goggles, he hurried over to where Hamilton was crouched near a large boulder and added his own eyes and ears to form a secure perimeter while the others began the ascent. Once everyone was with them, Hamilton gave Prentiss the order to deploy the drone.

Prentiss launched it and flew it up the steep hillside, turning it to the left to give them a bird's eye view of the target village. He and Hamilton watched the screen while Prentiss maneuvered their tiny spy from his remote control with the dexterity of a lifelong gamer.

"Two sentries posted, one appears asleep," Hamilton's

low voice said through Zaid's headset. The NIU had its own translator with them so Zaid didn't have to do the honors.

Not surprising one sentry was asleep, given the time of night and weather conditions. Only freaking lunatics would dare come to this remote place right now.

"Suspected cache location appears unguarded."

Bonus. Now if they could just get up there and take the villagers by surprise, they might not only find what they were looking for, but make it out unscathed as well. And if they were really lucky, they might even get a lock on The Jackal's location.

"It's a go," Hamilton said. "Let's move."

Good, because he hated waiting around out here in the open, exposed to both the elements and potential enemy eyes, and a brisk hike would at least keep their blood moving. It was freaking freezing even with all the layers and specialized material they wore.

Together the combined units made the two-mile hike up the steep switchbacks carved into the hillside, and paused just out of sight of the alert sentry's position. Hamilton waved Zaid over. He jogged to him, leaned in close so he could hear his team leader over the swirling wind.

"NIU will go in first. I want you with them, so you can translate what's going on for the rest of us."

"Roger." He motioned for the head of the NIU to join them and relayed the information, then waited for the Afghan force to move in. When their commander gave the order, Zaid stayed near the front of the column, weapon up and ready, scanning for threats.

"This is the police," one of the NIU members said in Pashto into a bullhorn as they reached the edge of the village.

The wide-eyed sentry stared at them in astonishment, and slowly raised his hands. His sleeping counterpart had dashed to his feet and grabbed for his rifle amidst the layers of robes he had wrapped around him, but froze when he saw how badly he was outnumbered.

"If you are armed, put down your weapons," the NIU member continued. "We are searching the village."

The second sentry dropped his AK like it was red-hot and stuck his hands in the air. While two members of the NIU engaged him to check for more weapons, Zaid stayed with the main force as they moved into the village, which was made up of a dozen or so dun-colored mud brick buildings.

Shouts of alarm and cries erupted from inside the dwellings. Zaid kept his weapon up, his finger on the trigger guard. They were here to seize drugs, weapons, cash, and hopefully net one very annoyed Jackal. The rules of engagement stated that they could only fire in self-defense or to protect the NIU members.

Through the confusion heightened by the darkness and swirling snow, men began to emerge from the buildings. Zaid watched their hands, assessing each man individually before moving to the next.

"Who are you? What are you doing here?" yelled one old man, his white beard and tunic blowing in the wind.

"We are conducting a search," the NIU spokesman answered.

"A search for what?" he demanded amidst a rumble of dissent from the other men now gathered in their doorways. "We are a peaceful village. No Taliban here."

The NIU member ignored him. "Stand back while we search each house."

Zaid passed on the info to Hamilton and the others via his headset. They all knew a little Pashto and Dari, but none were fluent except Zaid, who spoke both like a native thanks to his parents.

The teams moved quickly to check and secure each building before beginning the search while Hamilton and the NIU leader tried to get intel about The Jackal. Prentiss and Colebrook went with Zaid into one dwelling and together they swept the place in a few minutes. Several women were in the back room, comforting frightened children, and frantically covered their heads and faces with their shawls.

"Be at ease, sisters," Zaid told them. "We aren't going to hurt you."

But they were here to search every nook and cranny and get whatever intel they could.

He approached one woman, who was sitting on the floor with a crying infant in her lap, and hunkered down in front of her. "The Jackal. Have you heard that name before?"

She shrank away from him, hugging her child tighter to her.

"He's a dangerous man. There is a large reward for information leading to his capture. Have you heard anything about him?"

She shook her head, her body language screaming her fear and uncertainty.

Zaid moved to the next. "What about you? Have you heard something about The Jackal? Has he been here?"

"No," the woman said, completely hidden from view by her shawl. "Now leave us in peace."

The third woman also denied knowing anything about The Jackal. Zaid didn't buy it. Even out here people would know who he was. They might be telling the truth about him not being here, but Zaid wasn't leaving anything to chance.

All the intel said The Jackal had either been here within the past few days, or was about to move a shipment through here. And Zaid had noticed that all of the women had remained seated atop a threadbare rug on the floor with their children, rather than retreat to the corners of the room when he and his teammates had burst in.

With a few calm orders, he got the women and children up and moved to the front room of the tiny house, leaving the woven rug vacant. Lifting a corner of it from the dirt floor, Zaid found a sheet of plywood beneath it.

Bingo. "Got something," he said to the others, who came over immediately.

Holding a flashlight in one hand, he checked for anything that hinted at a booby trap before pulling the plywood aside, revealing a shallow, rectangular pit in the ground. A thin layer of plant material covered the bottom of it.

He reached in to grab some and brought it to his nose to smell it, then looked up at his teammates. "Hash." Only a tiny amount, though, not nearly enough to reach the arrest threshold. And definitely no Jackal hiding in the hole with it. "You guys find anything?"

"No."

Zaid relayed his findings to Hamilton, who reported the same from the rest of the team. "Anything?" Zaid asked him.

"A few old rifles, probably for hunting. Nothing to write home about. Target's not here, and neither is the dope. NIU's turned up nothing either."

Damn. The taskforce had seemed so sure that they were closing in on The Jackal, that this op might nail him. Agent Rabani was gonna be pissed that they'd hit yet another dead end even with Barakat's tip, and Zaid didn't blame her. He actually felt bad for her. She'd been working her ass off trying to get a break in this case, and because he liked and admired her, he wanted to see her succeed.

Setting aside his frustration, Zaid took pictures of the pit and checked a few crates stacked in the corner to make sure he hadn't missed something. Back outside, the bitter wind stung his face as he reconvened with his disgruntled teammates. Looked like this op was a total bust. "Maybe we're early."

"Maybe," Hamilton muttered, sounding totally unconvinced as he looked around at the NIU finishing their own search of the village. The wind continued to howl around them, buffeting against the rock wall the village was set into, slicing at their faces. "Go with the NIU and start questioning some of the elders. Find out what they know."

"You got it."

Within half an hour, it was evident that the elders knew nothing. Or at least pretended they didn't. If The Jackal had planned to use this village as a smuggling base, no one knew anything about it. Oh, they'd heard of him. Everyone had. But there hadn't been a shipment of drugs or any outsiders here recently, and none were expected.

Bullfuckingshit, but they'd definitely hit a dead end. All they had for their trouble was a small pile of weapons they'd confiscated, including a British Enfield left over from the 1800s. These people needed rifles to hunt to feed their families, so the NIU would only confiscate the handful of automatic weapons.

Zaid relayed the disappointing info to Hamilton, who gave a terse nod and reported it back to HQ. Agent Rabani would be there, waiting for word. She and her superiors weren't going to be happy that they were no closer to finding The Jackal's trail after all her work on this. She needed to have another talk with young Barakat and find out what the hell had gone wrong.

He shouldn't be thinking about her so much, and for sure not when he was on an op. Zaid sighed and looked around him at the pissed-off villagers all going back into their homes. Maybe they'd come too early. Maybe the smugglers hadn't been able to make it up the mountain in these conditions.

Or maybe Barakat had lied to their faces to throw them off The Jackal's trail, playing one side off the other and taking money from both.

Zaid wouldn't put it past the kid. Hell, after the things he'd seen and heard about over here over the past decade, nothing would surprise him in this country.

"All right, let's get out of here," Hamilton finally said, and pivoted to head out of the village.

Cold and discouraged, Zaid and the others started down the mountain with the rest of the unit. The reward for their efforts tonight was a long, cold hike to reach the exfil point, where they'd wait for helos that would fly them back to Bagram.

****

"The shipment made it across the border without incident."

The Jackal closed his eyes and let out a relieved breath at the news from his contact. "God is great."

"Yes, God is great. I wanted to alert you as soon as I knew."

He grunted. The intelligence planted through his network had worked, and led FAST Bravo to the wrong location. "Any further word on the boy yet?"

"Not yet. I'm working on it though."

"I should hope so." He knew which funnel the informant was working through. Now it was just a matter of time before he found out who it was. "Keep me informed."

"Of course."

Setting his phone down on the table, he rose and crossed to the window that overlooked the sleeping city. A gust of wind rattled the glass in its frame. Lights dotted the darkened landscape of Kabul spread out before him as snowflakes drifted past.

It looked so serene and peaceful right now, the darkness hiding the scars of war left carved on the land.

Deceptive. But he knew how fragile the illusion was. And how quickly a new offensive or suicide attack by the Taliban or any other insurgent group could shatter the stillness in an instant.

He was no stranger to violence and death. Anyone who posed a threat to him and his operations would earn a swift and violent end. He'd come too far and risked too much to turn back now.

A few more shipments, and with his cut of the profits he would have earned enough to get his son the things he needed. He would be able to get his entire family out of this country to start over somewhere new. Somewhere safe where they could live like kings without the fear of death hanging over them like a constant pall.

A small, rattling cough from down the hall broke him out of his thoughts.

On silent feet, he walked the length of the hallway. His wife emerged from their bedroom and opened the door opposite it. The soft glow of a lamp flooded the dingy hallway and the soft murmur of her voice floated out to him.

Reaching the other bedroom, he paused in the doorway to take in the scene before him. His wife sat on the edge of their son's bed, propping him up with a few pillows behind his back. The boy's face was pale and sweaty, a bluish tinge around his eyes and mouth. Just five years old. Far too young to know such anguish.

Those dark, sunken eyes swung up to him as another ghastly cough rattled that thin chest, and The Jackal's heart clenched with helpless grief. His boy had suffered so much in his young life. Too much.

Putting on a confident smile, The Jackal walked over and sat beside his son while his wife scurried off to get more medicine. "Is it bad tonight?" he murmured to Beena, placing a gentle hand on top of his son's head.

The boy nodded, his breaths raspy and strained, his

eyes pleading for an end to his torment.

Somehow he kept the smile in place. "Well, your mother has gone to bring you more medicine. That will make you feel better and help you rest."

Another nod, and Beena closed his eyes, as though they were too heavy to keep open.

The Jackal kept his hand on his son's sweaty hair, stroking his fingers through it gently. "It won't be long now. Another few weeks at most, and we can take you to a special doctor who will fix everything."

With a soft sigh, the boy slumped against the pillows.

The Jackal sat there in the pool of lamplight and stroked Beena's damp hair, unable to do anything more while he listened to each labored breath his son took. Anger and determination swelled until they all but choked him.

It wasn't right. Wasn't fair that his son should have to suffer like this simply because the procedure he needed wasn't available in Afghanistan. Not even from the American and British surgeons at the military bases.

His wife's soft footfalls reached him a moment before a gentle hand touched his shoulder. Her beautiful face was lined with worry and fatigue, her once raven black hair turned gray at the temples from the constant stress she lived with. She held the prescription bottle in her other hand.

"How much longer?" she whispered, the strain clear in her voice.

He didn't pretend not to know what she meant. How long until he had the money they needed to get Beena better. "Not long." He reached up to squeeze her hand in reassurance before pushing to his feet.

In the doorway, he paused to look back as she roused their son from his fitful slumber to give him the medicine.

Resolve hardened inside him. His son needed a life-saving operation, and he would make certain it happened, even if he had to work with the *Veneno* cartel to do it.

He didn't care who he had to work with or betray to make it happen.

Chapter Four

December twenty-fourth. Even without knowing the date, Zaid would have been able to guess it was Christmas Eve the moment he stepped into the squad room simply by observing his teammates.

The energy in the room was uncharacteristically low during this downtime before another team briefing. All the guys were quiet and subdued, partly because they were tired from the nonstop op-tempo over here, and partly because they were discouraged by the last two ops being total busts.

But more than that, Zaid suspected it had more to do with them being so far away from their families and significant others at this time of year. He missed his family too. And since FAST Bravo was only a few weeks into its four-month rotation, they had a long way to go yet before any reunions took place.

Jamie Rodriguez emerged from the small storage room at the back where they'd set up a laptop for private calls. They used their personal cell phones most of the time, but it was cheaper to use the laptop to check emails and do

Skype calls. "You need in here?" Rodriguez asked him.

"No, I'm good until everyone else has had a turn." The only people waiting for word from him were his parents back home in New Jersey, and since today wasn't that big a deal to them, Zaid could call them another time.

"You don't have a hot online date set up?" Rodriguez teased.

"Wouldn't tell you even if I did." And no, he'd given all that up months ago. He was sick of dating and things never working out. He wanted a meaningful connection he could build on with a woman he admired and enjoyed spending time with, not a string of hookups that went nowhere. He wanted it badly enough that he'd even jumped into online dating waters, something he'd sworn he'd never do, and had been matched up with a woman who seriously piqued his interest.

Still skeptical, he'd taken things slow with her, and after five weeks of chatting with her every day he was reasonably sure she was the real deal and had finally worked up the courage to ask her to meet in person when she came into town. She'd agreed and sounded enthusiastic about seeing him, and he'd eagerly anticipated it. Then, the night before they were supposed to meet, she'd canceled on him in a freaking text message and cut all contact.

Zaid had been bewildered, and yeah, hurt. More hurt than he probably should have been, considering they'd never actually met and hadn't even seen pictures of one another due to security concerns with their jobs.

Sure he'd withheld certain things from her, like his last name and what he did for a living, but he assumed she'd done the same and thought they'd had a real connection going. They had similar political and moral beliefs; they both valued family and wanted to make the world a better place. They both loved to read and liked a lot of the same books.

He had no idea what had gone wrong, but figured she'd either lost interest or found someone else. Or he'd misread her the entire time. Whatever the reason, he was in no hurry to put himself out there and get his heart stomped on again. Hence his dating hiatus. This deployment couldn't have come at a better time.

"Well you're no fun," Rodriguez said.

Guess not, or she wouldn't have cut contact with me.

Putting his hands in his pockets, Zaid tried to think of what he could do to raise spirits around here. As the team medic, it was his responsibility to look after the guys' physical injuries, but he also considered it his job to monitor and help them with personal things too. "How are things back home?" he asked Rodriguez.

"Okay. Charlie's good, still working hard on cracking more encrypted files on the *Veneno* investigation with her team."

Rodriguez's girlfriend was an analyst working the case back in D.C. The *Venenos* were a big freaking deal, and a global threat whose tentacles now reached all the way over here to Afghanistan. Rumors said The Jackal was involved with them somehow, shipping Afghan opium back to Mexico. "And your mom?"

Rodriguez hesitated, then lowered his gaze to the floor. "Not good."

Shit. Her MS was progressing much faster than anyone had expected. Now Zaid was sorry he'd asked. "Sorry to hear that."

Rodriguez nodded. "Thanks. It's not critical yet, but she's getting weaker every day, and losing more function." He blew out a hard breath and rubbed the back of his neck. "The holidays always make it tougher, especially when I'm so far away. At least she's got the rest of the family there with her, even if I can't be."

"Yeah." Zaid paused a beat. "Anything we can do?"

His teammate looked up and gave him a half-smile.

"No. But thanks for asking."

It had been worth a shot. "Sure."

Prentiss walked in and stopped when he saw them standing outside the storage room. "Y'all using the laptop?"

"No, go ahead." Zaid stepped out of the way and motioned for him to go in. "Got an important call?"

"Trying to set up one with Autumn, yeah. I want to make sure I get to talk to her either today or tomorrow."

His daughter. "Good stuff." Aside from their commander, Prentiss was the only one on the team who was a father. Zaid wasn't a parent and not likely to be one anytime soon even though he wanted that one day, but he could imagine how much it sucked to be away from your kid during such an important holiday—especially if it wasn't the first or even fifth time.

"My ex isn't making it easy, of course." Prentiss shook his dark head, frustration burning in his deep blue eyes. "She's a great mom, I give her all the credit in the world there, since she's basically a single parent while I'm gone. But when it comes to me?" He snorted. "She still doesn't seem to grasp the fact that I can't just schedule a call and always stick to it. That I can't opt out of a team meeting or mission to be on the call if something comes up."

"That sucks. Good luck." The guy lived for his baby girl, and rightly so.

"Thanks," Prentiss muttered, and walked past them into the storage room to shut the door.

"His ex is a piece of work," Maka said from over in the corner where he was busy loading his Nerf gun in gleeful anticipation of hitting another victim with a foam dart.

His latest coping mechanism to stave off boredom and pass the time while they waited for something from command. Zaid swore the guy had ADD.

"Never misses a chance to screw him over when it

comes to their kid." Maka shook his head and didn't bother looking up, intent on his work with the pile of darts in his lap. "Don't get why she's still so pissed at him about the breakup. They've been divorced for like, seven years."

Zaid snorted. "Says the guy who's never been through a divorce." Zaid hoped he never went through one. He was a one-woman kinda guy, and when he found The One, he would lock her down with a ring on her finger so the whole world knew she was his.

Unbidden, an image of Jaliya popped into his head. Now there was the kind of woman he'd be proud to settle down with one day. Smart, driven, sexy. They even shared the same religious background.

Not that he was ready to risk his heart again. Maybe after this deployment he'd feel up to putting himself out there once he'd been home for a while.

Maka looked up at him, his dark brows pulled together in a ferocious scowl. "I'm serious. She's nasty to him. Do you know how many kids out there would kill to have a dad who cared about them that much? Prentiss has done everything in his power to maintain a good relationship with his daughter since the split. But instead of trying to support that, his ex would rather sabotage it to get back at him out of some twisted sense of revenge. And who loses? The kid. Every damn time."

The impassioned speech took Zaid off guard so much that he didn't answer for a long moment, and shared a look with Rodriguez. Maka didn't open up about personal stuff too often, although the team knew he hadn't had it easy as a kid. It sounded like Maka had just exposed an old wound he'd kept hidden until now. "Was your dad like that?"

Maka's jaw flexed under the dark scruff and he looked back down at his foam ammo, shaking his head. "Are you kidding? My sperm donor didn't give two shits about me or my mom. Took off when I was a baby and never looked back. That's why I'm saying someone like Prentiss, who busts his ass trying to be there for his daughter, shouldn't have to fight for that relationship. It's not right, for him or his girl."

"No, it's not." And Maka was right. The daughter was the one who lost out when her mother tried to block Prentiss's efforts at keeping in touch. Using Autumn as a weapon was wrong, but sadly, all too common in divorces. "Let's hope things go smoothly for him this time."

"Wouldn't hold your breath on that one," Maka muttered, sliding the last of the foam bullets into his uzi-style Nerf gun. Sucker must have at least twenty rounds in it, after Maka's modifications. "Things have gotten worse for him since we got over here, in case you haven't noticed. Man, I'd love to meet her so I could give her a piece of my mind."

Zaid chuckled. "Are you kidding? One look from you and you'd have her in tears." Maka had a heart of gold, but he was huge and could be an intimidating son of a bitch to those who didn't know him.

Maka scowled. "I'm not that scary. Just don't like seeing my buddy getting a raw deal. Or Autumn either, for that matter. She's a sweetie pie."

Zaid smiled at the show of loyalty and protectiveness. Now that he thought about it, Prentiss *had* been even more withdrawn than usual this deployment. Things had always been rocky with his ex, but something more had to be up with them right now, because Prentiss was the only one who hadn't received a care package or parcel from home this week. Even Zaid had received a hand-written letter and a tin of cookies from his mom a few days ago, and they didn't even celebrate Christmas.

In fact, the only guy on the team who seemed remotely cheerful over the past day or two was Maka, prior to this conversation, anyway. Zaid nodded at the plastic weapon in his teammate's lap. "You better not try to shoot me with that thing."

A sly grin spread across Maka's face. "Oh, it's happening. But don't worry, you won't see it coming." He petted the plastic cylinder lovingly. "They never do."

"Don't forget, we shoot back," Rodriguez told him.

Maka shrugged a broad shoulder. "Just wanted to make sure I was loaded and ready to rock. Never know when the right opportunity will present itself."

Meaning, no one was safe, and they'd all be pelted with foam bullets at some point during this deployment. "Can't you read a book or something like everyone else, play some video games and pass the time in a way that won't wind up in a brawl?" Zaid asked.

"No."

Hell, now that he thought about it, maybe a little brawl would be good for them and their morale. Let some steam off. It wouldn't be long until they got another assignment, but the lag time in between was boring as hell.

The storage room door opened and Prentiss stepped out, looking ready to hit something. His gaze locked on Maka and the Nerf gun across the room, and his eyes narrowed in warning. "Don't even think about it."

Expression all innocence, Maka pointed the weapon at him and fired. A foam dart zinged across the room and pegged Prentiss center mass, dead in the middle of the star on his Captain America shirt.

"Asshole," Prentiss snarled, and took a menacing step forward. Zaid guessed the attempt to set up a call with his daughter hadn't gone so well. He almost hoped Prentiss and Maka did tussle. It would be good for both of them, and neither one of them would cross the line.

Hooting with laughter, Maka jumped up and ran out the door, whirling to fire another three rounds as he did. Prentiss ducked the first one, but the next two bounced off his shoulder. "Yeah, that's right, you pussy, run!" he shouted after Maka.

Deep laughter echoed back at them from down the hall as Maka went in search of his next unsuspecting victim. Zaid shook his head. "He's like a child."

"Yeah." A reluctant grin tugged at Prentiss's hard mouth as he stared toward the hallway after their teammate.

Rodriguez clapped Prentiss on the shoulder. "You can get him back while he's sleeping. When that guy's out, he's like a bear in hibernation." With that helpful suggestion, he walked out of the room.

Zaid looked at Prentiss. At least Maka's prank seemed to have lessened some of his teammate's tension. "So, how'd it go? You get it set up?"

"Dunno. Have to wait to hear back from the ex. I tried texting her and she won't respond." His expression was as sour as his tone, but the sharp frustration was gone.

Zaid checked his watch. They still had over an hour until the team briefing. He was looking forward to it and bet the others were too. It would give them something to do, and it would also give him a chance to see Jaliya again. She'd been as frustrated and annoyed as the rest of them about the lack of results from the past two ops. She and her team were working overtime to uncover new leads and find them another target to check out.

He had seventy minutes to kill before he got to look at that pretty face and tried not to let his mind wander off into imagining her naked. Or naked and under him. It was damn hard not to fantasize about it, even if he knew it would never happen.

Zaid glanced around the team room, now empty except for him and Prentiss. One of the guys had pilfered an X-Box system and set it up in the far corner. He raised an eyebrow at Prentiss. "Call of Duty until the briefing?"

This time Prentiss's smile was genuine, and full of appreciation. "Yeah, why not."

****

Even without seeing him, Jaliya knew the moment Agent Khan stepped into the downtown Kabul office the next day.

She'd been expecting him, yet something tingled low in her belly and a subtle tension took hold of her muscles, making her heart rate kick up a notch. She braced herself before turning, but it wasn't enough. His hazel gaze collided with hers from across the conference room, and the slight smile he gave her was so damn sexy her heart lurched.

Nuh-uh. You're working. And he's off limits. "Hello," she murmured, striving to be courteous and nothing more.

"Hi." Today he had on a tan tactical shirt that hugged his broad shoulders and chest, the short sleeves hugging the defined curves of his chest and biceps.

Yum.

"The others will be here in another minute," he added.

She nodded and put on a polite, professional smile, hoping he couldn't tell the effect he had on her. While she wasn't terribly experienced with men, she could tell Khan was interested.

He was subtle about it, though, respectful, and that made it twice as hard to ignore her own attraction to him. She was dying to know whether he was the same Zaid from the dating site. Online Zaid had been thirty-three, and this Zaid was around that age.

Not that she was going to pursue anything with him, because the whole idea was stupid. Getting involved with him would make her look completely unprofessional should anyone find out, not to mention that a potential relationship with him was an automatic dead end because she was based out of Kabul for the foreseeable future and he was only here for another three months.

"You been making any headway with finding your young informant?" he asked, folding his tall body into a chair on the opposite side of the table. The man had an air of authority and a natural magnetism that were impossible to ignore. Calm, self-assured, and she was pretty sure those hazel eyes missed nothing when he looked at her.

It made her feel naked, especially when they were alone like this, catching her off guard and rattling her a little. "Not yet." She set out the last of the folders and straightened, pulling her professional armor around her like a shield. "But we're following up a few leads."

"You think he was lying to us?"

"There's a good chance, yes." She'd known that going in, of course, and would weigh his intel carefully.

Agent Hamilton, FAST Bravo's team leader walked in, and gave her a friendly nod that she returned. "Sorry we had to push this back so late. Commander Taggart had Khan and me in another meeting."

"No, don't apologize. I'm glad you were both able to be here for this."

Agent Khan was here to help with translation during the presentation. And they would all be spending more time together in future because of the ongoing investigation with their informant, Barakat, who had seemed to miraculously vanish after their meeting.

Because the little tosser was most likely playing both sides against the other.

Jaliya still didn't know whether he'd fed them straight bullshit, or whether The Jackal had somehow been tipped off about the other night's op. Either way, their high value target hadn't been in the village when FAST Bravo and the NIU went in. It made her team —and by association, *her*—look inept. She wouldn't stand for it.

Commander Taggart and the rest of the taskforce arrived, including members of the NIU and two military officers, Colonel Shah and General Nasar. Four more

Afghan military officials took their seats next to the chief of special police in Kabul. With two members of her team beside her fielding questions and Zaid helping translate for the two Afghan officials who didn't speak English, she felt more at ease delivering the information she had to share.

"By this point we're all aware that recent operations to seize shipments and find The Jackal have been unsuccessful. The missing shipments we were assured were there, and the empty caches our teams have found are reason enough to suspect a problem within our intel network."

The whole time she spoke, she was acutely aware of everyone's eyes on her, but especially Taggart's and Khan's. Both secretly made her nervous, although for very different reasons. One seemed to scrutinize her capability as an intel specialist. The other made her feel intensely female. Desirable.

She cleared her throat and continued. "But based on recent information we have received, I'm comfortable in saying that we have a leak somewhere in our chain of informants. Or worse, within our own intelligence community. Whatever the case may be, we're certain that The Jackal is behind it." Her team was currently analyzing all the potential players involved, which more than doubled their workload.

With that she motioned for everyone to open their folders, and took them through all the intel she and her team had compiled, a page at a time. Efforts to find likely targets containing caches of drugs and weapons stemming from The Jackal were frustrated by teams coming up blank whenever they went out to search.

She was starting to wonder if the leak stemmed from someone in this very room.

As head of her division on the taskforce, it was her reputation at stake when the search teams came up empty in the field. She was the intelligence specialist assigned to FAST Bravo, and recent events had begun to make her look incompetent. That was totally unacceptable, and she would be damned if she'd let it continue.

No. When she found Barakat she would lean on him until he spilled everything in his devious little heart.

When she was finished with her presentation, Jaliya fielded a few questions from the taskforce representatives before giving her closing remarks. "Rest assured that my team and I are working around the clock to get to the bottom of this and find the source of the leak. I'll personally update the heads of the departments when I have any pertinent intel to pass on."

She and her team had already started combing through the movements of the taskforce personnel, just to make sure one of them wasn't involved in the leak. As far as she and her team could discern, the FAST and NIU members were all innocent. After all, they were the ones sent out to perform the ops. Their leaders appeared clean as well, or they wouldn't have been included in this meeting.

As soon as her team exposed the leak, they'd be one step closer to bringing The Jackal down once and for all.

"Any further questions?" she finished.

"You'll let the agency know if you need any more resources or assets to assist with the investigation?" Taggart's tone made it clear he wasn't asking. Rather, he'd just given her a politely-phrased command to bring more people on board.

She wasn't about to argue with him. They had more work than they could handle and her investigation had proven that Taggart was clean. "Of course."

Relieved the meeting was over, she gathered her files and tucked them into her backpack. When she straightened, her stomach did a little flip to see Khan standing next to the door, waiting for her.

She arched an eyebrow at him. Usually men only

singled her out if they were going to hit on her, and she was quick to put them in their place if they tried. She kept waiting for Khan to cross that line, but he hadn't yet. It made her wary. What did he want from her?

"Did you need something, Agent Khan?" she asked.

His gaze wandered over her face a moment before he replied. "No. And call me Zaid."

Okay, he was definitely attracted, but not being overt about it. Duly noted. She could play along for now.

She started toward him, her professional defenses firmly in place, ready to deflect the slightest hint of flirtation from him. "All right. Zaid." When she stepped through the open doorway, the others were already at the far end of the hall, giving them some privacy. "So, you're headed back to Bagram now?"

"That's the plan."

She could be friendly without encouraging him. She'd become good at that since joining the DEA. "How is your team doing? It's always hard to be so far away from family during a big holiday."

"They're okay. I think a few are a little homesick, especially one guy who has a young daughter back home. How are you doing?" he asked as he kept pace beside her.

She blinked at him. "Me?" No one ever asked her that around here. "I'm fine." She didn't celebrate Christmas, but the season still made the distance from her family seem sharper. They might not agree on a lot of matters, but they still loved one another and she missed them. It was lonely over here.

He gave a slow nod, his intent inspection of her face more intimate than she was comfortable with. "You do long deployments over here. How long this time?"

"Just under eleven months now, not including that whirlwind trip to D.C. in April." Where she'd first met him and his team at FAST headquarters in Arlington. The same night she'd canceled the date with online Zaid.

She was dying to know if it was him, but thought it best not to dredge it up in case it was. Talk about awkward. *Hey, um, sorry for canceling last minute like that, but I thought you were an asshole.*

"That's a long time. I remember how it felt doing long stints like that back when I was in the army. Ever get homesick?" He reached past her to get the glass door that opened up into another hallway. He had nice manners. She was all for opening her own doors in life, but she liked it when men showed that kind of courtesy that seemed to be dying out in today's society.

"Thank you," she murmured, and walked through. "Sometimes. My family's good about regularly sending me messages and emails, though, and I try to call home at least once a week. More if I can. You?"

"Same. Actually, my mom just sent me a container of my favorite homemade cookies."

Jaliya smiled. "That's sweet." Her family had just sent her a card and a framed picture of all of them taken when she'd been home last. It was on the bedside table in her hotel room.

Zaid shrugged, a slight grin tugging at his mouth. "She spoils me."

"And you love every second of it."

"Yeah, I really do."

She laughed and shook her head. "Why does that not surprise me?'

"Why should it? Everyone loves to be spoiled now and then. You saying you never get spoiled?"

"Sometimes by my mom. My father is…" What was the right word for him? "He's complicated. We tend to butt heads a lot." About pretty much everything except for the importance of education, hard work and family.

"And who usually wins?"

"Neither of us. I just carry on and do my own thing in spite of his disapproval." She'd gotten used to it over the years.

"Ah. Does he disapprove of a lot?"

"You could say I'm the black sheep of the family."

He frowned, eyeing her in surprise, as though he couldn't quite believe it. "Really?"

She nodded. "I know he loves me. Mostly he dislikes my choice of vocation, and my lack of conformity to his expectations about how I should practice my faith. I'm way too liberal and secular for his liking, not to mention stubborn. Although I get that part from him." She shrugged as if it didn't bother her, but a part of her would always hate feeling at odds with her father.

"Well, I know how that goes. My parents wish I was more conservative and traditional when it comes to religion too." He shot her a grin. "Although at this point, they've given up on trying to make me conform. I won."

She returned the grin as they continued down the hallway. It was easier for him to buck tradition because he was a guy. "That must be nice."

"Do you observe Ramadan?"

"I observe the fasting and charity, but the rest I'm not so strict about. You?"

"Same. Although when I'm deployed I can't always follow the rules. I need to eat and drink when I can so I'm mission ready."

That made perfect sense. "This year's going to be a bugger."

He rolled his eyes. "Tell me about it. Late May to the end of June? Worst time of the year for it to fall on. I'm dreading it."

"It's gonna be torture." A month of no food or drink— not even water—from sunup 'til sundown every day during the longest period of daylight in the entire calendar year was no joke.

"You can email me to whine if you want. Misery loves company."

She shot him a grin. Religion was such a controversial, intensely personal thing, and she didn't like having other people's interpretations of it shoved down her throat. So maybe she and Zaid had more in common than she'd realized. She and online Zaid shared that too.

They reached the end of the hall and Zaid opened the door to the building's underground car park. "You doing anything tonight?" he asked.

She glanced at him in surprise. He'd been careful not to stray into flirting territory thus far, but this was dangling right on the edge of it. "Working, trying to track down Barakat so I can drag him back here and get some real answers out of him."

"You gonna waterboard him?"

She gave a soft laugh. "I may have fantasized about it."

His eyebrows rose. "Wow. Hardcore."

Her lips quirked in a small smile. "Well, he's pissed me off. Lied straight to my face, the little wanker, and ran off with our money."

"Wow, wanker, huh? Is that like, a serious slur in England?"

"Deadly serious."

"Okay, but after you waterboard him. You're free then, right?"

She shrugged. "Who knows how long it'll take? I've never tortured anyone before."

"Still. You can't work *all* night."

"Sure I can." She'd pulled all-nighters quite a few times when an investigation became intense. Whatever it took to get the job done.

He gave her an exasperated look. "You must take breaks."

She thought about it for a second. "When I'm working on something important? Not really. Why, what are you getting at?"

"We're planning a get together tonight after dinner. Hamilton and I thought it would be a good idea to take everyone's mind off being away from home at Christmas. We're gonna break out a board game or two, have some pumpkin pie. You interested?"

She stopped walking. It wasn't what she'd expected him to say, and it sure didn't sound flirtatious. He hadn't asked her to go somewhere alone, just the two of them. "Really? You want me to come?"

"Yeah, I do. It'll be fun, and you deserve some downtime after the way this week's gone. Even if it's only an hour or two."

Huh. Sounded casual and innocent enough. She'd made up her mind not to fraternize with any of them, but she'd been working nonstop for so long and a tiny break like that sounded fun. And when was the last time she had any of that? "I do like pumpkin pie."

"Do you like it with whipped cream, or plain?"

"Whipped cream, spread over the top in a layer at least an inch thick. I can't stand it when people skimp on the whipped cream. I mean, why bother eating it then?"

"Okay, then I'll make sure we have plenty of whipped cream, and…" He narrowed his eyes at her thoughtfully. "Chocolate?"

Oh, she loved that even more than pumpkin pie. "Maybe I will come," she said, and resumed walking. "Where and when?"

"Seven, in the rec room at our barracks."

"Your barracks?" She raised her eyebrows at him and he laughed.

"Don't look at me like that. Bring someone from your team with you if it makes you feel more comfortable."

It would. She'd have to find someone to go with her. "And the others won't have a problem with me being there?"

"No, not at all. The more, the merrier."

"Okay. I'll see how things go with the case tonight. I've got someone out looking for Barakat now, trying to find whatever hole he slunk back into."

"Poor bastard. I kinda feel bad for him. Waterboarding by an amateur is almost worse than when it's done by an expert." Zaid looked around the rows of parked cars. The air temperature down here was warmer than outside. "Which one are you?"

"Over there." She pointed to where two members of her team were waiting with a driver next to a silver SUV. He walked her over to it. It was on the tip of her tongue to tell him it wasn't necessary for him to escort her, but she held back. His intentions seemed courteous and protective, not overbearing.

Her team members got into the back of the vehicle, still talking amongst themselves. Zaid opened the front passenger door for her and stepped out of the way to let her in. Her cheeks flushed even as she wondered why he was being so courteous. Because he was trying to win her over? Because he was being protective? She couldn't figure him out, and the devilish glint in his eyes told her he enjoyed whatever game he was playing.

"Thanks," she murmured, setting her backpack in the foot well before climbing up into the seat. The vehicle was armor plated with bullet-resistant glass. Couldn't be too careful over here. Americans and westerners in general had a lot of enemies.

"Welcome." Zaid waited until she put her seatbelt on and looked over at him before continuing. He was close. Close enough for her to see the flecks of gold and green in his eyes, and the thick fringe of black lashes surrounding them. "So, I'll see you later tonight then."

He was insistent, but she wouldn't make any promises. "If I can make it."

One side of his mouth tipped up in a smug grin, and it was so damn sexy it had her imagining what it would feel like to cup that rugged, dark-bearded face between her hands and kiss those smiling lips. "You'll make it."

She fought a smile at his confidence as he shut her door. It was impossible not to like him.

The driver started the engine and drove them out of the car park. When she glanced in the side mirror, Zaid was still standing in the same spot, and raised a hand in farewell.

For some reason the gesture tugged at a deeply buried part of her.

Purposely looking away from the mirror, she mentally sighed. He was a complication she hadn't foreseen, and one who, under different circumstances, she might have been tempted to try on for size.

Ten minutes later her vehicle was a few blocks from the hotel she and the others were staying at when a low rumble shook the ground. The driver stopped in the middle of the street and they all looked through the windshield as a huge plume of black smoke spewed into the cold, clear air.

"That's right near our hotel," Jaliya said, pulling her cell phone out of her pocket.

Before she could get it out, the driver's phone rang. He answered in Dari, and she listened to his side of the conversation, gaining enough information to understand that there was a major problem. Whatever had caused the explosion, it must have been big.

With the phone to his ear, the driver glanced at her with a frown. "There's been a suicide bombing outside your hotel. The entire area's on lockdown."

The blood drained from Jaliya's face. Some of her team were there.

She looked back at the rolling cloud of black smoke billowing high into the sky above her hotel, her gut telling her two things. The location and timing were too much of a coincidence for her to believe it had been anything but a targeted attack.

And that meant her team was being hunted.

Chapter Five

Heart pumping, Zaid jumped out of the vehicle as soon as the driver pulled up to the security checkpoint, Hamilton right behind him. A scene of total chaos met their eyes.

A block beyond the barricade, the hotel Jaliya and her team were staying at continued to billow huge clouds of smoke. The entire area had been closed off while emergency crews responded to the casualties and the fire. Sirens wailed as frightened civilians were herded away from the area, choking the streets and sidewalks and making it impossible to move.

Zaid showed the security personnel guarding the checkpoint his ID and spoke to them in rapid Dari, eager to get through the barrier and find Jaliya. Through Taggart, they'd received word about the bombing just as they'd left the outskirts of Kabul.

The initial report said Jaliya and her two teammates hadn't been at the hotel when the bombing occurred, but she hadn't answered her phone when he'd called her, and he wanted to see her with his own eyes to make sure she was okay. Besides, if the bombing had been a targeted attack on the hotel, she might still be in danger.

After talking to his superior on the radio, one of the guards finally let Zaid and Hamilton through the barricade. Together they hurried through the crowded streets to get to the hotel, where a tighter, interior security perimeter had been set up.

"Damn," Zaid muttered when he caught sight of the smoldering wreckage of twisted metal that marked the truck bomb. The front of the hotel was missing completely, wiped out by the blast. Paramedics and other first responders were busy dousing the flames and carrying victims out on stretchers.

"That had to be one big-ass bomb," Hamilton said. "Looks like it might have been a five-ton truck."

The location and timing of it worried Zaid. Impatient, he relayed his information to the men standing guard and waited to be let through. If the vehicle Jaliya was riding in was anywhere near here when the blast went off...

He scanned the crowds around him in all directions, searching for a glimpse of her.

"Taggart said Rabani and the others were okay," Hamilton said, correctly guessing the cause of Zaid's concern. "I'm sure she's fine."

Zaid didn't answer. He'd only relax once he saw her himself, and then make sure she was moved to somewhere secure.

This had the style of The Jackal all over it, and if Jaliya was in his sights, then Zaid wanted to get her to safety. He'd already lost one woman he cared about deeply, and he'd be damned if he would watch it happen to Jaliya without doing everything in his power to shield her. If that made him come across as an overprotective control freak, so be it.

He glanced to his left, then his right. On the east side of the street across from the hotel, the crowd shifted to let paramedics by with a stretcher and Zaid's gaze landed on a familiar female figure standing with her back to him, dressed in beige cargo pants and combat boots.

Relief swept over him in a warm wave. "There she is."

Without pause he jogged toward her, knowing Hamilton would follow. He didn't call out her name, not wanting to draw attention to her identity in case she'd been targeted and some of The Jackal's spies were among the crowd, watching. There was a slim chance this was unrelated to either The Jackal or Jaliya's team, but his gut said otherwise.

She still had her back to him as she spoke on her phone, her free hand covering her left ear to help her hear better. The smell of smoke and scorched metal hung thick in the cold air.

Zaid slowed as he approached, angling toward her so that she could see him in her peripheral vision. Her chocolate-brown gaze darted to him, and even though she didn't say anything, the relief on her face told him he'd been right to come.

Jaliya quickly finished her conversation and lowered her phone as she turned to him and Hamilton. "News travels fast."

"We heard a few minutes after it happened." Zaid scanned her quickly and didn't see any sign of injury. Or fear, even though she had to be shaken. He relaxed a fraction. "You all right?"

"Yes. We're all fine." She sighed and faced the burning building. "Security's locked everything down and won't let us in. The agency's working on finding a secure location to move us to. But I've got material related to a current investigation I need to retrieve from the safe in my room, and I'm not leaving until I get it. And after this, I won't let anyone from the hotel or their security touch it. Until I know what's going on and who detonated that bomb, I'm not trusting anyone here, not even the guards hired by the agency. I've tried to argue my way in, and called my boss to see what he can do to get me in there."

The sooner they got her away from here, the better. "Let me take a shot. Wait here." He motioned for Hamilton to accompany him to the side entrance, where more armed guards were stationed.

In Dari Zaid argued his case for gaining access to the building, and fed them a lie about being government security contractors guarding a state VIP. It was imperative that they clean out their client's room before either the police or military reached it, and if they weren't granted access before then, there'd be hell to pay.

After some arguing between themselves and their superior, Zaid pressed harder, promising severe consequences for them if they didn't let him and his team upstairs that instant. The guards weren't happy, but they grudgingly agreed. Zaid waved Jaliya over, who shot him a surprised look and followed him into the building.

"We've got fifteen minutes," Zaid told her, pulling his Glock from its holster on his hip as he reached the door to the stairwell. Hamilton and Jaliya both had pistols in hand, and kept watch while Zaid opened the stairwell and checked it. "Clear." He started up the concrete steps, maintaining his vigilance just in case anyone or anything was waiting to surprise them. "Where are we headed?"

"Fourth floor, number 416. End of the hall, near the far exit," Jaliya answered behind him, Hamilton watching their six as they ascended the stairs.

The stairwell was deserted, and when Zaid checked it, so was the fourth floor hallway. He strode for the door she'd mentioned, then held his hand out for her key card. "Stay put out here with Hamilton," he told her, then eased the door open. He swept the room, and, seeing no threats, swung the door wide open. "You'll stand watch?" he asked his teammate.

"You know it," Hamilton answered.

Jaliya quickly moved inside and Zaid shut the door behind her. She headed straight for the small closet opposite the bathroom and eased the folding door open, her weapon in her free hand.

With fast, economical motions she accessed the small safe and turned the knob back and forth to enter the combination. She let out a relieved breath when it opened. "It's still here." When she straightened and turned back to him, she held a flash drive and a file folder in her left hand.

"Need anything else? We've only got a few more minutes before our time's up." If they weren't out of here by the specified time, they'd have pissed off security agents coming in after them and Zaid would rather not be subjected to any more questions right now. His priority was moving Jaliya away from here as quickly as possible.

She was already hurrying to the dresser set against the wall opposite the double bed. "Just a few of my clothes and personal things."

In the midst of shoving a handful of what looked like lacy underwear into her backpack, a low rumble sounded below them. Both she and Zaid froze.

A moment later the rumble increased to a dull roar, and the floor shook.

Jaliya gasped and took a step back. Zaid immediately rushed to wrap a protective arm around her shoulders, ready to push her under the desk and cover her with his body. Another bomb? Debris falling from the hotel? But the floor stopped trembling a moment later and the noise ceased.

"God," Jaliya whispered, pressing a hand to her stomach in relief.

Hamilton pounded on the door. "You guys okay?"

"Yeah," he called back. "Just some rubble falling off the front of the building." He turned Jaliya around to face him and grasped her chin with his fingers to make sure she was coping okay.

She stared up at him with those gorgeous, thickly-lashed eyes, unmoving, only a few inches separating them. The sweet, clean scent of her filled his nostrils as he searched her face. She hadn't shown the faintest trace of fear until now, even though she had to be rattled. That bombing was too damn close and if she'd arrived a few minutes earlier she would have been caught up in the blast.

"You sure you're all right?" he asked her softly. Her skin was so damn soft, and her mouth was too damn tempting. The bravery she'd shown in the face of danger put a crack in the wall he'd erected around his heart. That combination of strength and softness sucked him right in.

She swallowed and gave him a tiny smile. "Yes."

He couldn't let it go. "Was your team the target?"

"I'm not sure."

"But you're not sure it wasn't."

She lowered her gaze, her chin still grasped in his fingers. "No."

He sighed. "As soon as we leave here, we'll get you and the others back to Bagram."

"That's not necessary—"

"I'm not leaving you in Kabul." He needed to know she'd be safe, and the best way to do that was to guard her himself until he got her to a secure location. "The agency can figure out where to put you after that."

He expected another argument, or even a show of annoyance from her, but instead her expression softened. "All right. Thank you."

He nodded.

Her lips twisted into a wry smile. "I'm sure you think I must be a sandwich short of a picnic to take on this job in the first place, huh?"

Her choice of words made him grin. "No." The grin

faded. "But I'll feel a lot better once I get you out of this city."

She searched his eyes, suspicion creeping into her gaze. "Why are you doing this for me?"

"Because I care about you." And he did. She'd flipped an invisible switch inside him. He'd sworn off relationships and women in general for at least a few more months, but somehow she'd shot that decision all to hell without even trying. He didn't want his heart stomped on, yet he couldn't stay away from her.

Surprise flashed in her eyes before she looked down again. "Well... Thank you."

Zaid didn't want her thanks. Something about her and this whole situation had triggered the protectiveness inside him and there was no shutting it off. Too many times over the past few weeks he'd imagined what it would be like to hold her. Taste her. Feel her arms twine around his neck as she reached for him.

He gentled his hold on her chin, cradling it. He'd whisk her out of this place in a minute. But first, he had to taste those soft lips.

In the stark silence he slid the pad of his thumb over the curve of her chin and up to that lush mouth he couldn't stop staring at or dreaming about. Jaliya's gaze darted up to lock with his, and the naked desire burning there sent a rush of heat through him, shooting straight to his groin.

Without giving either of them time to back out, he quickly holstered his weapon and took her face in his hands. A soft gasp fell from her lips and her lashes fluttered down as she put her hands on his shoulders and leaned closer.

That tiny signal that proved she wanted him destroyed the last of his control.

Bending closer, Zaid tilted his head and covered her mouth with his.

It was like touching a live wire. A jolt of pure

electricity arced between them. He angled his head and parted her lips to deepen the kiss, hungry to taste her, to touch the warm, sensual woman behind the professional front she always wore. Her hands tightened on his shoulders.

Zaid kissed her slow and firm at first, then gentled it, tenderly stroking the seam of her lips with his tongue. She made a small, hungry sound and opened for him, easing her body forward until her breasts pressed flush against his chest.

He groaned and eased his tongue into her mouth, tasting, caressing while her fingers bit into his shoulders and his swollen cock pressed hard against her lower abdomen. She tasted so damn sweet, and those soft curves molded to him were—

Hamilton banged on the door. "Zaid. We gotta go."

Jaliya instantly ripped her mouth away from his and stumbled back a step, looking guilty as hell. Her lips were wet and swollen and she was breathing faster.

Zaid clenched his jaw and bit back a growl of frustration. He shouldn't have kissed her, but he'd be damned if he'd apologize because he didn't regret it, and hoped she didn't either. But Hamilton was right. They needed to move. "Yeah, coming."

He drew a steadying breath in a futile effort to slow his heart rate, watching as she self-consciously smoothed her hands over her hijab that was still firmly in place. He wanted to pull it off her, run his fingers through the long, thick mass of dark hair he remembered from their first meeting back in Virginia. Wanted to wrap his hands in it and back her up against the wall, then kiss her until her knees gave out, until she was panting and trembling in his arms.

Until she was so hungry for him that she didn't want to let him go.

Which was insane. He didn't want to get crushed

again. "Ready?" he asked her instead in a voice like gravel, his entire body on fire for her.

She seemed to collect herself for a moment, then nodded and reached for her backpack without looking at him. "Yes."

Zaid followed her to the door, aching for more of what they'd just shared. He didn't want a relationship, at least not with someone who lived and worked thousands of miles away from him eight months out of every year.

But damn, now that he'd had a taste of her, he wished things could have been different.

Chapter Six

Hands on hips, Jaliya stepped back from the open folder on the desk and turned to look at the picture board she and her team had assembled on the back wall. All men who were reputed to be connected to The Jackal somehow. One of them might even *be* him.

Staring at the photo of the man at the top of the second column, a wave of cold swept through her veins.

"I don't like the look of it," her boss, David, said next to her.

"No. I don't either," she murmured, her eyes fixed on the image of the man in the dress uniform.

Since the hotel bombing four days ago, all evidence turned up by their investigation seemed to point to this man being involved. A local chief of special police with the insider knowledge, connections and means of carrying out such an attack, and he was widely rumored to be working with The Jackal.

With the amount of evidence they had compiled against him and the smokescreen surrounding some of his recent activities, as of right now he was her team's number one suspect in The Jackal investigation.

The problem was finding enough proof linking him to the bombing to pin on him and bring him in. Unfortunately, corruption within law enforcement, the military and the government were commonplace here, making her team's job even harder.

"Most of these tossers are bent as a nine-bob note," she muttered.

David chuckled. "I love your British expressions. They're so educational."

"You must know a lot of them by now," she said with a grin, still studying the board.

Trying to get someone to rat out a corrupt official was near impossible no matter how much money she waved at them, especially since she and her team were considered outsiders and not to be trusted by the locals.

Her being female made it even worse. Not to mention the risk of blowback that could be unleashed on an informer.

They had a list of other suspects as well, of course, their pictures all mapped out on the wall of their temporary "war room" here at Bagram, where she'd been since Agent Khan—Zaid, she corrected herself sternly— had escorted her and the others here right after the bombing.

Ridiculous, to think of him in any kind of formal way whatsoever after what had happened in her hotel room. She still couldn't believe she'd kissed him like that, stunned by her immediate and visceral reaction to the feel and taste of him.

The intensity of it had taken her completely off guard. She blamed it on a moment of weakness, a combination of curiosity, desire and adrenaline that had momentarily destroyed her common sense and objectivity.

While she was embarrassed about her lapse in judgment, she wouldn't go so far as to wish it hadn't happened. That kiss had been the most romantic, erotic of her life, and it had woken a kind of yearning inside her that she'd never felt before. But that's as far as things could go between them, and she'd have to make that clear to Zaid the next chance she had to speak to him in private.

The door to the war room opened and several Afghan military commanders walked in in full uniform. Colonel Shah and General Nasar. Their units had been assisting Jaliya's team with the investigation into the bombing, as well as searching for leads on The Jackal.

Shah was as rigid as ever in his bearing. He took one look at the wall they'd constructed and began demanding information about the bombing investigation.

Jaliya complied, mentally gritting her teeth at the disdain in the man's eyes as he listened to her. When she finished he conferred with David. Behind him, General Nasar spoke in a low voice to two of his men. He oversaw the operations of the NIU and had just returned from the site of the bombing in Kabul with an explosives team.

He didn't say much, preferring to observe and come to his own conclusions during meetings and briefings, and only offering his opinion if asked. Jaliya had worked with him several times on various things during this deployment. The DEA and other American assets frequently worked with him and his units in investigations and on operations.

Turning from Shah, her boss shook Nasar's hand. "General. Thank you for coming."

Nasar nodded and stood beside her to peruse the board, his hands clasped behind his back and his feet braced apart in parade rest position. Even in this casual setting, he was ever the soldier, his uniform and grooming impeccable, and his men were the same. He had a calmer, quieter demeanor than Shah.

"You'll note we've just added a new face to our list of suspects," David said to Shah and Nasar.

"Is this a joke?" Shah demanded, his flinty gaze cutting between her and David.

"No, it's not," she answered, tamping down the anger surging inside her. Did he seriously think they would make this up for fun?

Nasar made a sound of acknowledgment but didn't speak, still studying the photos on the board. Nine of them. A damn sight fewer than the twenty-seven they'd started with a few weeks ago, but still not narrow enough.

"All the threads we've gathered since the hotel bombing seem to lead back to him," Jaliya told the men, pointing at the police chief. "And we've managed to interview two men who claim to have proof of his involvement with The Jackal. Our legal team is working on putting together a case against him right now."

"The whole thing is ridiculous," Shah snapped. "He's no more The Jackal than I am," he said of the police chief.

"Until we can prove that, he stays on the board," Jaliya said, steel in her voice. Sod him if he didn't like it. She and her team were being thorough.

"It's an insult," Shah said, anger burning in his gaze.

Nasar turned his head and regarded her with his dark, deep-set eyes. He was one of the handful of high-ranking Afghan military officials who didn't seem to look down on her because of her gender, but she had no illusions that he liked working with her. "You have someone willing to testify against The Jackal?"

She cleared her throat. "Not yet." A wrinkle she was trying to iron out.

Both men had talked of having proof to indict The Jackal, yet neither of them could be persuaded to go so far as to give sworn statements or testify in court. Things worked very differently over here compared to in the U.S. A legal team was hard at work gathering enough evidence on The Jackal's crimes so that when he was identified and captured, they could extradite him to the States to face charges there.

Nasar nodded once, his response telling her he wasn't the least bit surprised, then turned his attention back to the board. She had the feeling that he'd already memorized every name and face on it. "A very serious accusation you're placing on him," he said of the chief of special police.

Shah folded his arms and gave her a hard stare.

"Yes. But there's too much evidence to ignore his involvement on some level. At this point he's our lead suspect," she answered calmly.

Out of the corner of her eye she caught sight of someone approaching the glass door to her right. Zaid and Agent Hamilton.

Her cheeks heated. When they entered the room she nodded at them by way of acknowledgment and quickly went back to studying the board while Nasar and Shah spoke to her and her boss.

The lack of progress was frustrating everybody.

Try as she might to be one hundred percent focused on the discussion at hand, part of her remained intensely aware of Zaid standing behind her and slightly to her right. It unsettled her. No matter how she tried she couldn't forget he was there. One hot kiss and her body had become a Zaid radar.

"I've heard enough. Until you have something more solid on a man of his position than mere suspicion, leave me to oversee my men," Shah said.

He'd just spun on his heel when Nasar spoke up. "I think Agent Rabani and her team are conducting a rather thorough investigation."

Shah snorted and walked out, and Jaliya couldn't help but smile at Nasar for the show of support. "Thank you."

He shrugged. "An intelligent man can see that." He and the other men left with David for another meeting on base, and Jaliya breathed out a silent sigh of relief when the door shut behind them. At least now she could relax her guard a little, without her boss and the others around.

Although nervous butterflies stirred in the pit of her stomach with Zaid so close. "Need me to go over any of that with you guys?" she asked him and Hamilton.

"No, I think we're good," Hamilton said. "I'm gonna follow them and listen in on the meeting with the NIU staff, so I'll see you later," he said to Zaid, and left.

Jaliya was torn about him leaving. Part of her was glad to have this chance to talk to Zaid in private, set things straight between them. The other was nervous as hell at being alone with him again.

Zaid stayed where he was, perusing the board one more time before settling that hot hazel gaze on her. "You find out anything more about the target of the bombing?"

He wasn't going to like it. She didn't like it either. "All the signs point to it being an attack on our team. Someone had apparently been asking about us while we were at breakfast in the lobby several hours earlier."

"Casing the place and trying to lock down your location."

She nodded. "Seems that way. They must have thought we were still in the building."

He eyed the board once more. "Looks like your team is making good progress with the investigation."

"We hope so." She really should talk to him about that kiss.

To buy her a few moments to work up her courage, she fiddled with some paperwork spread out on the long table beneath the board. Zaid stepped closer, standing near enough that she could feel his body heat licking along her side.

Without looking at him she opened a drawer and pulled out a stack of files she had to go through, all too aware of the way he watched her. "You're distracting me," she muttered and glanced up at him, annoyed that she couldn't concentrate with him around.

A slow grin spread across his lips. "Am I?"

"Very much so." And that was a first.

"I'd say I'm sorry, but then I'd be lying."

Fighting a smile, she picked up another file from the desk and attempted to kick her brain back into gear. If her team truly had been the intended target today, it meant someone knew not only about their movements, but their involvement with The Jackal investigation as well. And every time they left the relative safety of Bagram, they did so with targets painted on their backs. They couldn't afford to waste any time in finding the man responsible.

Zaid took another step closer, stopping mere inches from her back. Jaliya's spine snapped taut, every nerve ending in her body going haywire at his nearness. He was so close she could hear the slow, steady breaths he took. And when she inhaled, she got a breath of his clean, slightly spicy, masculine scent.

"What are you doing?" she managed without turning around, her voice a little breathless. *Besides crowding me and ruining my concentration.* If he thought they could pick up where they'd left off in the hotel, he was dead wrong.

"Reading over your shoulder," he answered softly, his breath caressing the sensitive skin of her cheek with every word.

Her nipples went rock hard and the muscles low in her belly clenched. *Time to go.* But first, she really had to make things clear. "About the other day," she began, unable to look at him. Four days ago, to be exact.

"I can't stop thinking about it."

At his low, impassioned words, her brain hit delete on the speech she'd been about to give him. The one about how things couldn't progress between them, for various reasons, blah, blah. Gone. She had nothing. Could only gape at him as every detail of the kiss came back to her in vivid color.

He laughed softly at her. "Okay, guess you weren't expecting me to say that."

"Um, no," she mumbled, scrambling to get her thoughts together. Reasons. She had reasons why they couldn't get involved. "Just to be clear, I won't sleep with you."

He jerked his head back slightly in surprise and raised his eyebrows. "I don't remember asking you to."

Bollocks. She was making a total ass of herself. "I just…" She cleared her throat again, her cheeks burning. "I thought I should tell you that up front. In case you thought otherwise." Because, *reasons*. Reasons that were hard to think of when he was standing right here in front of her, all hard-bodied, alpha male sex appeal.

He watched her closely for a long moment, a slight frown pulling the dark slashes of his eyebrows together. "Is there someone else?"

It took her a moment to understand what he was asking. Did she already have a guy. For a second she thought about lying, to make it easier to put distance between them. But she couldn't do it. "No. You?"

He shook his head. "No."

Why the hell did that make her so happy? "Do you date much?" It was embarrassing, how few words she could string together into a coherent sentence at the moment. She was totally fishing, wanting to find out more about him and maybe see if she could discern whether he was online Zaid.

He lifted a shoulder. "Haven't for a while. I even tried the whole online dating thing for a bit."

Her heart drummed fast against her ribs. This was the perfect opening for her to dig a little. "But it never worked out?"

"No." His gaze dropped to her mouth before coming back to her eyes, making her lips tingle. "There was someone I thought I had a real connection with a few months back, and then she disappeared."

She hid a wince, feeling half-naked under that stare. "Why, what happened?"

He gave her a funny look. "You really want to know about this?"

"Yes."

He relented and shrugged. "I dunno. She was overseas all the time on business, so we'd never met in person. We set up a meeting for when she came into town and then she cancelled on me the night before."

Oh, shit, he was talking about *her*. He was online Zaid. The blood drained from her face.

He cocked his head, his frown deepening as he watched her. "What's wrong?"

"Nothing." Whirling around, she frantically fiddled with the files, trying to look like she was busy organizing them when in fact her brain was in full panic mode. What now? "Were you upset?"

"A little, yeah. I thought we clicked. Didn't see it coming when she bailed on me like that."

"Maybe you came on too strong. Too macho or something, and scared her off." Dammit, she must have completely misunderstood his meaning in that email. Maybe he'd been teasing her, because the man she'd come to know would never have said it to be offensive.

"Too macho?" He sounded insulted. "I don't think so."

Now she felt awful, both for taking his comment the wrong way, and for cancelling on him like that. After getting to know him better over here, she realized that Zaid wasn't chauvinistic or controlling. But she didn't have the guts to come clean here and now.

"I've got a meeting to get to." She gathered up a couple of files and took her sidearm out of a drawer.

"With who?"

"A source. He says he's got some more info for me."

"And you have to meet him in person?" He followed her to the door. Yes, she was in full retreat mode, and didn't care. She needed time to think, to regroup.

"At this point, yes. I don't trust anything someone tells me over the phone or in a message. I need to look a source in the eye to know if they're feeding me a line of bullshit or not."

Five steps down the hallway, her phone rang. Her boss. "Rabani speaking," she answered.

"You're gonna have to postpone your meeting," David said, his voice tight with frustration.

"Why, what's going on?"

"Our number one suspect just got taken out. His vehicle blew up when he left the station about fifteen minutes ago. It was surgical. Nothing else around it was damaged except for a few windows blowing out on other cars parked along the street."

Jaliya stopped, rubbed at her forehead. Another targeted bombing. "You're sure?"

"Yeah, and since I doubt very much that The Jackal would blow himself up, we're at another dead end."

Oh, God, they'd have to go right back to square one again. "Dammit."

He grunted in agreement. "Meet me out front of my office in ten minutes. We're heading out to investigate."

"All right." She tucked her phone away and faced Zaid, who was watching her intently. "Our police chief suspect just got blown up on his way home from work."

Zaid's expression darkened. "So what now?"

"I go to Kabul, to try and find out what the hell is going on."

"You taking protection with you?"

She paused. "I assume so. David will handle it."

"I'll go."

He'd been acting overprotective since the bombing. Texting her to check on her. It was starting to annoy her a little, even though the sentiment behind it lit a warm glow inside her. She liked knowing that he cared. "No need. I'm sure David's got it covered."

He wasn't listening, already edging away from her back down the hall. "Gimme ten minutes. I'll go find us some backup." Before she could argue further, he turned and jogged away.

****

SA Reid Prentiss's stomach dropped as soon as he saw the email from his ex sitting in his inbox. He fought back an aggravated sigh and leaned a forearm on the table in the corner of the storeroom where the team had set up the laptop for everyone to use.

Change of plans, it read. Even though he could already guess what it would say, he opened it.

His jaw tightened when he began reading. As per fucking usual, Sarah had screwed with the timeline, and he had no doubt that it was on purpose. Last night he'd finally managed to get her to agree to a Skype call between him and their daughter at oh-nine-hundred Eastern time, so there would be no miscommunication, no chance of him missing it.

My parents have invited us over for a family get together before brunch, so we have to leave here before nine a.m. Sorry.

His jaw ached from the pressure of his teeth grinding together. *Bullshit you are.* Like she hadn't known about it weeks ago? This was par for the course with her. Had been since the day he'd left the marriage.

With a glance at the digital clock on the screen he mentally calculated the eight-and-a-half hour time difference back to D.C. The call he'd fought to set up in advance so he could at least spend some time with his daughter on Christmas Day would now be only a few minutes long—if he was lucky.

Anger and frustration swelled inside him, pushing his mood from bad to worse. He took a deep breath, deleted the email and opened Skype to place the call.

There was dick all he could do about his ex and the way she kept interfering with his attempts to maintain a relationship with their daughter. None of that was Autumn's fault, however. If all he got was a couple of minutes, he'd have to make the most of them.

His heart beat faster as he waited for someone to answer. Had Sarah assumed he hadn't gotten the email and decided to leave early? It would be just like her, using it as an excuse to punish him.

An image popped up on screen. Autumn's excited face appeared, looking far older than nine years old. "Dad! Hey."

And just like that, all his anger vanished. One look at his baby girl, and all was right in his world. "Hey, sweetheart. Merry Christmas."

"Merry Christmas to you too." She leaned closer to the screen, a frown pulling her dark brown eyebrows together. "What time is it there?"

"Just before five in the afternoon."

"Are you going to get a turkey dinner there?"

"I think so. We've been looking forward to it all day."

Her happy expression faded as she gazed back at him through the computer screen. "You look tired."

"I'm fine, sweetie. Did you get my present?"

"Yes, I've got it right here—I wanted you to see me open it." She leaned out of view to grab it. "Did you get mine?"

Now it was his turn to smile. "You sent me something?"

She sat up, giving him an offended look. "Of course I did." Then she lowered her voice, as if she didn't want her mother to overhear. "Max helped me mail it last week. It should have gotten there by now."

Hell of a thing, when the man who replaced him cared more about his relationship with Autumn than Sarah did. "That was nice of him. Don't worry, I'm sure it'll get here in the next day or two."

But Autumn looked genuinely distressed. "It was supposed to be there for today. We paid extra to make sure you got it." Her voice thickened.

"Baby, it's okay. Doesn't matter to me if it's late, it just means the world to me that you'd send me something."

She swallowed and wiped at her eyes before nodding. "I hate that you're all alone over there at Christmas."

His heart squeezed at her concern. "I'm not alone, I've got the guys with me."

A small smile curved the corners of her lips. "Yeah, but they don't get you presents."

"We make do. And we've even got a Christmas tree set up out in the squad room. Wanna see?"

"Yeah."

He lifted the laptop and shoved open the storeroom door so he could pan the camera around to show her the tree. A sturdy broom handle formed the trunk, and it was studded with toilet brushes that had been duct-taped to it—Reid hoped they were unused—with khaki-green shirts and socks rolled up over the "branches" to make it look green. Someone had pilfered a strand of white lights to wind around it, and they'd even hung grenades from the branches as ornaments.

"Pretty awesome, huh?"

Autumn laughed. "That's the ugliest Christmas tree I've ever seen."

"What? We think it looks festive. Kai and Logan put it up the other day."

"Are those…grenades? Real ones?"

Using them broke about a dozen base rules, but what

the hell. "Yep. I think they add a nice touch." He couldn't help but grin at her horrified/fascinated expression, proud that she could identify them in the first place. His baby girl took an active interest in him and what he did for a living. And he'd already put the fear of God into her about drugs and boys. "The team's real busy over here, lots to keep us busy, so don't worry about me."

She rolled her eyes, looking so much like her mother in that instant that it startled him. "I always worry about you, Dad."

A wave of emotion hit him. How could he not love this child with every fiber of his being? "I know you do. But I promise I'll be okay. You know I hate you worrying about me. I just wish I could have spent Christmas with you." He hated being away from her for big events and holidays.

"It's okay. You can't help it."

Reid's throat thickened. It was little things like that, little comments that showed a maturity well beyond her years, that hit him hardest. She never played the pity card or laid guilt trips on him for being away from her so much.

Did she really understand why he was so dedicated to his job? Did she secretly feel like he was always letting her down, or choosing his job over her? The last thing he wanted was for her to constantly stress about his safety.

He swallowed the lump in his throat. "Why don't you open your present so I can see?"

Her expression brightened. "Okay." She set the parcel on the desk and began tearing at the paper to reveal the books he'd bought her. "Wow, you got me the whole Harry Potter series!" she cried.

"Only the best for my little bookworm. And there's something taped to the top of the box, too."

She tipped it toward her and tore off the envelope he'd attached. When she saw the brochure inside it she gasped, her whole face lighting up as she looked back at the computer screen. "*The Wizarding World of Harry Potter*!

You're taking me to Universal *Studios*?!" Her eyes were huge with surprise and hope.

"Yes, ma'am. Orlando, sometime this spring, just you and me. We can hit Disney World while we're there too. I'm back home at the end of March, so we'll set a date for sometime in April. Not Easter, because that would be too busy." Not to mention impossible, since Sarah always insisted Autumn be with her family for the long weekend. "That sound okay to you?"

"Yes! I'm so excited—you're the best dad *ever*." She clutched the brochure to her chest like it was the most precious thing anyone had ever given her and beamed at him.

He winced internally as her words struck him in the heart. *I'm doing my best, baby girl.* But maybe his best wasn't good enough. "Anyway, fill me in on the latest with you. You excited about going skiing over the break?"

"Not really. I'm glad I get time off school, though. You got my pictures from the Christmas play, right?"

He'd replied to her email as soon as he'd received it, but maybe Sarah hadn't told her. "I did, and I wrote back right away. You looked like an *actual* angel."

She laughed. "Dad, all four of us did."

"Nope. The others looked like girls dressed up as angels. You looked like a real one. And you sang like one too."

Her cheeks flushed and she glanced away almost bashfully, but Reid could tell she was pleased by the compliment. He considered it one of his most important tasks as a father to make sure she had a solid sense of confidence and self-worth. "Yeah, okay."

He propped his chin in his hand. "What else have you got planned for the holidays?"

"Oh, you know, the usual. Gifts at Gram and Gramp's after breakfast, then church and over to Uncle Tom's after that. Tomorrow we're going to see Max's parents, and then we—" She stopped and looked behind her as someone entered the room.

Reid fought to keep his expression neutral when he caught sight of the light brown hair and familiar profile at the back of the room. Sarah.

His ex said something to Autumn that he didn't catch, and stood there with her arms folded, a cold expression on her face.

"But Mom, we've only been talking for a few minutes. Can't I have a little more time?"

Sarah gave an emphatic shake of her head. "No. I told you what time we had to leave. Now say goodbye and get in the car. Hurry."

She walked out of view without so much as a *hey, Merry Christmas* or *kiss my ass* to him, and Reid wasn't sorry to see her go. He had to work to put on a smile for his daughter as she turned back to him with a crestfallen expression that broke his heart. "Sorry, Dad. Guess I have to go."

"It's okay." It wasn't okay, it was total bullshit, but again, that wasn't Autumn's problem. He got that Sarah hated being a single parent while he was away; he just wished he could figure out a way to make peace with her so they could all move forward in a healthy way. "It was good to see you and hear your voice. I miss you like crazy."

Autumn's face crumpled and her voice turned rough. "I miss you too, Dad."

Aw, shit, the sight of her fighting back tears just sliced him up inside. "Don't cry, baby. We'll set up another call in a few days or something, okay? And you can always email me."

She nodded, visibly fought back her tears. "Okay. You be safe."

"I will be safe. Promise. Love you, and have a good Christmas."

Her expression was pure misery, nothing like what a little girl's face should look like on Christmas Day, when she should have been beside herself with excitement about what presents might be waiting for her at her grandparents' place. "You too. Love you."

"Bye, sweetheart."

"Bye." She ended the call and the screen went blank.

It felt like his only lifeline to her had just been severed.

Reid closed his eyes and scrubbed a hand over his face, all his emotions tangled in knots and topped off with an avalanche of guilt. He loved his job, loved being part of the team, but at times like this he was never more aware of the damage his career did to the person who mattered to him most.

Autumn was growing up way too fast, turning into a young woman right before his eyes, and too often he only saw it as an observer from thousands of miles away. How many Christmases and birthdays had he missed already that he would never get back?

Too many.

Then he thought of Sarah and her coldness and the rage began to simmer just below the surface. He got why she hated his guts, and why she hated what he did for a living, because in her mind he'd placed that above his family, and that's what ultimately had led to their split.

But they'd been divorced for nearly seven damn years, and since she was supposedly so happy with her new boyfriend Max, then why the hell couldn't she let it go and at least try to be civil? And why use Autumn as a weapon when their little girl wound up suffering as much as him?

"Fuck," he muttered, Autumn's devastated expression burned into his mind as he shoved back from the table and stood. What he wouldn't give for a bottle of Jack right now.

His mouth watered at the idea, his brain lighting up

even all these years later in anticipation of what it could never have again. Alcohol had damn near destroyed his life and he knew better than to give into temptation, even once. One drink was one too many for him now, and he fought that battle every damn day.

"Hey, how's Autumn?"

Reid swung around to find Zaid standing in the doorway of the squad room. "Sad," he muttered, hating himself and this whole situation with Sarah. It wasn't right. "She misses me, and she's worried about me, when all she should be thinking about is what presents she's going to get, or what games she'll play with her cousins this afternoon."

Zaid winced in sympathy. "Sorry, man. You weren't on long with her."

"No. Sarah made sure of that." And if she tried to stop him from taking Autumn to Orlando for a father-daughter trip… Exhaling, he headed for the door and squeezed past Zaid into the hallway.

His teammate followed him out. "Wanted to talk to you about something," Zaid said.

Reid stopped and turned to face him. "Sure, what's up?" He was closest to Zaid of anyone on the team, and Reid had taken to hanging with him whenever he could.

Zaid was a good guy, he cared about everyone on the team, and bonus, he didn't touch alcohol because of his religion. Maybe it made him a selfish prick to use Zaid that way, but it helped to be around someone who never drank. If Zaid suspected that was part of the reason Reid had been spending so much time with him over the past eight months, he'd never said anything.

"A situation's just come up with the investigative team looking for The Jackal. You up for a private security detail for the next few hours?"

Beat the hell out of feeling sorry for himself on Christmas while his daughter was on the other side of the world, and having a duty to perform would help take his mind off everything for a while. "Yeah, sure. Who's it for?"

"Agent Rabani and her team."

Reid wasn't positive, but it sure seemed like his buddy had a thing for her. There was no other explanation for the whole protective routine he was pulling today. Whatever Zaid needed, Reid was more than happy to be his wingman. "Okay. Where we headed?"

Zaid grabbed the door handle and paused to look at him. "Kabul. The guy they thought might be The Jackal just died in a targeted hit outside the police station."

Chapter Seven

The vehicle he and Prentiss rode in jostled over the uneven road as Zaid drove into Kabul. It was full dark now, and that made their presence here even riskier given the present circumstances. Men with evil on their minds loved to come out after dark.

Jaliya and her boss were in the vehicle in front of them. In addition to their driver they also had an armed security agent with them. Along with Zaid and Prentiss, that gave them three hired guns to watch their backs.

Zaid got the feeling that his insistence on accompanying them here had annoyed Jaliya, but he didn't care. He'd rather be here to guard her and risk being overbearing and overprotective than sitting back at base waiting on another assignment with his team and leaving her safety in someone else's hands. Screw that. Thankfully, Taggart had granted him and Prentiss permission to do it.

The flash of emergency vehicle lights up ahead was visible from more than a block away as they approached the special police station. Zaid turned right to follow the other driver toward the main building.

After parking along the curb beyond the security gate he and Prentiss hopped out with their M4s. They maintained careful watch over the area as Jaliya and her boss—both armed with pistols tucked into thigh holsters—met with the acting deputy police chief outside the taped-off perimeter set up outside the headquarters.

The cold air carried the stench of scorched metal from the car burning somewhere behind the building, but he couldn't see it as the acting deputy chief began to lead Jaliya and her boss to the other side of the compound.

To stop them from rounding a blind corner without checking what was on the other side first, Zaid intervened. "Hold it."

The chief and Jaliya looked back at him in surprise but he ignored them and motioned to Prentiss. Together they rounded the corner of the building and swept the area out back where the targeted vehicle sat smoldering. He already didn't like Jaliya being exposed out here; trusting that the cops had cleared the compound properly wasn't happening.

There was no way he was letting either Jaliya or her boss near the explosion site until he was certain it was safe. If militants were responsible for the bombing, it was feasible that more IEDs might be planted nearby. Hitting first responders as they were attending to victims or clearing the site while large crowds gathered around seemed to be a favorite tactic.

His boots crunched over the gravel in the back parking lot as he turned the corner and got his first good look at the vehicle. The fire was long out but the twisted hulk of burned metal that had been the victim's ride was still smoldering next to the small crater beside it.

Looked like the bomb had been small, and either attached to the undercarriage or maybe planted in the ground beneath it, set off remotely or by pressure plate.

Zaid was betting on the former. Whoever had killed him had probably been watching from somewhere on the street, waiting for the vehicle to drive over the IED. One touch of a button on a cell phone, and boom.

Three fire crews stood next to their rigs in full gear while EOD teams scoured the area, looking for other devices. Ten yards from the ruined vehicle, an ambulance crew was busy loading a body bag into the back of a government vehicle. The charred remains of the former chief of special police.

"Got anything?" he asked Prentiss after he'd scanned the surroundings and satisfied himself that everything was secure.

"Negative. We're clear."

Zaid turned around and headed back to where the others waited around the side of the building. "Okay. We're good. Go ahead."

Jaliya gave him a small smile of thanks and nodded before following the deputy chief toward Zaid. "Could anyone on the force have been behind this?" she asked the man in Dari. "A rival maybe, someone who had a grudge against the victim, or someone who didn't like his political views?"

"No," the deputy chief said, his voice adamant. "Absolutely not. He was well-respected by his men and everyone at this office. No, this was done by an outsider."

She translated for her boss before continuing with the questions. "So then why do you think he was targeted? Could he have been involved with something he shouldn't have been? Maybe something to do with The Jackal?"

The man paused and threw her a look of complete disgust. "No. They killed him because he stood up to them. He was a good man. A hero to his people."

Zaid slanted a glance at Jaliya to gauge her response. She was watching the man closely, but her expression gave nothing away about her inner thoughts. She was too smart for that.

He turned his attention back to his security work as she and her boss continued to question the deputy chief. The ambulance holding the deceased's body drove off.

Zaid kept his back to the group behind him and watched everyone else, taking note of their positions and their movements. He was relieved when Jaliya and the others finally turned back and went inside the building, though he kept watch from inside as well, not about to let his guard down. For all they knew, someone within these very walls had helped plan or maybe even carried out the attack.

Jaliya, her boss and the deputy chief disappeared into an office a couple minutes later, leaving him and Prentiss standing guard out in the hallway.

Prentiss looked over at him from the other side of the door. "Think the vic was The Jackal?"

"No clue." Was possible though. Maybe there was some serious infighting going on in The Jackal's ranks.

The minutes ticked by as he and Prentiss stood sentry in the hall. What he wouldn't give to be a fly on the wall inside that office right now, while Jaliya kept peppering the deputy chief with questions, trying to piece together what had happened, and maybe even catch the other man in a lie.

Zaid wanted to know what was going on as badly as she and her boss did. If the dead guy had been The Jackal, then problem solved for the moment. "Guess we'll find out within the next few days. If his network and shipments are disrupted going forward, then it was him. It's possible he's already got a few lined up that can still take place without him coordinating everything. But if he's dead, sooner or later, there'll be a major disruption in the chain of command and the operations."

The death of a leader like that always left a vacuum in his absence. Maybe it would allow Jaliya's team enough time to track down someone in the network before someone else took over the operation, and collar the organization once and for all.

Prentiss nodded and went back to scanning the hall as uniformed cops passed them with hard looks they both ignored. "And if it's not him? They got any other promising leads?"

"They've got a few others." He'd seen the pictures on the wall earlier. "Not sure how promising they are, since I didn't get all the details."

His buddy's mouth twitched in the hint of a grin. "Bet Agent Rabani would tell you if you asked."

Zaid shot him a hard look but Prentiss didn't make eye contact, so he let it drop, not wanting to talk about her. Prentiss was observant, and it shouldn't have surprised Zaid that his buddy had picked up on Zaid's interest in or protectiveness toward her, but Zaid didn't want anyone talking about her or speculating about what was going on between them. He wouldn't allow her reputation to be tarnished.

After about forty minutes, the door finally opened and Jaliya and her boss came out. Zaid looked at her, taking in her self-assured gait and posture. The woman moved with a confidence that was damn sexy. "All done?"

She nodded. "For now. You guys ready to head back?"

"Sure. Just let me contact your driver." Zaid pulled his cell out and dialed the guy, double checked to make sure everything was still secure outside. "Yep," he told the others, "we're good to go."

Outside on the front steps of the building, Jaliya's phone rang. Zaid paused to look back at her. She pulled it out and stopped when she glanced at the screen, the overhead lights showing a slight tension taking over her body.

He moved fast, grasping her arm and pulling her into the shadows beside the building, his only thought getting her out of the light so she wasn't an easy target for anyone lurking out here and hoping to take a shot at her.

Her dark eyes flashed up to his, a little annoyed. "I need to take this," she argued, trying to pull her arm free as she raised the phone to her ear with her free hand.

"You can take it once you're off these steps," he told her, and hustled her down and into the relative safety of the shadows. She followed, barely paying attention to him.

"Barakat," she said, causing Zaid and her boss to look at her sharply. He'd called her? There was no way she'd given him her personal cell number. Maybe she'd had another number forwarded to it. And this must be important, for him to miraculously overcome his earlier dislike of her. "Where are you?"

Zaid kept moving her toward the vehicle. The driver had pulled it up to the main gate and waited with the engine running.

But Jaliya dug in her heels and twisted away from Zaid a few yards from the main gate. She shook her head adamantly at him when he tried to grab her arm again, and began speaking in rapid Dari.

Zaid and Prentiss immediately went back into sentry mode, watching for threats while she continued her conversation. Her voice was clipped, her posture tense. "No, he's not all right," she told Barakat. "His body is on its way to the morgue right now. What do you know about it?"

Her boss stood a few paces from the gate, eyes glued to her. "Where is he?"

Jaliya shook her head at him and continued to talk. "No. No deal. The intel you gave us before? Useless. We sent a team out to the site you gave me and there was nothing there." Her mouth compressed into a thin line as she listened to whatever Barakat said next. "I don't think so. You expect me or anyone else to listen to you after what happened? No. Your words carry no weight with me."

A tense pause followed. Jaliya's gaze flicked between Zaid and her boss. "All right, I'm willing to meet with you. Right now. At a location of my choosing." She named an address Zaid wasn't familiar with, but he guessed it was somewhere in the city. "Twenty minutes. Come alone. If you don't show up, or if you feed me more lies once you get there, I promise you'll wish you'd never taken my call that first time."

She hung up and strode for the truck, an air of palpable excitement radiating from her. "He's meeting us in twenty at a café a few miles from here."

Her boss raised his eyebrows. "Us?" He shook his head. "I'm due back at Bagram within the hour, so I'm already going to be late as it is. With this assassination under investigation, I can't push back the meeting."

"But he says he's got intel that could help our investigation. He said The Jackal is still alive."

David cursed under his breath. "And what if he's straight up lying again, just to get more money?"

"Or trying to lure you in for a kidnapping or targeted hit?" Zaid said, unimpressed by Barakat's sudden change of heart about "helping" them.

She turned her head to stare at him, her expression unflinching. "I need to meet with him. I want to see his face and read his body language."

In other words, she was going with him, or without him. His choice.

Her boss's gaze shifted to Zaid and Prentiss. "Can you go with her?"

What? Zaid stared at him. He was seriously going to allow her to jeopardize her safety for a meeting with this little asshole?

"We've got our own security with us, so you and Prentiss can stay with Jaliya. If your team can spare you a while longer," David added.

Since the guy outranked him, Zaid kept what he was really thinking to himself. "You sure about this?"

David glanced at Jaliya, then back at him. "Yeah. You guys will escort her to the meeting. If it feels off, get out of there. If it feels okay, make it fast, find out what the kid knows—if anything—and leave. Call me with an update as soon as you're done. If he really does have something for us, I want to move fast."

"Okay." Jaliya looked over at Zaid. "Where did you park?"

Zaid couldn't believe they were doing this. He wanted to put her in the truck and drive her straight back to Bagram. But if she insisted on going through with this meet, then he was going with her. "You good with this?" he asked Prentiss.

His buddy nodded once. "Yeah. I'll call Hamilton, let him know what's going on and see what he says."

"Okay." He waited while his teammate made the call. There hadn't been anything scheduled when he'd left base, and neither Hamilton nor Taggart had called them back in, but something might have come up in the past couple hours.

Prentiss ended the call and put his phone in his pocket. "Got a green light."

Guess we're doing this, then. Zaid turned to Jaliya, trying to be all business and ignore the invisible pull she had over him. "Stay close to me, and don't get in the truck until we check it."

She frowned at his brusque tone, but didn't argue. "Fine."

His senses were on high alert as he, Jaliya and Prentiss headed for the truck, parked outside the main gates behind the other agency vehicle. He made Jaliya stay back about twenty yards on the sidewalk while he and Prentiss checked to make sure no one had tampered with the vehicle or rigged it with wires or explosives. Only when he was satisfied that he wouldn't blow them up by turning the ignition did he go back for her and escort her to the rear driver's side door.

Once she was settled he scanned the street before climbing behind the wheel and starting the engine, while Prentiss rode shotgun. "Where are we headed?" he asked her.

In the rearview mirror her dark eyes sparkled with excitement in the glow of the streetlights, the thrill of the hunt revving her up. They were more alike than he'd realized, and she was unlike any woman he'd ever met. More daring. Ballsy, even. On her, it was sexy as hell.

"Go north for two blocks, then take a left," she said.

Zaid followed her directions, winding them through the darkened streets of the crowded city center while Prentiss kept watch of what was going on around them. "You think the kid knows anything?" he asked Jaliya. Zaid had his doubts. Serious doubts, and he just hoped the kid wasn't luring them into a trap of some sort.

"He'd better."

Yeah, no joke. "How do we know he isn't working for someone else now?"

"We don't." She gave him a little smile, her dark eyes holding a distinct gleam of anticipation. "Thanks for this. I feel way better with you guys coming with me."

Her admission surprised him a little, because she always seemed so fearless. "Welcome. But just so we're clear, I'm not leaving you alone with him at any time." He didn't care if she didn't like it. That's how it was going to be.

"Good. I need the intel he has, but I don't trust him."

Neither did Zaid. And even though he disliked this situation, he had to admit he admired her bravery and dedication. "Are you always this determined?"

Her lips twitched as she stared out the windshield. "I

think so, at least when it comes to getting what I want."

Wish you wanted me that badly. He didn't dare say it aloud.

"I usually do, though. My father says I've always been headstrong."

She claimed to have lots of friction with him, but she sure talked about him a lot. Whatever their history, she obviously loved and respected him a great deal. "What does your mom do, anyway? I never asked."

"She teaches classical studies at a college. Yours?"

"We're blue collar all the way. My mom has a cleaning business and my dad's a mechanic. Their English still isn't the greatest, even though they emigrated from here to the States when my mom was pregnant with me."

Jaliya nodded. "Learning a new language as an adult is hard."

True.

"Wait, your old man's a mechanic? Then how come you suck with mechanical stuff?" Prentiss asked.

"I don't suck at it, I'm just not as talented with machines as I am at patching up human bodies."

Prentiss chuckled under his breath. "If you say so."

Okay, a change of subject was in order before his ego took a beating in front of the woman he was trying to make an awesome impression on. Zaid glanced up to meet Jaliya's eyes in the rearview. "Were your parents born in the U.K.?"

"My mom was. Dad's family was originally from right here in Kabul."

He shook his head. "Man, the changes our parents have seen here over the last few decades must have been mind-blowing."

"Yeah, the country's barely recognizable to the one they grew up in. It's one of the reasons I took this job. I hate what's happened over here and I wanted to make a difference."

"Trying to make the world a better place."

Their gazes connected in the mirror once more, and at his words her expression froze for an instant before closing up. Almost as though she was hiding something. "Exactly," she murmured, looking away.

Make the world a better place. His gut tingled as that same phrase echoed in his mind, from a conversation he'd had months ago with the woman he'd met online.

He dismissed it and picked up the thread of conversation. "Me too. Prentiss, what about you? Why'd you take on this gig?"

"I get to play with some pretty cool toys in this job, and my teammates rock even if the assignments don't always. Also, drugs suck."

They totally did. "Right. Don't do drugs."

Even painkillers could be the start of a slippery slope for a lot of people. For that reason he never gave a patient a higher dosage than absolutely necessary during treatment and transport. Not unless they were going to die and the only act of kindness was to pump them so full of meds that they didn't suffer in their last few minutes on earth. His hands tightened around the steering wheel as ghostly faces flashed in his mind.

Pushing them aside, he glanced in the mirror again. Jaliya was watching him, the touch of her gaze a low-grade tingle beneath his skin.

"Do your parents support your job?" she asked.

"In FAST, you mean? Or the agency in general?"

"Both."

"Yeah, they do. They're proud that I'm trying to make a difference for the people here and back home by cutting off funding to terrorist organizations and cartels. But they don't love how dangerous it is." He took in her profile for a second as she gazed out the window before focusing back on the road. "Why, you don't think yours support your job?"

She made a face. "They like that I'm fighting for what I believe in, but they'd always hoped I'd pick something more academic." She tossed a grin at him. "More white collar."

"So they're snobs," he teased.

She laughed and he smiled in reflex. "When it comes to professions, yes, I guess they are. Mostly I think they just worry about me all the time. They want me to be safe, and to them that means a comfy, boring desk job back in the States."

I want you safe, too. It's why I'm here. But he would never want her to give up a job she was so well suited for and obviously loved, even if it was dangerous. He might not like that she was in danger, but he'd learn to deal with it.

"I guess that's just something parents never stop doing—worrying about us." He loved her laugh. And her voice, her cute British accent. Her dedication to her job and that she was a team player.

"Maybe. And, I guess you've probably noticed by now that I hate any kind of misogynistic bullshit."

"I had, yes," he answered with a straight face.

"I noticed that too, by the way," Prentiss said with a wry smile.

She gave a soft chuckle that went straight to Zaid's gut. "My parents and sisters share my view on that, but they hate that I'm so vocal about it. They think I should fight quietly and not be so...brash about it."

"But then you wouldn't be you," Zaid said.

She turned her head to meet his gaze in the mirror then, and for a split second there was such unguarded gratefulness on her face that it sent a wave of tenderness through him. He wished they'd been alone and not riding in a vehicle so he could hug her.

"That's exactly it." She paused a moment, as if searching for the right words. "I tried to fit into their mold when I was younger, I really did, but I felt suffocated. We all love each other, even if my father can't say the words, so that made it easier when I broke with tradition and went my own way."

The friction with her father was starting to make a lot more sense now. "How many sisters?"

"Two. I'm the middle."

He grinned. "It's always the middle child."

She shot him a playful glare. "What are you, then, the perfect eldest?"

"Nope. Only. Perfect? My mom thinks so. Although my cousin did come to live with us for a few years when I was in my teens, and she was like a sibling."

"Was?"

His stomach muscles grabbed. "She…passed away the year she was supposed to graduate." He'd never gotten over it. Or over the feeling that he could have—should have—done more to save her.

"Oh, I'm so sorry. What happened?"

Prentiss already knew the story, so Zaid didn't mind telling her with him here. "Her ex wouldn't take no for an answer, refused to believe they were done. So he ran her car off the road and shot her twice in the chest as she lay there pinned in the wreck."

"Oh my God, how awful. Is he in jail?"

It had been the darkest time of Zaid's life, knowing that he hadn't done enough to protect her. "Yes. I think about her all the time. She had the purest heart of anyone I've ever known. Maybe she was too good for this earth."

"That's the nicest compliment I've ever heard someone give another person."

Well, it was the truth.

They lapsed into silence for a few minutes as he drove them deeper into the city.

"We gettin' warm yet?" Prentiss asked finally, checking the GPS on his phone.

"Take a right at the third street up," Jaliya said.

Zaid did, and she swiveled in her seat to peer out her window at the buildings they passed. "Just up here on the right, about twenty metres—yards, I mean. Yes, there he is." She pointed.

Zaid glanced over in time to see Barakat appear out of an alleyway and walk toward the building. He watched carefully to make sure no one was with him. "I want to drive around the block first, see if we have any other company." Both his and Prentiss's phones had tracking beacons in them, so Hamilton or Taggart would be able to follow their position, just in case.

"All right." She unbuckled her seatbelt and got to one knee to reach for the opposite door, ready to open it. He wouldn't have been human if he didn't steal a glance at her sweet, round ass in the rearview mirror as she did.

Jerking his gaze back to the road, he continued past the café, turned left at the next street and doubled back around, checking for a tail. At this time of night there weren't many people walking around—all of them men—but nothing tweaked his internal radar. Barakat was slouched against the far brick wall of the café, watching them when Zaid pulled up.

"We good?" he asked Prentiss.

"Yep."

Jaliya opened the rear passenger door. "Get in," she told him in Dari, pistol in her free hand.

Zaid lowered his right hand to the sidearm on his hip and kept careful watch while the kid got into the back, even though Prentiss already had her covered. Zaid didn't question the territorial urge he felt toward her.

As soon as their passenger was aboard, he hit the gas. "Where we headed?" he asked Jaliya in English.

"Wherever. Just keep driving around while I talk to him." She turned to Barakat, and when Zaid flicked a glance in the rearview mirror, the kid was looking nervously at her weapon. "What have you got to say for yourself?" she demanded in Dari.

"I didn't lie," he insisted. "I did not," he said more forcefully when she raised an eyebrow at him. "I was told The Jackal would be in the village that night."

"Well, he wasn't. And not only that, we reviewed satellite imagery of the area for the week prior and every day since our last meeting, and he still hasn't shown up. No weapons or drugs, either."

Barakat folded his arms across his chest and seemed to curl into himself as he leaned against the corner of the door, keeping as much distance between himself and Jaliya as possible. "He should have been there," he muttered.

Jaliya let out an irritated sigh. "What about tonight? Have you heard anything about who planted the bomb?"

"It was The Jackal."

"How do you know that?"

He shrugged. "Everyone knows it's true."

Zaid mentally rolled his eyes. Seriously? That's the best the kid could come up with in terms of evidence? Zaid had half a mind to pull over right there and throw him out on his ass.

"Why would he want to kill such a high-profile victim? He was the chief of the special police," Jaliya said.

"Because he was working with The Jackal. And The Jackal was afraid he would talk."

Whoa. Zaid met Jaliya's eyes in the mirror for a moment before she focused back on Barakat. Prentiss would only be picking up words and phrases from the conversation at most, but he would be able to tell from her tone that Jaliya wasn't taking any bullshit.

"You have proof?" Jaliya demanded.

"I overheard a conversation. I recorded it on my phone." Barakat held it out to her.

She took it. "Who else is working with The Jackal?" she pressed.

"Lots of people. I don't know how many."

"How many people in a position of authority are working for him?"

"All of them."

It confirmed what Zaid already suspected, and what Jaliya must have as well—that The Jackal had his hooks into the majority of officials in Kabul and beyond. It was the only way he could have pulled off smuggling operations on that scale without anyone stopping him. Corruption was rife in this country. It was one of the main factors hampering their efforts at uncovering and locating The Jackal.

"Who is The Jackal, Barakat?" Jaliya's voice was hard as iron.

"I don't know," he muttered. "I only heard rumors in the last few days."

"I want names. Whoever you heard about, give me their names."

A long, tense pause followed. "I don't know if any of it's true."

"I'll find out whether it is or not. Their *names*, Barakat. The more you give me, the more I give you in terms of money and protection."

"Hey, two o'clock," Prentiss murmured to him.

Before Zaid could answer, a small, beat-up pickup zipped out into the intersection ahead of them and stopped perpendicular to them, blocking the road. Zaid hit the brakes, a warning prickle lifting the hairs on his nape. He glanced in the rearview mirror but there was no one behind them.

Prentiss sat still beside him, his attention riveted to the pickup.

"Barakat, did you tell someone you were meeting me?" Jaliya demanded, her voice stern.

"No, I swear."

Zaid paid only partial attention to the conversation, half-turning in his seat to look through the rear window. The street behind them was clear and there was no one on the sidewalks. When he looked frontward again the pickup driver had turned the truck to face them head on, and was speeding toward them down the center of the street.

Prentiss was already lifting his M4 from the foot well. *Shit.*

Either the kid was lying, or someone had followed him here without Barakat knowing. Either way, Zaid was getting them the hell out of here.

"Hang on," Zaid muttered, swiveling in his seat to look over his right shoulder as he hit the gas. The engine responded with a throaty roar and shot them backward.

Prentiss peered out the windshield. "He's gaining on us."

Zaid didn't answer, all his concentration on reversing to the nearest exit off this street as fast as possible without getting into a wreck. His boot had the accelerator pinned to the floor. The SUV's engine screamed as he raced through the darkness, turning the wheel sharply to avoid cars parked along the curb.

"He's pulling a weapon. Down!" Prentiss barked.

Zaid vaguely saw his teammate reach back to push Jaliya downward, but she was already shoving Barakat flat onto the back seat. Zaid scanned for an exit, but the nearest street to turn onto was still at least forty yards away.

"Shooter," Prentiss warned.

A heartbeat later bullets pinged off the front end of the armored SUV. Sparks flew, little flashes of light in his peripheral vision.

Dammit...

A round struck the windshield, cracking the glass but

not punching through it.

Screw this.

"Hold on tight," Zaid warned as the upcoming street loomed closer.

A moment later he hit the brakes and wrenched the wheel to the right, swerving them backward in a tight arc onto the cross street. He didn't have time to shift into drive and pull out to get ahead of the pickup—it was nearly on top of them.

"Want me to take out the driver?" Prentiss asked.

"No." If it had been just the two of them Zaid would have driven straight at the fucker so Prentiss could smoke him, but he wouldn't put Jaliya and her informant at further risk. The safest option was to lose the shooter.

Zaid hit the accelerator again, rocketing them backward down the darkened side street. It was narrow, with a crap ton of obstacles in their path. The back bumper smashed into a garbage bin, knocking it flying. He veered left to avoid another vehicle, just as the bright beam of a headlight cut down the alleyway in front of him.

"He's gonna fire again," Prentiss said.

Two more bullets struck the windshield.

Jaliya popped her head up, staying out of Zaid's line of sight as she peered forward between the front seats. "Any other vehicles with them?" Her voice was surprisingly calm.

"Negative," Prentiss answered, his hands steady on his weapon, no doubt itching to roll down his window and shoot back.

The alleyway opened up into a street. Zaid floored it, hoping to gain some distance on the pickup.

"He's falling back a little now," Prentiss said.

Zaid didn't let up on the gas, kept going until a car pulled out behind them. He slammed on the brakes and veered left, narrowly missing it, and careened up onto the sidewalk. Something else crashed off the back bumper, but now he could see an upcoming street.

As soon as he reached it he swerved backward into it, shifted into Drive and slammed his foot down on the accelerator, hunkering in his seat to see between the cracks in the windshield. The SUV lurched forward in a powerful surge that shot them into the darkness.

Prentiss slung around to look behind them but Jaliya beat him to it. "I got him," she said, peering out the rear window. "He's still coming, but you've got almost a block on him now."

Time for some slick evasive maneuvers.

Zaid took a hard right at the next street, the back end sliding on the pavement as he made the turn, then a sharp left two streets after that.

"He missed the turn," Prentiss said.

Not trusting that the threat was over, Zaid sped through the darkened warren of streets, zig-zagging back and forth in an effort to lose their tail.

"No sign of him now," Jaliya said thirty seconds later, her voice full of relief.

Zaid wasn't counting on their hostile welcoming committee giving up so easily. "I'm getting us the hell out of here."

"Good plan," Prentiss muttered as Jaliya let out a sigh of relief.

In the rearview mirror Zaid glimpsed Barakat finally sitting up. Jaliya was glaring a hole through the kid, and when she spoke her normally sexy voice was like ice. "We'll take him with us back to base," she said to him and Prentiss in English, "and find out whether that welcoming party was meant for him, or for us."

Chapter Eight

Jaliya's insides were still buzzing with the aftereffects of adrenaline from that car chase back in Kabul when she finally got Barakat settled in an interrogation room at Bagram seventy minutes later. He claimed he was innocent of any wrongdoing and had nothing to do with the attack, that he'd told no one about their meeting, for fear of reprisal for colluding with the enemy.

She didn't trust him, but her gut told her he was telling the truth about that at least. He'd been visibly terrified when the shooter had opened up on the SUV, flinching every time a bullet hit it, cowering flat on the seat with his arms over his head while muttering prayers to himself.

Not exactly the actions of someone who had expected the attack. So someone had either followed him to the meeting, or they'd followed her, Zaid and Prentiss there.

On the hour-long drive here, Barakat had given her another tip her team was investigating right now. Another possible suspect in the frustrating game of *Find The Jackal*. And another possible location for a large shipment, headed through Kandahar this time.

If, and only *if* her team could back up the intel about Kandahar, they had to get teams down there to check it out tonight.

When she was a few steps from the main door, David came through it with Colonel Shah and one of his men. "Jaliya." He seemed to sag a little in relief, then raked a worried gaze over her. "You really okay?"

"We're all fine." Thanks to Zaid and his expert driving. She hadn't had a chance to thank him for it. "I've got our young friend waiting for you in the usual room." She nodded behind her.

His expression hardened. "Good. I'll see you in the briefing room when we're done. Everyone's on the way there."

"Perfect." Her blood was up. So much so she barely felt the cold as she exited the building and headed back to her temporary quarters.

She wanted answers. If tonight's attack was linked to the hotel bombing, then it meant someone wanted her dead. She was going to disappoint them.

"Jaliya."

At the sound of that familiar, deep voice behind her, she stopped and spun around. Zaid was striding toward her at a rapid pace, probably just having filed a report at the vehicle depot, detailing the sequence of events tonight, and the damage to the SUV.

"Hey." Her pulse accelerated at the sight of him.

He rushed up to her, his tall form throwing a long shadow over the cold, frozen ground. "Are they questioning him now?"

"Yes. Meanwhile, our teams are being assembled in the briefing room. We're trying to verify whether his story about Kandahar has any truth in it. If so, you guys are going to have to move fast."

He nodded and ran an assessing gaze over her face for a moment, then glanced left and right before grasping her hand. "Come with me." He tugged.

"Where are we going?" she blurted, trailing after him. They had an important meeting to get to.

He didn't answer, just led her to a shadowy area between two small buildings and crowded her against the wall of one, moving in tight until his body was pressed to hers from chest to pelvis.

The breath backed up in her lungs, and any protest she might have made died in her throat. With him this close and her still revved up from earlier, she craved his touch and the feel of his mouth on hers. Reaffirming that he cared, proving that she was safe. She curved her hands around his thick shoulders and peered up at him in the dimness.

A tiny amount of illumination cast by an overhead light somewhere far to the left lit his profile and glinted off his dark beard, allowing her to see his taut expression and the intense gleam in his eyes. Hunger.

A surge of desire swept through her, sweet and hot, spreading out from where his hips pressed into her lower belly. The thick outline of his erection made her pulse thud and her mouth go dry.

He didn't say a word and he didn't need to—the look on his face mirrored everything she was thinking, feeling. They wanted each other, and all the reasons they shouldn't get involved didn't mean anything now. She didn't dare speak for fear of shattering the spell and the heady rush of anticipation that made her skin prickle with a million goose bumps.

Staring into her eyes while the tension between them intensified, his body heat wrapping around her in a sensual cocoon, Zaid raised one big hand to cradle her cheek. The show of tenderness in the face of all that hunger undid her.

"Wait," she blurted. She couldn't kiss him again without telling him the truth. It would be wrong otherwise.

He froze and searched her eyes questioningly. "What?"

"It was me you met online. I used my middle name for my profile. Yasmine."

He stared down at her in bewilderment. "You…?" He seemed at a loss for words, and she didn't blame him. "Are you serious?"

She nodded and bit her lip, waiting for him to say something else. Praying he wouldn't be too mad.

Confusion filled his expression, and the spark of anger that ignited in his eyes made her wince inside. "What the *hell*? Why didn't you say something before?"

She groped frantically for a way to defuse this. "I didn't know for sure until we talked this afternoon, and then I wasn't sure what to say."

"But you suspected? All this time and you never said anything?"

It sounded really bad, she had to admit. "Yes. And then I felt too awkward to tell you. I'm sorry." The sorry was important, and she hoped he believed it was sincere.

His brows crashed together in a fierce scowl, her apology doing nothing to neutralize the situation. "Why? Why'd you bail on me like that? I thought we had something real happening."

God, her reasoning sounded so stupid now. "We did. Then you wrote something and I…jumped to the wrong conclusion."

"Huh?" He scowled harder. "What did I write?"

She blew out a breath. "That the man should wear the pants in the relationship."

He stared at her in stunned silence for a moment, then exploded, "I was *joking*."

She winced. "I know that now, but I didn't then. I thought you were like the guys my dad kept trying to push on me. Controlling and conservative and…"

His jaw flexed, the angry gleam in his eye making her want to squirm. "A dick."

She gave him a sheepish smile. "Yeah. But now I know you're not like that."

He shook his head and pulled in a deep breath, as though having trouble putting it all together. "So you're saying I lost the chance of getting together with you months ago because of a misunderstanding over a goddamn *joke*?"

Okay, he was still mad. Maybe if she apologized again— "Yes. But we're together now."

As soon as the words came out she cursed silently. Crap, she hadn't meant to say that. She was supposed to be distancing herself from him, not giving him the green light to move forward in whatever this…thing happening between them was.

She rushed on. "And I really am sorry about all that. Truly." She gazed up at him in earnest, hoping he would get over it. She couldn't bear him being angry with her. Not after everything that had happened.

The anger faded and his expression softened. "Yeah. We're together now," he murmured, studying her face intently before settling his gaze on hers once more. "And if you think I'm letting you walk away from me a second time, you're dead wrong," he muttered, and brought his mouth down on hers.

Even though she was hoping for the kiss, the bolt of hunger that shot through her took her completely off guard. Her knees wobbled, her entire body melting until only the wall at her back and Zaid at her front held her upright.

He wasn't gentle. And she didn't want him to be.

As though driven by a need to claim her, reassure himself that they were both whole and alive after the attack, he plunged his tongue between her lips, taking total possession of her mouth. She didn't resist, needing that same reassurance, because it was Zaid. The man who made her feel safe, who made her heart and body sing.

Strong hands curved over her shoulders and slid down her back, learning her shape, pulling her closer so that all her curves were melded with the hard planes of his body. Jaliya moaned into his mouth as sensation splintered through her, every nerve ending exploding to life, her nipples hard and aching, wetness forming between her thighs.

Even in her relative inexperience she recognized this for what it was: a claim being staked. If she'd been clear-headed and enacting her original plan to keep her distance, that possessiveness would have made her bristle. Instead it made her melt, and there was no way she could think with the feel and taste of him making her mind go blank of everything but the deep, pulsing need inside her.

Desperate for more of him, she clung to the hard planes of his back and shoulders as she stroked her tongue against his, letting herself get lost in him, in this moment. He made it way too easy to forget the rest of the world. To forget that they had only a short time left together, and how much it would hurt when he left.

When he broke the kiss to stare down at her a minute later, one hand cupping her nape, she was dizzy and weak, her body on fire as she gasped for breath. All she could think about was finding a private room where she could peel his clothes off and explore that hard, powerful body with her hands and mouth.

Holy crap.

Breathing hard, her heart knocking against her ribs, she playfully narrowed her eyes at him and tried to dial back the hunger roaring through her. "Still not sleeping with you." The words were too breathless to be convincing, but she still felt the need to say them. Just so he didn't think she was caving on her principles.

His teeth flashed white in the dimness as he grinned.

"Glad you're sticking to your guns. But I'm still gonna do everything in my power to change your mind on that."

She huffed out a weak laugh, both relieved and disappointed when he released her and stepped back. Clearing her throat, she reached up to make sure her hijab was still in place for the meeting they had to hurry to. Wearing it gained her at least a modicum of respect from the locals.

She drew in a deep breath, let it out slowly to calm herself. "Well. That was quite an eventful evening. Thank you for getting us out of there so fast."

He stroked his thumb across her cheek. "I'm just glad you're safe now."

His words hit a deeply buried part of her that she guarded closely. The truth was, she wouldn't have felt that safe with anyone else. Even while the bullets had been flying, she'd been scared, but she'd had complete faith in Zaid's ability to get them clear of the threat. And she'd been right.

When he kept staring at her she flushed and struggled to gather her scattered wits. "Well. We'd better get to the briefing." They all had more work to do tonight. Finding The Jackal was her team's number one priority.

He nodded once and they crossed the base together while she stemmed the urge to reach for his hand, to link their fingers together just to feel connected to him. When they got into the briefing room, everyone was already there except for David and the two men he'd taken with him to question Barakat.

Zaid joined his teammates on the far side of the room to talk amongst themselves while Jaliya, Commander Taggart, Colonel Shah and General Nasar gathered around a table strewn with intelligence reports and satellite images. The reports coming back from her team said that Barakat's intel seemed solid. A few helo crews were present as well, including SA Tess Dubrovski, who

Jaliya had met twice before, and her copilot. They'd be flying the FAST and NIU teams to the insertion point.

When she had verified all the latest intel and had everything ready to go, she put two fingers in her mouth and let out a shrill whistle to get everyone's attention. Barakat better not be playing them, or he'd be sorry.

"Thank you all for coming on such short notice," she began. "Since you've already been briefed on the latest intel, let's get right to it. Our informant has identified the site of a drop scheduled to happen at oh-two-hundred hours, down near Kandahar, and our team has pieced together intelligence saying the same. If we're right, this is going to be a big one. No word on whether The Jackal will be handling it himself, but if we can capture some of his men, we may be able to find out who he is and get a lock on his location."

Right now there were just too many unknowns for them to narrow down their list of suspects any more. They needed a big break, and they were sure as hell due for one.

Using the maps and satellite imagery she outlined the village and the routes leading to and away from it, then spoke to the helo crews. The urge to look at Zaid was strong, but she squelched it.

"Your insertion point will be here," she told the pilots, indicating a spot on the topography map on the table. "The teams will insert and approach the village on foot. You're to fall back and wait within easy reach of the village. If all goes smoothly and the village is declared secure, you'll extract them from there, along with any prisoners and contraband seized."

Hopefully a crap ton of drugs and at least someone who knew The Jackal personally.

Commander Taggart took over from there, going over the operation in detail with his team while General Nasar and Colonel Shah watched on, saying little as one of Shah's men translated for the NIU. "The NIU will take care of the arrests while you carry out the search and seizure," Taggart told FAST Bravo.

Jaliya listened to his instructions while the low-grade buzz of nerves that always hit her prior to an operation she was involved with intensified in the pit of her stomach. Against her will, her gaze strayed to Zaid on the other side of the table.

He was focused on his commander, both hands braced on the tabletop as he leaned over it, the stance emphasizing the muscles in his arms and shoulders. Muscles that only a matter of minutes ago had held her tight against his equally hard body.

A large knot seemed to lodge in her chest and her mind began working overtime. Was this intel accurate? Had Barakat told them the truth, or had he just made up a story to get her off his back? That risk always came with the territory. Everyone on the taskforce understood it, even though her team had agreed this target looked solid.

Zaid and his teammates, along with the NIU and the flight crews, were executing this op based on her recommendation, and acting on the intel she'd provided. She wasn't directing it or solely responsible, but she was responsible enough. If anything went wrong, or if this one ended in failure like last time…

She shook away the thought and attempted to quiet her busy mind. Zaid and his team were pros. They would be careful, and this time, the drugs and weapons would be there.

Right at that moment Zaid glanced up and caught her looking.

Jaliya lowered her gaze and fought the blush working up into her cheeks. Her personal feelings for him didn't matter here. She couldn't give him any more focus than she would give any other member of the taskforce, or she would risk others figuring out that something was going on between them. Also, she didn't want to distract him when his and his teammate's lives depended on planning this op carefully.

Taggart addressed the flight crews next, reiterating some of what Jaliya had said earlier, and adding a few more things. "Any questions?" he asked as he finished.

Agent Dubrovski shook her head, her honey-blond hair wound into a sleek knot at the nape of her neck above the collar of her flight suit. "No, sir." She and the others left for the flight line, where the crew chiefs were already busy checking and readying both Blackhawks.

Jaliya answered some questions from the FAST Bravo guys, and one from General Nasar about the expected size of the anticipated shipment, conscious of Zaid's eyes on her the whole time.

After the NIU left to get kitted up for the coming op, FAST Bravo conducted their own meeting. Jaliya stood off to one side, remaining out of their way but close by if any of them needed her to clarify a point.

It was fascinating to watch them. So different from the conventional units she'd worked with before, their process very similar to SOF units. Less authoritarian, more democratic.

Rather than having Taggart or even Hamilton dictate how things would go, all the members were involved in the discussion, and even though the chain of command was clear and everyone deferred to both Hamilton and Taggart, each man had his say.

"All right, boys," Taggart finished a few minutes later, straightening. "Go suit up and be ready to hit the flight line at oh-one-twenty."

The team filed out of the room after its commander, but Zaid hung back, waiting by the door for her when she'd gathered up all her files. "Will you be watching from the TOC?" he asked her.

She wanted so badly to pull him back into the room and slam the door shut so they could be alone for even another minute, just so she could kiss him again. Run her hands all over the hard muscles beneath his shirt. Tell him without words how much she cared about him, that she would worry about him when he was out there, and silently beg him to come back unharmed.

But that would take her one step closer to the point of no return with him, and that was a place she couldn't go. She wasn't ready to make herself that vulnerable to him, or to risk losing her heart when their lives and careers were too different to make any hope of a relationship possible.

"Yes." She would be there the entire time, and not leave until they'd landed safely back at Bagram. They were risking their lives because she and her team had convinced command that this operation was necessary.

She prayed they were right.

He headed for the exit with her, his sheer presence and masculine energy holding her spellbound. "So, we didn't get to have our game night."

"I'd forgotten all about it."

One side of his mouth tipped up. "Well, we kinda had a lot on our minds tonight. Anyway, the guys never got around to it anyway. You busy tomorrow night? They're planning for it after dinner. It'll be like a secret date," he added, his eyes brimming with amusement.

She really shouldn't. Especially not with whatever was happening between them increasing in intensity. Certainly not when her job required her to provide intel that sent him and his team into potentially deadly situations each time they went on an op to investigate her team's findings.

He gave her shoulder a friendly nudge. "What, you already got a better offer or something?"

That made her grin. "Not sure yet." She should have just said no, made some excuse. But she couldn't. She was already too addicted to him to stay away. And on some level that scared the hell out of her, but at that moment she just didn't care.

"It'll be fun," he coaxed.

Probably, but all she cared about was being able to spend time with him. "No promises. But I'll see what I can do."

His answering smile made her heart squeeze. "I'll look forward to it." He stopped to open the exterior door for her. A blast of cold air slapped her in the face, instantly clearing her head. In the space of a heartbeat she was back in work mode.

The wind was picking up again. Might affect visibility for the flight crews, and the team members on the ground once they inserted.

Stepping through the doorway, she paused. She was heading right to the TOC, and he left, to join his teammates. Walking away from him felt wrong on a visceral level. She simply couldn't do it.

She turned to face him, let her eyes drink in every rugged, masculine detail of his face. Just in case. *You'd better come back to me.* "Be safe out there."

He gave her a soft smile that made the ache beneath her ribs even worse. "I will. And because I'm guessing you're not the kind of girl who gets all mushy over flowers, I'll bring you drugs and weapons when I come back instead."

He was so damn cute. "You guess right. And you sure know how to sweet talk a girl."

His hazel eyes heated with the promise of what was to come. "Sweetheart, you ain't seen nothin' yet."

With that he turned and jogged away, leaving her staring after him with an unfamiliar ache of longing filling the center of her chest.

****

Man, it was colder than a hair on a polar bear's ass out here.

Zaid dropped into a crouch behind Kai, using his buddy as a human windbreaker while they waited in position for Hamilton's next command. As usual the team leader was up front with Freeman, scouting out what was happening in the village from their vantage point on top of a low rise about two hundred yards away.

They'd inserted a couple klicks to the west along with the NIU guys, using a ridge in the topography to help muffle the noise of the helos' rotors, and then covered the distance to here in under ten minutes. The NIU force was fanned out ahead of them, ready to lead the charge into the village. As planned, the Blackhawks had pulled back to another location, where they would await the order for extraction from the target once the op was over.

On one knee, Zaid shifted his grip on his rifle and scanned the dusty terrain through his NVGs. It was slightly warmer out than during their previous op, but the slicing wind made it feel way colder. Thankfully Kai's big frame blocked the worst of it for him as they waited, the other five guys behind Zaid.

He had a good feeling about this one. Nothing he could point to with certainty or even give a reason for; more like a gut-deep knowledge that this time their efforts were going to pay dividends. Jaliya had grilled Barakat on the drive back to Bagram, and relayed everything she'd learned to her boss over the phone en route. By the time they'd made it back, the wheels for this op had already been set into motion.

But he hadn't been able to focus on any of that with all the emotions swirling through him, too caught up in the need to touch her. Hold her. Taste her.

Make her his.

He still couldn't believe she'd broken contact with him all those months ago over a goddamn joke. There was no way she could have misunderstood what that kiss tonight had said, however.

He wanted her, plain and simple. All of her, everything she had to give. He refused to be the only one risking his heart here. So he would break through whatever barriers she put between them to make that happen.

"Okay, listen up," Hamilton said through their headsets, jerking Zaid back to the present. "We've got movement in the southeast part of the village, and HQ confirms there are five vehicles on site. Two old five-ton, three pickups. Minimal number of men with them, maybe a dozen total."

Zaid couldn't wait to get in there and ruin the party with his teammates. To jam a monkey wrench in the guts of The Jackal's smuggling machine and bring that bastard to justice.

"We're going in in two teams. NIU's ready to go. Let's move."

Zaid's blood pumped hot and heavy in his veins as he stood and followed Maka over the other side of the rise. Prentiss hustled past him to get his part of the team in position, and together they started for the unsuspecting village.

The NIU got there first. Sporadic fire erupted from the men manning the trucks, but they were quickly subdued by the NIU's immediate and decisive response.

For the first time, Zaid's confidence about the raid wavered. Was that it? A shipment big enough to fill two five-tons, and that was all the resistance they mounted? Something was off.

When he and his team reached the village, they immediately moved to assist the NIU in securing the village. The Afghan unit had wounded two men and were in the process of cuffing another nine.

Zaid broke off with Maka to check the first house they came to. A young family of four sat huddled on the dirt floor in the front room, hands on heads. Zaid found a hunting rifle in the bedroom and took it outside, explaining to the husband that he would return it when the teams left the village.

"Village secure. Let's see what we've got," Hamilton said.

Zaid and Maka went through the little house, found nothing, and moved to the next one. The NIU was already tearing apart the five-ton trucks while Freeman and Prentiss went through the pickups.

In the second house, Zaid found a small cache of weapons. A dozen pistols and four rifles hurriedly wrapped in a rug and tossed into the corner, probably moments after the NIU had arrived. "Anything?" he called out to Maka, who was in another room.

"Yeah, got something."

Zaid walked through the mud-brick doorway to find his buddy pulling black plastic-wrapped bricks out of an old wooden crate. "How much have you got?"

"Five. They find anything in those trucks?"

"Hope so. Here, gimme those. I'll take them to Hamilton and see what I can find out." He took the bricks to his team leader, who was standing beside one of the five-tons talking with the NIU commander. "Maka found these in the second house," Zaid said, pointing.

Hamilton grunted. "Nothing else?"

"Few weapons." He looked back at where everyone was still conducting the search. "How we doing so far?"

"Not as well as we thought we would. Trucks are empty. Whatever they were carrying is long gone."

That didn't make any sense. "Has to be around here someplace. They must have buried it all."

"If they did, let's hope we find it."

The search of the village turned up more weapons and bricks of hash, but nothing on the order of what they had expected. An expanded search of the immediate area turned up no sign of buried contraband.

The good news was, they had more than the fifty kilogram arrest threshold of hash, meaning they could arrest the men they'd cuffed and bring them in for questioning. The drugs themselves didn't matter, but the information they stood to gain from the prisoners did.

Zaid stayed with Hamilton and the leader of the NIU to question the prisoners, trying to find answers. Upon separate questioning, the men who'd come in with the trucks all told the same story, insisting that they had been hired to drive the vehicles here and await further instructions.

"From The Jackal?" Zaid demanded of one, the youngest of the prisoners, a teenager barely old enough to grow a scraggly beard. His threadbare clothes and worn footwear told Zaid he was just a poor farm kid.

"Yes."

And the little bit of money dangled in front of the kid had been more than enough to make him jump at the offer, no matter that it could have cost him his life. "You saw him?"

"No. I only know that was the name of the man who was going to pay us. But he was here."

Zaid's attention sharpened. "When?"

"Tonight. Before we got here."

He exchanged a loaded look with Hamilton.

"Get me the village elder," his team leader growled.

Zaid found him in one of the houses and brought him back for questioning. The man had a snow-white beard and looked like he was in his seventies, though he could have been much younger. Eking out a life here in this harsh terrain took its toll on people.

If the elder had seen The Jackal in person or knew who he was, he wasn't saying, either too afraid or paid too well to snitch. But from what Zaid could deduce, the smuggler could have been here as little as a few hours ago.

Throughout the questioning, Hamilton stood listening with his arms folded across his chest, his expression giving away nothing. "Put a hood on him and take him over to the others, then get samples of those bricks," he muttered to Zaid before walking away, pulling out his sat phone to contact HQ.

Zaid escorted the bound and hooded prisoner over to wait with the rest of them, all lined up against a rock wall. Leaving the NIU to guard them, he and his teammates began to collect samples of the hash before throwing it all into a pile and burning it.

In the darkness they waited for the Blackhawks to arrive. Zaid loaded the samples and confiscated weapons onto his team's bird and jumped aboard as the NIU hustled the prisoners into two of the others. Frustration was starting to take its toll on them. It felt like they were playing a losing game of whack-a-mole out here, wasting their time—not to mention money and resources—for no reason.

Part of the job, man. Comes with the territory. You'll get a big score next time.

Sometimes hope was the only thing that kept him from feeling his team's efforts were completely useless over here.

Cold, clean air rushed through the Blackhawk's open doors as the helo lifted into the sky for the trip back to base. Zaid stared out at the barren landscape passing beneath them and thought of Jaliya. Hopefully she and her team would at least be able to gain some valuable intel from the prisoners they were bringing in.

Time was slipping away from them. Only nine weeks more, and he'd be heading back home. That left him with one hell of a conundrum.

Because unlike all of his previous deployments over here, this time he'd be leaving his heart behind when he left. The countdown was on to make her his before that happened.

Chapter Nine

"Go get 'em, tiger," Zaid murmured as he pulled the door open for her.

Jaliya shot him a grin and continued past him and Prentiss where they would stand guard outside the hotel dining room doors until she'd finished.

Their team had returned safe and sound after the op last night, bearing prisoners who had given her team the tip that had led to this hastily arranged meeting. And since FAST Bravo had some downtime this afternoon, Zaid and Prentiss had kindly volunteered to escort her here for this lunch meeting and act as her personal security detail.

Given the circumstances, she was nervous about it, but having Zaid nearby made her feel safe and bolstered her courage. Her boss had increased her responsibilities and given her more operational latitude over the past few weeks, because he'd said she'd earned it.

She was determined to prove he'd made the right decision. She was going to uncover the identity of The Jackal if it was the last thing she did, and cut off a major stream of revenue for terror groups in the region.

While she did that, it was nice to know she had two men she trusted watching her back outside the hotel dining room.

So resolved, she strode into the posh restaurant with her head held high and the need for vindication burning inside her. With the special police chief's murder in Kabul last night her team's list of possible suspects involved with The Jackal had led her next to this man, a local politician.

In the interest of time efficiency, David was meeting with another suspect, a wealthy businessman whose office was only a few blocks from here. They were going to meet up and discuss their findings after they finished their individual appointments.

While Jaliya didn't dare to hope that the man she was about to meet might actually be her elusive quarry, she had enough evidence to at least link him to The Jackal. He absolutely knew something important about their target. Whether or not she could pry it out of him was another matter.

She spotted him seated at a table over in the corner, a tall, slim man dressed in a dark suit. She headed straight over. "Thank you for seeing me," she told him in English, pasting on a smile as she approached his table.

He rose from his chair, his dark brown gaze raking over her long-sleeve sweater and cargo pants in stark disapproval before he also put on a smile. "It is my pleasure. Please, sit." He gestured to the chair opposite him.

Her research had shown Mr. Yasin to be a proud, calculating man who surrounded himself with sycophants to constantly stroke his ego, as so many politicians did. He was dirty for sure. Just how dirty, she intended to find out.

Yasin sat back down and regarded her with a slightly patronizing expression, his thin lips all but disappearing into the neatly-trimmed beard he wore. "So. To what do I owe the pleasure of this meeting?" He folded his hands on top of his menu and waited for her response.

She'd set up the meeting with his assistant just that morning, so he wouldn't have had much time to investigate who she was. *Commence phase one of ego stroking.* "I've heard a lot about you since I arrived in Kabul months ago. Because of that, I wanted to meet you in person."

He leaned back slightly in his chair and draped an elbow over the back of it in a pose redolent with self-assurance. "Then I'm glad we had this opportunity." He signaled a waiter over and addressed him by name before looking at her. "Shall I order for both of us?"

He probably thought he was being intriguing and sophisticated, when all it did was make him look even more like a controlling asshole. "Thank you, yes." *Commence phase two.*

She continued to make small talk with him while they waited for their meals, putting him at ease and making him drop his guard. The whole time they ate, he talked about himself and what he'd done for the city, going on about how everyone else was corrupt and not to be trusted, while he was the shining example and the only man who could bring peace and security back to the city.

It damn near turned her stomach, but she kept taking bite after bite, nodding when appropriate and making sure to appear she was hanging on his every word.

As soon as the waiter cleared their plates and brought Yasin a cup of tea, she put her Ms. Nicey-Nice persona away.

"That was delicious, thank you," she said, placing her napkin on the tablecloth.

"You're most welcome. I can't tell you how much I've enjoyed our time together."

Phase three. Flatter his ego before dropping the

hammer. "I know you're a busy and important man, so I won't take up any more of your time than necessary."

"Not at all. It's not often I get to enjoy lunch with such charming company." An indulgent smile crossed his face and she mentally rolled her eyes at his overinflated sense of self-importance before continuing.

"I'll be blunt about my reason for asking you to meet. I wanted to find out what you know about The Jackal."

His smile faded, a trace of anger flashing in his dark eyes before he masked it with amusement. "I know the same as what everyone else in Kabul does. Terrible, the things he's done."

"Yes, terrible." She didn't trust this man's word one bit, but she wanted to feel him out before she showed her cards. "I understand your office has made attempts to locate him over the past forty-eight hours."

"Of course. It's my job to ensure the security of my constituents and foreigners such as you who stay in our beautiful city. Any means I have at my disposal to bring someone like him to justice, I will use."

Uh huh. She kept her expression impassive and dropped the hammer. "Does that include refusing the donations he has contributed to your office?"

The amusement bled away, leaving a cold expression that even eight months ago would have put her stomach in knots. But she had a lot more confidence in her abilities now than she had back then. "We received anonymous donations," he said in a clipped tone. "There is no evidence to support any of it coming from him."

Now she gave him an indulgent smile. "Mr. Yasin, please. We both know exactly who it came from, because your office and mine have both traced the funds back to companies linked to The Jackal's reputed network. I've seen the wire transfer records myself."

His eyes hardened and his jaw flexed before he answered. "I see you are no ordinary reporter. What agency are you working for?"

"It doesn't matter. What matters is that you understand both your government and mine have been watching you closely. Your office received a donation from that same shell corporation as before after the hotel bombing the other day, and again this morning. Curious, that you should have received another deposit into your business account the day after an important public servant was assassinated." She cocked her head and eyed him. "Don't you think?"

"I *think* that you have no idea what you're talking about," he snapped, his cheeks reddening above the line of his beard.

"No?" She quirked an eyebrow. *You're such a cockwomble.*

"No."

"Well. I suppose we'll just have to leave it to the investigative journalist I spoke with to get to the bottom of it. He seemed incredibly keen to begin work on the story when I met with him this morning."

When the color drained from his face, she knew her threat had hit home. He was dirty and now people outside of his corrupt little circle knew it. Once exposed, his credibility in this city—in all of Afghanistan—was shot to shit. And that likely put him square in The Jackal's crosshairs.

"Well, thank you for lunch." She stood and pushed her chair back, satisfaction surging through her veins. "I'm fortunate to be in a position to provide you a certain amount of…protection, should you decide to cooperate in our investigation. If you decide you want to make a deal, your assistant has my contact info. Think about it. "

Giving him a tight smile, she grabbed her coat and headed for the door, doing a mental fist pump. That dumbstruck and stricken expression on his face had been priceless. She'd bet a year's salary that he'd call and ask for a deal within the next twenty-four hours.

Already riding high on the wave of her success, the sight of Zaid waiting for her outside the dining room doors made her heart flutter.

"All done here," she said.

He gave her an assessing look before nodding and transitioning back into sentry mode. "Prentiss is bringing up the SUV. I told him we'd meet him at the corner."

"Sure." She followed him outside, her mind churning. Yasin was pretty adept at covering his tracks. She and her team had to be better at uncovering them before he could destroy whatever remaining evidence linked him to The Jackal.

She and Zaid were a few steps down the sidewalk from the hotel when a familiar voice came from behind her. Jaliya glanced back to see Yasin and his security agent emerging from the lobby onto the front steps. Yasin's face was dark as a thundercloud, his strides quick and angry as he started down the steps.

Someone shouted. She stiffened and whipped fully around, caught a glimpse of two men as they burst out of a vehicle in front of the hotel, automatic weapons in their hands. A ragged gasp locked in her throat.

Yasin froze on the steps. His bodyguard reached back to shove him to the ground and reached for his weapon, but it was too late. The gunmen opened fire.

Strong arms grabbed her around the shoulders and yanked her sideways as the bullets flew. She bit back a cry and braced for impact, but Zaid twisted them and managed to get a hand up to cradle the back of her head before it could bounce off the concrete. They hit the sidewalk together and he rolled on top of her, covering her with his body as they hid behind the flimsy cover of a bench.

Screams and shots filled the air. She made out the sound of pistols returning fire and the automatic weapons stopped. Tires squealed. Then an eerie silence took over.

Her heart thudded in her ears and her lungs were tight. After a few moments of quiet Zaid lifted his head to glance behind her. "Don't move from here until I tell you to," he muttered, and rolled off her to crouch behind the bench, drawing his weapon.

Jaliya rolled to her stomach and peered beneath the bottom of the bench, uncaring about her scrapes and bruises. Yasin and his bodyguard lay sprawled on their backs on the hotel steps, their blood running in crimson rivulets down the treads. People were racing out of the hotel to help them. One of the gunmen lay dead on his side on the sidewalk, his weapon still in his hands.

She swallowed, shock rolling through her in a dark wave. The Jackal? Had he known about the meeting? Had he or his men followed her here?

Beside her, Zaid was already on his phone to Prentiss. "Meet us one block north." He shoved his phone back into his pocket, reached out to grab her under the arms and hauled her to her feet. "Let's go." His tone brooked no argument and she had none anyway.

Her mind was in a fog as she jogged behind him, his hand locked securely around hers as he led her alongside the hotel to the street behind it, and turned left. They'd just assassinated Yasin in broad daylight, in plain view of no fewer than a dozen witnesses. Would they have killed her too if Zaid hadn't tackled her?

Cold seeped into her bones. If she'd been a few seconds slower, she and Zaid might be lying in their own blood on those steps right now too.

Barely aware of moving, she blinked as the SUV suddenly appeared before them at the end of the alley. Prentiss brought the vehicle to a rocking stop.

Zaid ripped open the back door before shoving her into it. He was right behind her, sliding into the back seat before slamming the door shut. Prentiss took off, speeding them away from the scene.

Jaliya gripped the door handle and tried to steady herself. *I'm okay. I'm fine. Zaid's okay too.*

"You get a good look at them?" Prentiss asked.

"A good enough look," Zaid responded, looking all around them as his teammate drove. "Two gunmen and a driver. Driver and one of the shooters got away."

"Get the plate?"

"No." He was so calm. But she wasn't. Not inside, at least. Inside, she was shaky as hell.

Zaid reached for her hand and wrapped his fingers around hers. She was cold, her breathing slightly choppy. "You okay?" he asked quietly.

She met his gaze and nodded. "I'm okay."

No she wasn't. She was shaken, but putting on the best brave front she could. And she was too smart not to realize that her involvement in this investigation might have just put her square in The Jackal's crosshairs. She might even have been one of the intended targets back there.

"We'll get you back to base real soon," Zaid murmured, rubbing his thumb across her knuckles.

She nodded, still not trusting her voice.

Her hands were clammy, her lips stiff. What she wouldn't give to feel Zaid's strong arms around her right now. If they'd been alone she would have crawled right into his lap and burrowed into him, because then she'd feel truly safe.

Squeezing his hand once instead in silent thanks, she let out a slow breath and turned to stare out through the windshield. "So he definitely wasn't The Jackal." She hadn't thought Yasin was, but now yet another lead had been violently eliminated—this one right in front of her.

"No."

She clenched her jaw tight and took a deep breath. Zaid was still holding her hand tight. She didn't plan to let go until she had to. "Well. I guess the good news is, our list is one suspect shorter now."

Two lead suspects killed within the space of a few days. There had to be a leak somewhere. But where? They had to completely lock down the flow of information to try and isolate the source within the taskforce, reducing their group to only U.S. personnel and a few select others they trusted.

Now it was a race against the clock to find the leak before someone else wound up dead.

Chapter Ten

Jaliya paused outside the door to the team rec room that night as the sound of male banter came from inside, and questioned her decision about coming here. She'd dragged a male analyst from her team with her just in case, even though she had tons of work waiting for her on her desk. She should have stayed in her makeshift office here on base and attempted to make a dent in the paperwork instead of doing this.

But after witnessing the assassination earlier, she hadn't been strong enough to stay away. The part of her that ached to be close to Zaid again had compelled her to come, even if she'd only be able to interact with him in a non-intimate way. Seeing him but not being able to touch him would be torture, but not seeing him at all was unbearable.

"Are we…going in?" Her analyst prompted, sounding confused.

"Yes." Raising her hand to knock, she jumped back when the plywood door suddenly swung open.

A big man wearing an AC/DC shirt and jeans stood

there, blinking at her. Agent Logan Granger. His reddish-brown beard made him look like a Viking, or maybe a Highland warrior.

He seemed surprised to see her standing there, whether because he hadn't known she was coming, or because she wasn't wearing her hijab. "Hey. Are you guys…here for game night?"

She flashed him a smile. "And pie. If that's all right. Agent Khan invited me earlier."

"No, yeah, of course. Come on in." He stepped aside to let her pass. "I was just on my way to grab some munchies. I'll grab some pie if I see any."

Once inside the room, Jaliya scanned it and felt totally out of place. The entire FAST Bravo team was there, minus their commander, and a couple other guys she recognized as SOF operators from around the base.

She was the only female here. That was…awkward.

She got a few curious glances but the room was so full she couldn't see Zaid. Damn, she should have brought a female analyst with her. This place all but reeked of testosterone.

Then, over in the far corner of the room where a long table had been set up, she finally spotted Zaid. He looked up and caught her eye, then stood, and the smile he gave her made her heart swoon.

"Hey, you made it," he called out over the noise, causing all his teammates to look over at her.

"I did." Probably a mistake, but no point dwelling on it now, and she felt better just being able to see him.

He waved her and her colleague over. "Come on, I saved you a seat." He patted the back of one between him and Prentiss.

"I'm gonna go grab something to drink," her colleague said.

"Sure." Even though a large part of her wanted to turn around and head right back through the door, she walked over and sat down between Zaid and Prentiss.

"How's it going?" Prentiss muttered as he raised his coffee mug to his lips.

"Good." Still a little rattled by the shooting whenever she thought about it, though. "You guys got the whole night off?"

"So far," Zaid answered. "Can I get you anything? I'm betting you haven't eaten. Granger just went to grab snacks."

"Yes, I just saw him as I came in. I'm okay, thank you. Maybe some tea, if you have some?" She'd kill for a cup of Earl Grey.

His slow smile heated her insides. "So very British. I can find you an iced tea. Will that work?"

She barely kept her horror from showing. "Sure." She loathed the icky sweet bottled American version, but she just couldn't force herself to drink any more water today, and even a fake, sugary form of tea was better than coffee. Vile stuff.

"Okay, hang tight." He walked off, leaving her with Prentiss and six of the other FAST Bravo guys as they gathered around the table.

"So, Rabani. Sure you're up for this?" Hamilton asked as he pulled in his chair, his dark gray eyes filled with mischief. All the guys were in jeans and T-shirts rather than the usual tactical stuff she normally saw them in.

"I'm not sure. What are we playing?" If it was strip poker, she was outta here.

"Our own version of Taboo. Ever played the regular one?"

"A long time ago." Growing up, her family used to play games together in the evenings and on weekends. She missed it, and being over here for so long made her miss them all the more. It had been over a year since she'd been back home to Michigan.

"Well, you've never played it like this," Hamilton said

with a wink, and downed the rest of his water.

"Why, how do you guys play it?"

"You'll see. Just waiting on Maka to get us a buzzer."

"Okay." She glanced around, found that her analyst had abandoned her for the SF guys on the other side of the room, who were all transfixed by whatever military video game they had going on there. So she might as well have come alone.

She made polite conversation with the others and Zaid finally came back a few minutes later with a bottle of iced tea and some baked goods wrapped in a paper napkin. Cookies and bars. "I saved these for you," he said as he set them in front of her. "My mom made the spice cookies. Might be a little on the stale side now, but should still taste pretty good."

He was so sweet, and so was his mother sending him homemade treats. Her family sent her care packages filled with books and treats too, but never any baking. "Thank you."

"Hey, is that one of my mom's blondies?" Granger accused as he came back to the table carrying a box filled with bags of crisps—chips, she corrected herself—and at least a dozen packages of red licorice.

"Yep, and I saved it for Agent Rabani," Zaid said, sliding into the chair beside her. Lord, he smelled good. And every time he shifted his right arm brushed against her left one, sending sparks along her skin.

Jaliya set the light-colored brownie back down on the napkin. "Do you want it?" she asked Granger.

He waved the offer away. "Nah. Just, if I'd known he still had one, I would've stolen it from him."

"They're that good, huh?"

"*Best.*"

Well that demanded a taste test. She broke off half and held it out to him. "I'll share with you."

He huffed out an embarrassed laugh and shook his

head. "No, it's okay."

"I can't deprive you of the whole thing knowing it reminds you of your mom," she insisted, waving it at him.

Grinning, Granger took it from her and raised it in salute. "Thanks."

She bit into hers the same time he did. "Oh, yeah." She chewed it, savoring the buttery, sugary flavor, and moaned. "Oh, God, she used real butter."

He made a rumbling sound and nodded as he chewed, taking the chair at the head of the table. "*Lots* of butter."

The second bite was even better than the first. She hummed in pleasure and belatedly caught the way Zaid was staring at her as she ate—as though he was imagining taking a bite out of *her*. Blood surged into her cheeks and she hoped no one noticed. She'd done more than her fair share of fantasizing about tasting him too.

"Okay, I found it. Game on," Agent Maka said as he strode up to the table holding something she couldn't see in one hand. He folded his huge body into the last empty chair, hiding whatever he held under the table.

She started to bend over to peek beneath it, but he cocked his head and raised an eyebrow at her, so she stopped. "So, how do we play?" she asked.

"We all came up with a bunch of words to guess and wrote them down on slips of paper," Zaid said, reaching out to shake the helmet on the table that was full of little folded bits of paper. "We break into teams of two and each team gets a turn. One player pulls a word from the helmet and has to get their partner to say it without using the word itself, or the five other words listed on the paper. The team that wins the most rounds is the champion."

"And someone from another team watches from behind the person giving the clues," Maka added with a sly grin. "If they say a word on the paper, they're done. Next team gets to go."

Jaliya nodded, all the rules coming back to her now.

"Am I going to know these words?" Because considering all the acronyms and pet names they probably had for things, she might not.

"Good point. Yeah, you should. At least most of 'em."

"And I guess you guys have some kind of buzzer or whatever, to alert us when someone messes up?"

Agent Maka's face broke into a wide grin. "Yes, ma'am, we do."

"Okay, so, teams," Zaid instructed. "Rabani's with me. You guys pick whoever you want."

A flurry of movement followed as the team members repositioned themselves across from their partner. Zaid flashed her a grin as he dropped into the chair opposite her, and she smiled back. He was quite something to look at, and this gave her the perfect opportunity to do so without raising suspicion that something was going on between them. But man, what she wouldn't give for the long, tight hug she'd been craving from him since the shooting.

"I probably should mention that I'm kinda competitive," Jaliya said.

His eyes glinted with humor as he gave her a pretend shocked look. "No way!"

She laughed softly and settled back to await the start of the game. "Whatever. Like any of you aren't just as bad." Probably worse, actually, considering the grind to make it into the FAST program.

"Okay, ladies first," Zaid announced, then held her gaze and murmured, "Ladies should always come first."

Her face heated even more as the rest of the guys chuckled, but she folded her arms across her breasts and raised an eyebrow, not about to be cowed even though all she could think about now was the two of them rolling around naked together, and wondering about all the things he might do to her to get her off.

Though if he'd known how inexperienced she actually

was, she doubted he would have teased her like that in front of everyone. Her one and only sexual partner hadn't been able to make her come at all, so the only orgasms she'd ever experienced were self-induced. Something told her that wouldn't be the case with Zaid. Her insides clenched, arousal stirring inside her.

"Really. A gentleman then, are you? Glad you feel that way." She gestured to the helmet, anxious to change the subject because it was already hard enough to sit across from him and not think about sex without him stirring her up even more. "So. Let's start building some points, shall we?"

He nodded once. "Right on." Reaching into the helmet, he pulled out a yellow slip of paper and read the clue, then held it shielded in one palm while Maka perched on the edge of his chair to peer avidly over his shoulder.

"Go ahead," Maka said when Zaid gave him the side-eye.

Zaid turned his attention back to the clue. "This is a word for someone who you use during an..." He paused, frowned before continuing. "The kind of work you're doing right now."

"Good catch," Agent Maka murmured, eyes still fixed on Zaid's paper.

Jaliya didn't have any ideas yet and motioned for him to continue.

"It's a term for that kind of person. For their role when you're trying to figure out stuff on a case."

"A witness?"

"Like our young friend we drove back from Kabul the other day."

"Informant!"

He smiled and met her gaze. "Yeah." Next to him, Maka looked disappointed. "Okay, our turn again." Zaid pulled another clue from the helmet. Everyone else was busy watching, while digging into the box of junk food Agent Granger had brought in. As Zaid read the clue, he winced a little. "Ah…okay. Another word for a small, domestic pet."

"Guinea pig. Hamster. Rabbit."

"Likes to catch mice."

"Cat!"

He made a circular motion with his hand, urging her to continue. "Cruder."

Oh. "Pussy." They *would* put that one in there.

"Yeah!"

Two chairs down from him, Agent Rodriguez shook his head and helped himself to another handful of nacho chips. "You guys are getting all the easy ones."

"Haters' gonna hate," Zaid said without looking at him, reaching for another clue. "Okay, this is the term for the force generated by a…" He seemed to struggle with coming up with a hint that wasn't on the paper. "A vehicle that inserts us by air."

A force generated by an aircraft. "Yaw."

He shook his head.

"Thrust. Pitch."

Another shake. "Different kind of air vehicle. Rotary—"

Expression full of glee, Maka shot his hidden hand into the air and a deafening blast shrieked through the air. Jaliya jumped a foot, clapping both hands over her ears as the air horn assaulted her eardrums. She stared at him, wide-eyed, until he released the trigger a few seconds later as he smirked at Zaid. "You're out."

Zaid glared at him. "I didn't say a taboo word."

"Did too. Rotary has rotor in it, which is on the list. And so does rotor *wash*, the answer. Hence, you said a taboo word. Hence, you're out, brah." He held the air horn in Zaid's face and gave it another short blast for good measure.

Zaid shoved the thing aside and tossed the scrap of paper down. "Whatever. Rule Nazi. Here, give me that thing." He snatched the air gun from his teammate and gestured to the helmet. "Your turn." He narrowed his eyes in playful warning. "And I'll be watching *carefully*."

"Yeah, go ahead, you might learn something." Looking way too pleased with himself, Maka pulled a clue and gave hints to his partner for the game, Agent Rodriguez.

As the game got back underway, Jaliya glanced across at Zaid. His gaze was locked on his teammate's paper, but it slid her way after a moment and he spared her a wink before focusing on the list of taboo words. She bit her lip to keep from laughing, the crazy humor of it making her glad she'd come. This was going to be quite an experience.

Maka and Rodriguez's turn came to a screeching halt when Zaid stuck the air horn next to Maka's ear and pulled the trigger. "Hey! No need to deafen me." He snatched it from Zaid and handed it to Agent Freeman.

Freeman and his partner went next, and the game continued to move around the table amidst much excited banter and arguments between the team members.

An hour later she and Zaid were two points in the lead when the blast of the air horn ended the game suddenly in the middle of Hamilton and Colebrook's turn.

"Yes!" Jaliya cried, jumping out of her seat to do a little victory dance, and pointing a taunting finger at the rest of them.

Maka pointed the air horn at her and pulled the trigger. Jaliya's laugh was drowned out by the blast and she stuck her tongue out at him. "Sore loser?"

"No. Wish I'd gotten to use this more though." He laid his weapon on the table. "So what now? Poker?"

"I'm in for some poker," Prentiss said.

"Me too," said Freeman. "Colebrook, you in?"

"Yeah, for a while," Colebrook said, leaning back in his chair to stretch his arms over his head. "Gotta call Piper soon though."

"Awwww," the guys all chorused.

Colebrook grinned and threw them a mock scowl. "Screw off."

Zaid took a pull from his water bottle. "What about you?" he asked her.

Poker was definitely not her thing. "It's been fun, but I'd better get back to work. Thanks for having me though," she said to everyone.

"Anytime," Hamilton said, raising his bottle of water in acknowledgment. "Maybe we'll do a rematch."

Flashing Zaid a smile, she pushed her chair back and stood. He did the same, coming around the end of the table to meet her. "You sure you don't wanna stay a while longer?" he asked. "We could watch a movie or something if you don't want to play cards." He nodded to the TV mounted on the wall on the other side of the room. A three-person couch sat in front of it.

As much as she'd love to snuggle up and watch a movie with him, that wasn't going to happen with all the onlookers in here, and she had work to get done before she could turn in for the night. "Thanks, but I really need to make a dent in my mountain of paperwork." Clues to ferret out, evil drug-smuggling overlords to expose.

"Okay. I'll walk you back."

She opened her mouth to tell him that wasn't necessary, then changed her mind and gave him a nod before heading for the door. Even if a few minutes alone with him were all she could have, she'd still take it.

Chapter Eleven

Once back in her empty office across base a few minutes later, Jaliya's heart thudded harder when instead of saying goodnight and leaving, Zaid walked inside and closed the door behind him. There was no doubt as to what he wanted, but she was already in jeopardy of letting him in too far and had to somehow bolster her lagging defenses, no matter how much her body craved that hug she'd been dreaming about all day.

Fortunately for her, she had the honest excuse of needing to get her files done before she could go to bed. Prepared to kiss him and then say goodnight so she could get to work, she pushed up her sleeves as she turned to face him and hid a wince as a bit of her sweater pulled away from the scrape where it had stuck to on her elbow. She was sore all over.

Missing nothing, Zaid reached one hand out to gently capture her wrist, his gaze flicking up to hers before he pushed the sleeve up past her elbow and turned her arm slightly to examine it. "Did this happen when I tackled you earlier?" he asked softly, his touch and gentle tone sending a flush of warmth across her skin.

"I'm lucky it's not far worse than a few scrapes," she said.

He frowned at it. "It's weeping. You should have covered it with a bandage. Did you clean it out at least?"

"No, I didn't have time." She'd been too busy trying to track down Barakat and get answers about the assassination today. So far the team didn't think she'd been one of the targets, but they were no closer to discovering The Jackal's identity.

"You got a first aid kit in here?"

"That's not necessary, I'll just wash it in the shower after I—"

His eyes flashed up to hers, and the words died in her throat. He was so close, his strong hands cradling her arm so gently. It was as if he couldn't stand the thought of her suffering even a scraped elbow. "Have you got one here?"

Got one what? Oh, a first aid kit. "Yes."

"Then I'll clean and dress it for you. Easier for me to reach it than you."

She didn't need to be babied, even if the idea of being taken care of by him was way more appealing than she wanted it to be. "Zaid…"

He rubbed his thumb along her inner forearm. Just that tiny, simple touch had goose bumps flashing over her skin and her nipples tightening. He had the ability to undo her with a single touch, and it was both thrilling and terrifying.

"I hate seeing you bleeding, even this tiny little bit." He dropped his gaze to where his thumb stroked her. "I don't like how close those bullets came to you today."

"Well I didn't like how close they came to you, either."

His eyes warmed as he half-smiled. "I'm going to take you worrying about me as a positive sign that I'm starting to work past your defenses."

She wasn't even sure if she had any defenses left

against him at this point.

With her heart threatening to turn into a pile of mush in the middle of her chest, she reached to the side and pulled the kit out of her top desk drawer. "Here."

He opened the kit, eased one jean-clad hip onto the edge of her desk and gently took hold of her arm to clean the scrapes. "Anywhere else?"

Her cuts and scrapes were nothing, but she knew he wouldn't believe her if she said no. She let out a sigh and gave in. "My other elbow, my right knee and my right side."

With a gentleness so at odds with a man of his size and skill set, he carefully cleaned her scraped elbows, wiping away the dried blood and dirt before applying a thin layer of antibiotic cream and a bandage over each.

"This feels really weird," she murmured as he put on the last bandage. It wasn't hard to see why Zaid was FAST Bravo's medic. All the team members had combat medicine training, but not as in depth as Zaid. He truly cared about people, wanted to help them, and it showed. His teammates clearly adored him. She was starting to adore him too.

"What, me putting bandages on you?" He didn't look up from his work. "Your dad's a doctor. He must have done this for you a lot when you were a kid."

"Yes, but that was different."

"Different how?"

"It just is." The way Zaid tended to her now made her heart flutter and her throat tighten. She wasn't going to admit that aloud, though.

He finished with her other elbow and reached for the hem of her shirt before meeting her eyes. "May I?"

She raised it for him, baring a few inches of skin above the waistband of her pants. The scrape across her ribs was bigger. Not as deep, but the larger surface area affected made it painful, and her sweater had been sticking to it too.

"Ouch, that's some pretty good road rash I gave you," he murmured, reaching for more antiseptic wipes.

"I'd rather have some road rash than a bullet hole any day of the week."

He smirked and began carefully wiping at her scraped flesh. "So, since we're here alone," he began in a tone that told her she probably wasn't going to like his next sentence. "Can I ask you something?"

Her stomach muscles tightened with a mix of dread and anticipation but she answered anyway. "Sure."

"Why are you so dead set against sleeping with me? I'm just curious."

"You're asking me this while you're at eye level with the bottom of my boob?" she said with a laugh, trying to shake the tension. She had on her plain black bra, and wished it had some lace or something to sexify it.

One side of his mouth lifted in a half-grin. "I guess I am, yeah. It's a damn nice view from down here, other than the scrapes I'm cleaning."

Her cheeks flushed. "Maybe it's because all you're offering me is sex, and I'm not that kind of girl."

Now he looked up at her, his eyes alight with interest as they pinned her in place. "Why, do you want something more?"

She'd set that trap without even realizing it.

If she were smart, she would make a hasty tactical retreat and get off this shaky ground. It didn't matter if she wanted more than sex from him, or that she liked him enough to want a relationship. It couldn't happen.

"Stop looking at me and I'll answer your first question." When he did, she pondered her response for a moment, and ultimately decided just to be straight with him. "Like I told you, I came from a fairly conservative home. And so I was raised to be a good, modest girl."

Thankfully he kept his eyes on her scrape as he

answered. "Meaning, no sex before marriage."

He didn't sound judgmental, so she relaxed a little more. "Right. But as you know I'm the black sheep, and what's a black sheep without a checkered past to go with it, right?"

He paused to look up at her again but she frowned and waved him away, exasperated. "If you really want me to answer the question, will you at least not look at me while I do? It's hard enough as it is."

"Sorry." He went back to his work, a slight grin tugging at his mouth. God, he smelled good. "Go on."

She cleared her throat. "There was a guy, in college. I met him in third year. By this time I was in full rebellion and independence mode, determined to blaze my own trail in the world. Of course I thought I was way smarter than my parents, and so their rules and expectation about me staying a virgin until I got married were archaic." She paused a moment. "He was a good person and he treated me well. We'd been dating for about six months, I guess. I thought we were in love. Or rather, at least I thought I was in love with him."

He stopped wiping at her side, which was a relief because it was stinging like hell. She fought not to squirm. "But you weren't?" He leaned closer still and blew on the scrape gently, and the intimate action sent her thoughts up in a cloud of smoke, leaving her frantically chasing after them.

"I didn't figure that part out until after we slept together a couple times."

Zaid didn't say anything else, no rebuke or smart remark, and his silent absorption of her story allowed her to continue.

"Suffice it to say, the whole experience was a massive disappointment for me. Wasn't at all how I thought it would be. It was awkward and not pleasurable in the least." She'd felt completely cheated, and then wondered

KAYLEA CROSS

if something was wrong with her.

Zaid eased back and resumed wiping with the antiseptic pad. "Pretty sure my first thought the exact same thing," he said in a dry voice. "Takes guys a while to figure out what they're doing."

Oh, but I bet you're more than willing to put the effort in to learn. Jaliya smiled at the top of his head. "I doubt it was anywhere near as bad as my experience." She sighed, mentally shaking her head at her twenty-year-old self. "I felt terrible about it afterward. The guilt was way worse than I thought it would be. Part of me was convinced I'd sealed my fate in hell. The other was horrified that I'd given my virginity to a man who I not only wasn't married to, but who I really didn't love."

But the worst part by far was admitting that her parents had been right about warning her not to sleep with him. She hated it when they were right and pulled the whole, *we tried to warn you but you wouldn't listen* routine.

"You were how old?" Zaid asked.

"Old enough to know better. Anyway, I vowed to myself after I broke up with him that I wouldn't have sex again until I got married. Then my dad started shoving guys he'd hand-picked at me, and I hated it. So I also swore I wouldn't date a Muslim guy ever again."

He glanced up, his eyes brimming with humor. "So basically you're telling me I have no prayer."

She smiled at him, fighting the urge to stroke her fingers through his short hair. "None." But it was a lot of fun to imagine what it would be like with him. To imagine what it would be like to be in a relationship with him.

He made a low sound. "Well. Lucky for me, I pretty much ignore the odds when they're stacked against me."

A thrill raced through her at his words. It made no sense, considering what she'd just told him. But oh, she loved the idea of him wanting her enough to pursue her and not give up. Though she was having a hard enough time convincing herself to keep her distance as it was. "Is that lucky?"

His gaze flicked up and caught hers, and for a moment her heart faltered. "I think so. For the both of us. And for the record, I never said I only wanted sex. You assumed that part. It's a bad habit of yours, apparently, assuming things. You should work on that."

Okay, he had her there.

She opened her mouth to respond but the look on his face stopped her cold. Staring into her eyes, he took her right hand in his, and slowly raised it to his lips, killing whatever response she might have made.

Jaliya's breathing halted at the sheer heat in his eyes, her toes curling in her boots when the warmth of his lips brushed across the sensitive skin of her inner wrist. He didn't just want sex? How much more did he want? And didn't he realize that was impossible, given their jobs?

His lashes lowered as he lingered there, the kisses growing longer and firmer. Her fingers twitched, restless with the need to stroke his thick, dark scruff, then dig into the muscles at his nape and drag him up to kiss her properly.

Zaid inched his lips higher, blazing a heated trail all the way up to her inner elbow. She sucked in a breath when the hot, damp stroke of his tongue lit nerve endings she hadn't even known she possessed on fire.

But instead of continuing upward, he reversed course, retracing the path he'd made. Slowly he kissed his way back down her inner arm, each touch of his lips and the erotic caress of his tongue making her blood race and her heart pound.

By the time he reached her open palm, she was having a hard time keeping her breathing steady, her mind already having made the mental jump to picturing them in bed together and him being this attentive to all of her body.

Her utterly naked body.

She sucked in a breath as he gently sank his teeth into the base of her hand, then he kissed each fingertip before lowering her hand, still keeping hold of it. "What about now?" he whispered, his eyes gleaming with a hot mix of desire and mischief. "Still a firm no on the sex part?"

She was dizzy. Overheated. And unbearably aroused. She was tempted to push him flat on her desk and crawl on top of him. "Still no." It sounded like she had severe asthma.

Zaid laughed softly and shook his head once. "Can't blame a guy for trying."

No. And she loved his version of trying. A lot. She wanted him to do it more, only on her face and down her neck to every part of her that was now aching and throbbing way worse than the scrapes he'd just cleaned. Except she didn't want just sex.

There had to be more than that between them before she would ever consider sleeping with him. She might have broken free of her conservative upbringing, but casual sex would never be okay for her. Maybe it was partly her religion, and maybe it was just the morals ingrained in her from her upbringing, but that's who she was.

Clearing her throat, she looked down at the floor and changed the subject. "I had fun tonight. Thanks for inviting me." It hadn't been a smart move on her part, to participate with them on a social level and muddy the waters in what should be a strictly professional relationship, but guess what? She wasn't perfect. And she didn't regret a moment of it.

"Thanks for coming."

Her eyes darted up to his. *Coming.*

That's all she could think about right now, him making her do just that, and her returning the favor. God, how was she ever going to live with herself for holding back when she wanted him this much?

A sharp knock at the door made her jolt and pull her hand from Zaid's. The door opened and her boss popped his head in. "Hey." He looked from her to Zaid and back again. "Any progress on those files yet?"

"Not yet." Not with Zaid making her work ethic fly out the window and setting her entire body on fire. "Any luck finding out about the shooting?"

"Got the names of the shooters, but still trying to figure out whether they're linked to The Jackal." He nodded at the pile of folders on her desk. "Text me if you find anything." After shooting Zaid a hard look, he left.

Zaid waited a few seconds to make sure he wasn't coming back, then stroked a hand over the side of her face and over her hair. "I'd better let you get to it."

"Yes," she murmured, disappointment flooding her. It was definitely best that he leave now, though, before she did something else she would regret.

"Good luck. See you tomorrow sometime?"

She wasn't sure how much longer the agency would keep her here at Bagram. As soon as they found her team a secure location in Kabul, they'd be moving. "Sure."

His hand tightened around a fistful of hair for a moment, then he leaned in and kissed her softly. Slowly. As though savoring the feel of her lips beneath his, until she swayed toward him and had to put a hand on his shoulder for balance.

His thick, heavy arms wrapped around her, pulling her tight to him. Giving her the hug she'd been craving so badly. She let out a shuddering sigh and cuddled in close, savoring the sense of instant security.

He rubbed his bearded cheek against hers, gave a soft growl that sent shivers through her. "I want you so damn much," he whispered fervently.

She closed her eyes and pressed her cheek to his, savoring the faint scratch of his short beard. *I want you too. So. Damn. Much. But I can't give you what you want unless there's more.*

Either way, the logical part of her brain knew she couldn't have him. Not if she wanted her heart intact when he went back stateside in a few weeks' time.

Without warning he pulled away, but his gaze was so full of heat and need it sent an arrow of pain through her. "Good night."

She forced a smile while her entire body screamed at her to take what he was offering. "Good night."

When he walked out and the door closed behind him, it felt like the room became a vacuum, sucking the air from her lungs. Her knees gave out and she dropped into her chair, staring sightlessly at the mound of paperwork in front of her. She felt cold and…empty now that he was gone.

She blew out a shaky breath. How the hell was a man like that still single? What was wrong with all the women back in D.C.? "They're either stupid or crazy," she muttered to herself, and forced herself to reach for the first file.

No, *she* was crazy, for not taking what was right in front of her. Even though it would be smarter to steer clear of that temptation.

One thing was for certain: if Zaid were hers, she'd never let him go.

****

Another day, another enemy eliminated.

The Jackal paused at the base of the back steps to his home and gazed upward. Warm light spilled from his son's window that overlooked the garden. And suddenly he was both terrified and exhausted.

Because of the mounting pressure from the investigation about him and the proximity of the threat bearing down on him and his network, he'd been forced to intensify his response. Taking out two targets in as many days was risky, but necessary if he wanted to keep his identity hidden from authorities. Anyone who posed a risk of exposure would be eliminated immediately.

He stared up at the bedroom windows, his heart heavy and aching. His wife and son had no idea what he'd done and would continue to do in order to secure the surgery.

Just a little longer. Please. Just let me stay hidden in plain sight a little longer.

The phone in his pocket vibrated, startling him. His heartbeat quickened when he saw the area code of the unfamiliar number, and he walked through the wrought-iron gate into the garden before answering. "Hello?" Was this it? The news he'd been waiting, praying for?

"My friend, how are you?" a familiar voice said in accented English.

For a moment he couldn't believe his ears. This had to be it. There was no other reason for this man to contact him personally. "I'm anxious to get my son better."

"I know you are. That's why I'm calling."

He held his breath, waiting. *Please…*

"I'm told you're under siege there. That must be hard."

Not surprising that the man knew about what was going on. He had spies everywhere, even here in Kabul. "Yes. I don't know how much longer I have before—"

"I've found a surgeon who is willing to perform the surgery with his team."

The Jackal squeezed his eyes shut. He rubbed at the sudden sting there, fighting back tears of relief. "That's good news. But we don't have a donor."

"I'll find one. Children die every day all over the world. It's just a matter of finding one we can use. I have people keeping their ears to the ground for us."

He shook his head, his voice hoarse. The lack of control terrified and infuriated him. "How? How do I know I can trust you with this?"

"Because good or bad, I'm a man of my word. Ask anyone who's done business with me, and they'll tell you."

"I already did." He'd done it way before he'd agreed to this dangerous arrangement. But desperation drove people to do things they would never dream themselves capable of. He was living proof.

A low chuckle. "Of course. Well. Have you got the money?"

He'd been told that given the situation, if he was short money when the time came, the head of the Veneno Cartel would likely pay the rest himself. But he wasn't counting on that. "Most of it."

"Ah. The shipments are flowing nicely. I'm told that almost ninety-percent of the product is making it through the border and onto the ships."

"Yes. And I have more coming soon."

"I'm glad to hear it. I love doing business with you, Fahim."

He flinched at hearing his name said aloud and automatically looked around him. Not that anyone standing nearby would be able to overhear the conversation, but if anyone was monitoring the cellular signal, they might have heard it. And people were hunting him.

A long inhalation followed, as though the man on the other end of the line was taking a drag of something. Not drugs. Fahim had been told that *El Escorpion* never touched any of his product, but that he had a penchant for Cuban cigars. "How's your boy doing?"

"He's weakening." And it killed Fahim to watch it.

"I'm sorry to hear it." He sounded so sincere, but then *El Escorpion* had children of his own, so maybe he meant it. "Go. Spend some time with him before he goes to sleep. I just wanted to let you know I'm working on it on my end. As soon as something comes up, I'll let you know."

But what he'd really called for was to check to make sure The Jackal hadn't been identified yet. At the end of the day, this was merely a business arrangement for *El Escorpion.* Where for Fahim, it was his son's *life.* "Thank you."

"You take care, my friend."

My friend.

Fahim set his jaw and slipped the phone back into his pocket, unable to shake the feeling that he was being watched. He wasn't *El Escorpion's* friend and never would be, even if he managed to conjure the miracle of saving Fahim's son.

No, this was business, nothing more, and it was as ruthless as the drug trade he was now too deeply ensconced in to escape. He was only useful as long as he kept the opium flowing to Mexico.

For his son, he would ensure that it did.

Fahim wiped at his eyes to hide all traces of fear and sadness from his face before climbing the back steps and letting himself in through the kitchen door. His boots were quiet on the tiled floor as he made his way to his son's bedroom.

When he reached the doorway his wife and son both looked up at him with tired smiles. The boy was in his mother's lap, his dark head resting on her shoulder as she read him a book.

"Ah, that one again?" Fahim asked with an indulgent smile.

"I love it," Beena rasped out from beneath the oxygen mask. His face was ashen, a bluish tinge to it, his little chest laboring as he struggled to breathe.

Fahim's heart cried out in agony at the unfairness of it, but he kept his smile firmly in place. "Would you like me to read it to you tonight?"

Beena nodded, his eyes brightening.

"All right." He traded places with his wife, pausing to grasp her hand as she passed him. She stopped and looked down at him, concern darkening her eyes for a moment, but he merely squeezed her hand once and released her.

He lifted Beena into his lap, anguish slicing through him as the slight weight of his son's too-thin body snuggled into him. Such trust and innocence. Relying on his father to provide for and protect him.

Fahim would not fail him.

Clearing his throat, Fahim started the story from the beginning, his mind on his son and the people who threatened to unravel it all.

The entire American team had to be dealt with. He wanted to do it immediately but killing them now would look far too suspicious so soon on the heels of the other two assassinations, even if he staged it to look like an accident somehow. So no matter how he hated to wait, he'd have to.

Just a little longer.

Chapter Twelve

"**B**lade one in position. Moving in on target."

The silent tension in the cramped room sharpened at the SF team leader's words. It had been two days since the assassination in downtown Kabul, and Jaliya's team had uncovered yet another target to raid.

She leaned closer to the computer to watch the live feed from the soldier's helmet-mounted camera, showing the desolate nighttime landscape in the mountains outside of Jalalabad in neon green. Sergeant Bowen was his name.

She'd met him several times now, and he and a few of his teammates had been in the room during the game night with FAST Bravo last week. She knew his face, what color his eyes were, and that he wore a titanium wedding band engraved with a message from his wife.

It was so much harder to watch an operation unfold in real time when she knew people in the unit involved.

It was even harder tonight, since this was the first time that military action had been carried out based directly on *her* intelligence. Through her network she'd received a tip late this morning that The Jackal would be checking on this shipment tonight personally. The source was credible, and she had high hopes that tonight would prove The Jackal's undoing. They'd also tightened security in an effort to stop or at least isolate the suspected leak.

As she watched the soldiers on screen, her mind flashed to Zaid and the rest of FAST Bravo, who had been sent to check out a different village close to the SF team's target. They'd texted back and forth since the other night in her office, but hadn't seen each other since.

It was impossible not to worry about him and the others, especially when she had no information on their op or movements. All day she'd been focused entirely on planning this op, and Commander Taggart was monitoring his team from another room.

No matter how hard she tried, she couldn't stop thinking about Zaid. In a matter of weeks since FAST Bravo had been over here, he had managed to steal his way into her heart. If anyone suspected there was something going on between them, it could be disastrous for her position. She'd done her best to hide her feelings and tried not to pay him more attention than the others when they were in a meeting or briefing, but she wasn't certain she'd pulled it off.

It was unsettling to feel so intensely about a man when she couldn't have him. Not for anything more than a short-term fling, anyway. Wondering what he meant by wanting more than sex was driving her crazy, but that was a conversation she wanted to have face-to-face, in private.

Well, you can't always get what you want.

Yeah. Wasn't that the truth?

With a mental headshake, she focused back on the screen as the SF team approached the remote village. Everything was so quiet, the team having maintained the element of surprise. The target convoy in the village consisted of seven heavy trucks. Was The Jackal in one of them? Her pulse beat faster.

"Contact, eleven o'clock," Sergeant Bowen suddenly called out.

Fear slammed into her.

Jaliya gripped the edge of the table harder and stared at the screen, her heart surging with a mixture of alarm and dread as the sharp crack of gunfire filled the audio feed.

The steel door behind her opened quietly. She spared a brief glance over her shoulder to see Taggart step inside before looking back at the screen. The SF team was taking enemy fire from the village.

"Engage all targets!" Bowen yelled over the noise of battle.

The volume of fire increased sharply, a staccato beat that matched the clatter of her heart against her ribs. Her hands turned clammy and cold and she was vaguely aware that she was holding her breath as she watched the footage from Bowen's helmet cam.

On screen the world tilted and rolled as Bowen hit the ground with a harsh grunt. Jaliya's stomach clenched.

He didn't move.

Everyone around her was deathly quiet, only the crack of gunfire filling the room. She stared at the screen, unblinking, horror washing through her.

Get up. Please get up...

"Bowen's down," another voice said over the radio.

The army colonel next to her cursed under his breath and shifted restlessly, his eyes glued to the screen.

Through Bowen's helmet cam, tracer fire arced through the darkness like swarms of lethal fireflies. Satellite imagery on the flat screen mounted on the wall above them showed thermal images of the battlefield, the enemy swarming out of the trucks and houses in the village.

Too many. Far more than they'd anticipated.

Ice shot through her veins as she realized the intel she'd received had been wrong. That the information they'd based this entire operation on had been wrong.

The SF team continued to return fire in the face of the overwhelming enemy force attacking them. She couldn't believe what she was seeing. Had thought the intel was reliable after the bad tip she'd gotten last time.

"Fall back," one of the men ordered sharply.

Jaliya let go of the table edge and straightened, unable to stem the urge to press a trembling hand over her mouth as she watched the tragedy unfold via satellite imagery, helpless to stop it.

Three more SF soldiers fell. Their remaining teammates laid down suppressive fire and rushed in to save them, risking their own lives to pull them out. One fell next to his wounded teammate during the recovery attempt.

Jaliya bit her lips together, horrified.

"Be advised, we've got seven wounded, three critical," a breathless voice reported.

"Jesus Christ," someone muttered next to her.

It was a bloodbath. And she'd sent them straight into it.

Everything in her wanted to turn and run out the door, flee from this horror and the weight of responsibility crashing down on her. She refused to obey her instinct, made herself stand her ground and watch the carnage she had created unfold in front of her.

Men shouted orders and reported in to the TOC. The soldier handling comms in the room responded at a rapid clip, relaying critical information. "Two medevacs have been dispatched to exfil point delta, ETA thirteen minutes. Gunship en route. Retreat to that position and await—"

"Negative," one of the soldiers responded, "we don't have thirteen minutes. Two of our critical are bleeding out."

Jaliya swallowed convulsively as her stomach twisted. Those men were bleeding out because of her. Dying right there on the screen in front of her.

She couldn't bear it.

"FAST Bravo's en route back to base. They're still close enough to get in there and help," Taggart said from behind her.

The colonel hesitated for only a split second before waving him forward to set it in motion. Jaliya backed out of his way, cringing inside, alternating between shock and wanting to throw up.

Taggart's voice registered above the pop of gunfire as the SF team battled to reach the wounded and get behind cover. The minutes ticked by in a surreal haze while she stood there frozen at the back of the room, unable to move, unable to do anything to fix this horrible situation.

After an agonizing wait, a gunship arrived on station and opened fire on the enemy position. Jaliya felt nothing but numbness as the thermal images on screen fell like leaves in a windstorm.

Then SA Hamilton's familiar voice came over the radio, breaking her out of her trance. "FAST Bravo in position. Moving in now to assist."

She bit down on the inside of her cheek as the screen split into two feeds, the second showing FAST Bravo moving from a Blackhawk toward the pinned-down SF team. Without knowing who was who, she watched the men who raced for the wounded, knowing one of them was Zaid.

Three Bravo members each stopped next to a wounded man while the rest of their teammates and the gunship kept firing at the scattering enemy. Finally, the medevacs arrived. In the ensuing confusion Jaliya lost track of which unit was which.

But the damage had already been done.

"This is SA Khan."

Her head snapped toward the radio at the sound of Zaid's voice.

"All three criticals are onboard the medevacs and en route back to base. Crews have alerted the surgical team to be ready to receive them as soon as they land at Bagram."

Hearing his voice speak those terrible words made the backs of her eyes burn.

Oh God, I'm sorry. I'm so, so sorry.

Futile, useless words. Weak words that had no place here. Sorry wouldn't fix anything. Sorry wouldn't make this okay or absolve her of the guilt slowly crushing her.

She bit down harder on the inside of her cheek and blinked fast, determined not to let a single tear fall. This was on her and she would stand here and watch what she'd caused, listen to each horrible update until every last man had been safely evacuated from the battlefield.

On screen, FAST Bravo and the tattered remnants of the SF team continued to engage what was left of the enemy as the Spectre gunship made another pass overhead and fired at one of the trucks that was attempting to flee.

A bright flash lit up the feed as the vehicle exploded. Two men jumped out of it, both on fire, and flailed for a few moments before dropping to the ground.

Jaliya watched it all, unable to feel even a little triumph. She just hoped one of them was The Jackal.

Silence enveloped the room for a few moments, before SA Hamilton spoke again. "Be advised, we're moving in to secure target."

Another wave of fear hit her as the men emerged from behind cover and started toward what was left of the convoy. FAST Bravo moved in with the remaining SF soldiers, checking the trucks before entering the tiny village.

David glanced back at her and she yanked her hand away from her mouth, straightening her spine. Whatever happened to her after this, she would take it without flinching.

"All remaining trucks are filled with ammo. We've got eight prisoners, five of them with non-life threatening injuries," Hamilton reported. "Khan's questioning them now."

A few minutes later, she got the answer they'd all been waiting for.

"Our HVT's not here," Hamilton said. "They're saying one of the KIAs from the destroyed truck was one of his lieutenants."

"Copy that," Taggart told him, his voice filled with frustration. "Sweep the village and report back with an update." He straightened and moved back from the desk, allowing the others to take over again. When he turned his head to look at her, Jaliya swore she saw condemnation in those turquoise eyes.

She jerked her gaze away and focused on the feed in front of her, feeling small and helpless. It seemed to take forever for the men to sweep the village and take samples of the drugs they found before destroying them and the weapons. This time at least, there were a lot of both.

Except the Jackal hadn't been there. Even though he'd been directly involved with the shipment.

Jaliya squeezed her eyes shut for a moment. *Damn*. So close. But the price paid in American blood to find out he wasn't there would never justify the cost of the op.

People began leaving the room, brushing past her without a word, and she was too afraid to look them in the face. She stayed where she was until every last man on the battlefield was aboard the helicopters and on their way back to base.

David stopped next to her on his way to the door and put a hand on her shoulder. She tensed, barely resisted the urge to wrench away. "We were close," he murmured, squeezing gently. "Closer than we've ever been to him before. That's something."

Jaliya didn't answer. She couldn't, her throat was too tight.

David released her. "Come on," he urged, nodding toward the door. "Let's go get you some tea."

"No," she rasped out. "I'm not leaving until I get an update on the wounded."

He stared at her for a long moment, but when she didn't budge, patted her on the back once before leaving.

Now it was just her and four men connected to the SF team in the room. "Is there any word on the wounded?" she made herself ask.

The colonel removed his headset slowly and met her gaze. "Yeah. We're down to just one critical. The two others didn't survive the flight back to base."

Jaliya hitched in a breath as pain stabbed through her chest. The floor seemed to tilt beneath her feet for a moment before she turned and shoved the door open, then blindly raced down the brightly-lit hallway.

Chapter Thirteen

Hamilton and Taggart were waiting for him when Zaid stepped out of the O.R. back at Bagram. It had been a long, shitty night, and while he wanted a shower and a hot meal before hitting his bunk, he wanted to see Jaliya more.

If he was right, she'd be blaming herself for what happened, even though it wasn't her fault, and she hadn't been the only person involved in the taskforce's decision to green light the SF team's op.

"Well?" Taggart said, hands on hips.

Zaid had tended to two of the wounded on the flight back to base, and stayed with them right up until the anesthetist put them under in the operating room. "One will probably lose his lower leg." He'd done everything he could to stop the soldier from bleeding out during the flight here. But the bullets had shredded the calf and tibia so badly that no orthopedic surgeon would be able to put it back together.

Taggart cursed and shook his head. "And the others?"

"Still in surgery." He stripped off the bloodstained

latex gloves and tossed them into a nearby trashcan, then grabbed a handful of paper towels and started scrubbing at the blood smeared on the front of his uniform. Little good it did him.

"What are their chances?" asked Hamilton.

Giving up on trying to wipe the blood off him, Zaid tossed the paper towels and stripped the fatigue jacket off. "Good. They're all expected to make a full recovery. We'll know more in a few hours. Surgeon said he should be done by oh-five-hundred."

"You go clean up," Taggart said. "I'll get an update and pass it on to you if anything happens."

Zaid inclined his head. "Thanks, I—" He broke off when Jaliya stepped around the corner and paused. Her dark gaze darted between the three of them before settling on him.

She twisted her fingers together, the haunted look on her face twisting his heart. "The third critically wounded. Have you heard anything?"

Ah, shit. Taggart had said she'd been in the TOC the entire time. She'd seen it unfold in real time. He nodded, wishing he could somehow shield her from the truth, or at least soften the blow.

"Is he…"

He really didn't want to say it in front of Hamilton and Taggart, but he wouldn't lie to her. "He didn't make it," he said gently.

She stared at him for a split second, then her expression turned stricken and she whirled away.

"Jaliya—"

She'd already disappeared around the corner.

"Shit," he muttered, and started after her.

"Gimme that," Hamilton said, holding out his hand for Zaid's bloody uniform jacket. "She doesn't need to see it."

Zaid tossed it to him and went after her. She was

already halfway across the road when he shoved the front door open. "Jaliya!"

She didn't stop, didn't even slow as she held up a hand to ward him off and kept hurrying away.

Dammit. "Jaliya, wait." He ran faster, barely noticing the cold, his only concern for her.

She broke into a jog and ripped the door open to her temporary quarters. It slammed in his face as he reached it.

Cursing, Zaid wrenched it open. The hallway was empty. She must already be in her room.

He kept his steps quiet as he hurried across the linoleum floor and stopped at the door to her room. He knocked softly. "Jaliya."

No answer.

"*Jaliya.*"

"No."

To hell with that. She was hurting and there was no way he was walking away from her right now, even if his actions confirmed to Taggart and Hamilton that they were together.

Pulling a ballpoint pen from his pocket, he took it apart, then set about picking the lock on her door. Within thirty seconds he had it unlocked and pushed it open.

Jaliya spun away from him to face the far wall, her spine rigid, her long, inky hair spilling down her back in thick waves. Her hijab lay crumpled on the floor next to her bed, and with each choppy intake of breath, her shoulders shook.

Zaid's heart squeezed. "Hey."

She didn't respond, didn't move as he shut the door and crossed the room, but flinched when he put his hands on her shoulders. "Don't," she begged, shrugging away as though she couldn't bear his touch.

No. No way he'd let her suffer through this alone. He'd vowed not to get involved with anyone, but it was way too

165

late for that now. She needed him, end of story.

"Come here," he murmured. Ignoring her protests, he spun her around and wrapped his arms around her, pulling her tight to his chest.

JALIYA'S INITIAL REACTION was to struggle. She started to bring her hands up, ready to shove him away. Zaid just held her tighter, those strong, hard arms banded around her back. And when he slipped one hand into her hair to bring her face against his shoulder, something inside her broke.

She bit her lip as a sob tried to tear free. Instead of pushing away she burrowed closer, reaching around his ribs to grip handfuls of his sand-colored tactical shirt.

"It's my fault," she gasped out, speaking the terrible, painful truth aloud.

"No it isn't."

"Yes, it is. I sent them out there."

"A dozen other people signed off on the op too, including their CO. They all knew to expect armed resistance."

"But I got it wrong." Her voice was muffled by his chest. "I didn't realize how outnumbered they'd be."

"You couldn't have. No one could have. Shit happens all the time on ops. They were as prepared as they could be, and you gave them the best intel you had available."

"I got them attacked, and some of them *killed*. And The Jackal wasn't even there," she finished, her voice shredding as she pressed her face against his pec.

She was directly responsible for those men suffering and dying, and it confirmed her worst fear. Her father was right; she didn't have what it took to do this job, and it had taken losing those men for her to get past her stupid fucking pride and realize it.

"You didn't get them killed. Every one of those men knew the risks when they went out there tonight. And

166

every single one of them would do it all again tomorrow. It's their job." Just like it was his. "They signed up for this. Don't take their bravery away from them. They died doing what they believed in."

He laid his cheek on the top of her head, one hand stroking through her hair. She didn't deserve the comfort or his care, but he didn't seem to understand that. "We all know the risks and what can happen out there. It could just have easily been my team when we went out to search our target tonight."

"Oh God, don't. Don't say that." She hugged him closer, unable to bear the thought of him being wounded or killed in the line of duty, much less on an op planned based solely on her intel. "I couldn't take it if anything happened to you. You hear me?"

"I hear you. And here I am, safe and sound."

Yes. This time. And as selfish as it made her, she was so damn grateful he hadn't been one of the men bleeding out on the flight back to base.

His arms were so strong around her. Protecting and comforting her. Somehow he'd escaped injury during the dangerous rescue and was holding her now.

Jaliya sucked in a shuddering breath and fought to stop the burn of tears, pulling his scent into her nose. Sweat and soap and…Zaid. She'd remember his scent for the rest of her life.

Need sparked low in her gut. There was no stopping it, and this time, she didn't feel like fighting it.

She'd been angry at first when he'd followed her here and barged in. Now she was glad. She needed a distraction from the turmoil inside her, and he was certainly…a huge distraction.

It was more than that though, even if she wanted to convince herself otherwise. She'd never wanted anyone the way she wanted him, and the attraction was growing stronger no matter how much she tried to convince herself to squelch it.

They had such a short amount of time left together—he could be sent elsewhere at a moment's notice. And every time he and his teammates went outside the wire, there was a chance that they wouldn't come back at all.

Jaliya shuddered and pulled in another deep breath, savoring the feel of him. She was tired of fighting the pull between them. Sick to death of repressing her needs and desires because of a deep-seated sense of guilt and some stupid vow she'd made to herself years ago to stay celibate until she at least got engaged.

The only man she wanted was right here in front of her, and she was done pretending she could live without satisfying the raging need he ignited in her blood.

Gathering her courage, she eased her grip on his shirt, flattening her hands against his broad back, and raised her head to look into his face. His gold-flecked eyes searched hers, one hand smoothing gently over her hair. The concern and tenderness on his face undid her.

Pushing up on tiptoe, she angled her head and fused her mouth to his.

Zaid made a low, hungry sound in the back of his throat and fisted his hand in her hair, forcing her head back more as he took over. Desire exploded, blasting throughout her body in a dizzying wave.

All that mattered was this. Them. Finally being able to give reign to the hunger she'd been suppressing, finally getting to taste and touch the man she'd been fantasizing about for so many weeks.

They were plastered together from chest to groin, but it wasn't good enough. She gripped the sides of his head in her hands and pushed her tongue against his, conveying her urgency and desperation without a single word. He didn't pull back or ask questions, just grabbed her by the hips and hoisted her off her feet.

Jaliya moaned at the show of raw male strength and

wound her legs around his waist, stopping the kiss and releasing his head only long enough to peel her shirt over her head and fling it behind her. Then she sought his sexy mouth once more, vaguely aware that he was moving them backward.

With one hand holding the back of her head he bent forward, lowering her onto the hard cot she'd been sleeping on the past few nights. She kept hold of his shoulders and tugged him down on top of her. Zaid groaned deep in his chest as he stretched out on top of her, his tongue sliding against hers.

Her breath caught and sensation zinged through her when his weight lowered onto her, pressing her down against the blankets. The pressure of his erection between her open thighs made her shudder, the acute ache sharpening. Then he nipped at her bottom lip and kissed a path over her jaw to the side of her neck.

"Sweetheart, are you sure?" he murmured.

She loved that he'd asked. "Yes." She needed him. Didn't want him to stop, no matter what she'd said before.

Jaliya tipped her head back to give him more room, gasping at the wet stroke of his tongue and the scrape of his scruff against her sensitive skin. By the time he reached the base of her throat her breasts felt swollen, her nipples tight and aching.

Dragging his tongue across the upper swell of her right breast, he shifted to his knees to straddle her and reached beneath her to undo her bra. She shrugged out of it and tossed it aside, a thrill rushing through her when he paused to stare at her naked breasts.

His eyes darkened and his jaw grew taut. Those big strong hands slid up to cup the tender flesh, his thumbs sweeping gently over the rigid peaks. A moan slipped out of her as pleasure shot through her. She arched her back, silently asking for more, and she bit her lip as he lowered his dark head.

The moment his lips closed around her nipple she grabbed hold of his head and bit back a whimper. His hot, wet tongue circled it, soothing and tantalizing as he sucked. She locked her legs around his and lifted her hips, desperate for more pressure between her legs.

But Zaid apparently wasn't in the mood to be rushed. His hands held her in place as he sucked and stroked and teased her nipple, then switched to the other.

"Zaid," she panted, wanting so much more and impatient to get it.

He made a low sound and continued to torment her, ignoring her restless movements. Finally, when she couldn't stand the burn a moment longer, he sat up and reached for the top of her pants.

She helped him, undoing the button and yanking down the zipper while he unlaced her boots and tugged them off. Shoving her pants down her legs, she kicked them off, leaving her in just her panties. Before he could touch her she reached for the hem of his T-shirt, needing to be skin on skin with him.

He reached one hand between his shoulder blades and peeled it over his head and she stopped, spellbound by the ridges and hollows of muscle beneath the dusting of black hair and smooth, bronze skin. Setting her hands on the curves of his pecs, she explored him, drinking him in, reveling in the sheer masculine strength of his body.

"God, when you look at me like that…" He trailed off and grasped her hands in his. Jaliya looked up at him, her heart tripping when she saw the naked longing on his face.

Without a word she curled a hand around his nape and brought his mouth to hers. Zaid gobbled her up in a greedy, savage kiss that thrilled her to her toes.

She was so wet, on fire for him, and the ache between her legs was driving her insane. Her fingers tangled in the waistband of his pants but he drew them away and pushed her flat on the cot as he came down on one elbow beside her.

His hand drifted up her bare calf to her inner thigh, his light touch sending shivers through her. He angled his head to watch and inched the pads of his fingers over the smooth skin of her thigh, stopping at the edge of her panties.

She held her breath, waiting, praying for him to touch her where she needed it most, and finally he brushed his fingertips over her covered mound. She hissed air between her teeth and closed her eyes, rocking her hips up to meet his hand.

"I've wanted to do this for so long," he whispered against her neck, hooking his fingers into her panties and slowly dragging them down her legs. The wash of cool air against her heated folds increased the pulse there.

"Then do it," she said, her voice unsteady enough to take the bite out of the demand.

One side of his mouth kicked up and his gaze settled on hers as the heat of his palm covered her mound.

She closed her eyes and bit her lip, the slight amount of pressure he applied the sweetest torment. And then he began gliding his fingers up and down the seam of her folds and she could barely breathe, a tiny whimper breaking free of her throat. She needed this, needed it so badly she ached.

The cot shifted. She forced her heavy eyelids apart in time to see him ease onto his knees beside the cot, his expression absorbed as he continued to stroke and tease the slick flesh between her legs. He was so unbelievably sexy like that, intent on his task, utterly in control despite the flush of arousal on the tops of his cheeks and the ridge of his erection pressing against the front of his pants.

He eased a finger into her just as his thumb swept across the swollen knot of her clit.

"Ah!" she gasped, automatically lifting her hips as pleasure seared across her nerve endings.

"You're all soft and wet for me," he whispered, repeating the motion before pulling his finger out and adding a second.

The sweet pressure inside her expanded, her clit throbbing now. "Zaid..."

"Stay still," he commanded, his free hand gripping her outer thigh and shifting it to open her wider. Holding her immobile.

Her legs trembled, all the muscles in her belly pulling taut as he lowered his head toward her. She closed her eyes and grasped the blanket in both hands, managed to stifle a cry of mingled relief and passion when the heat of his mouth touched her most intimate flesh. He kissed her there, his fingers moving slow and steady as his tongue swirled hot, melting circles around her swollen clit.

Oh God, oh God...

She couldn't speak, could barely breathe as his slow, erotic kisses and caresses drove her out of her mind, pushing her higher and higher. Then his free hand eased up her ribs to cradle her breast, his fingers squeezing her hardened nipple just as his lips firmed around her bundle of nerves and sucked gently.

A breathless mewl broke free as the orgasm loomed, her entire body strung taut, thighs trembling. His tongue slid across her clit, his fingers rubbing against some magic spot inside of her while he played with her nipple, and suddenly she couldn't take any more.

She released the blankets and grabbed his head, holding him to her as her climax hit, wave after sweet wave of heated pleasure flowing through her entire body. Heart thundering against her ribs, she sagged against the cot with a ragged groan and tugged at his head to make him stop. He paused only long enough to press one last kiss to her slick folds before lifting his head, and the gleam of victory in his eyes was unmistakable.

She had no words. But as sated and relaxed as she was,

she still wanted more.

Sitting up, she sought his lips with her own, tasting herself on him as she reached down to undo his pants. This time he didn't stop her, wrapping one big hand around her nape and shoving his pants down to his thighs with the other.

Jaliya tried to draw him down on top of her but he made a sound of protest and grabbed her hand instead, pulling it down until she could wrap her fingers around the hot, rigid length of his erection. He groaned into her mouth and tangled his fingers in her hair, pushing into her grip, his fingers locked around hers.

Wanting to draw out the pleasure as he had for her, Jaliya slowed the kiss, sliding her tongue against his as she pumped her fist. His hand tightened in her hair, the slight burn adding to her excitement. He was so hard and thick, straining in her grip. She swirled her fingers around the head of his cock as she worked him, watching his face.

His jaw tightened and his eyes grew heavy-lidded. His breathing sped up and turned shallow. The muscles in his chest and abdomen tightened.

She leaned in to kiss that sexy mouth, her hand moving slow and steady on his rigid length. His tongue plunged between her lips, a low growl emanating from his throat as he pumped into her fist, reaching down to close his hand around hers, squeezing tight. Triumph shot through her when he kicked in her hand, warmth spurting over their joined fingers and onto her stomach.

Zaid broke the kiss and leaned his forehead against hers with a satisfied groan, their fingers still locked together around his erection. They stayed like that for some time, both of them content to bask in the afterglow and savor the closeness.

Finally he kissed her slow and soft on the mouth and drew away. "You okay?" he whispered.

She nodded. "You?"

He laughed softly. "Yeah. I'm okay." He kissed her forehead, and the tenderness of it made her heart squeeze. "Stay here," he whispered, hitching up his pants as he stood.

Suddenly cold and strangely self-conscious without his arms around her, she drew up one knee and grabbed his shirt from the floor to cover her breasts. He crossed the room to grab some tissues and came back to the bed, giving her a sensual smile that made her insides curl before sitting on the edge of the cot and wiping her stomach clean. She avoided his gaze, unsure where to look or what to say now that it was over.

"Hey." He gently grasped her jaw in his hand and lifted her face. "Having second thoughts already?"

What? "No, not at all. I just wondered if maybe you did."

Something possessive flared in his eyes. "No way. You're mine."

She loved the way he said it, and the sentiment behind it. Even if this could only last a short while longer.

He stroked her hair back from her forehead. "You really okay with this?"

"Yes. Thank you."

He chuckled. "Trust me, I should be thanking you. Although technically you still haven't had sex or slept with me."

That made her smile. "No, I haven't, have I?"

"No. So your honor is still intact."

She'd wondered why he hadn't entered her. Now she knew why, and it turned her heart over to know he'd wanted to protect her that way even in the heat of passion. "You make me lose my head."

"Yeah? Well that's only fair, since you do the same to me." He gathered her clothes from the floor and handed them to her.

She tugged them on quickly, relieved when she was

covered once more. "Here're yours." She held out the shirt she'd been holding to her breasts.

He lifted it to his nose and inhaled. His eyes went smoky. "Mmmm, smells like you."

She flushed. "Shame, to cover up such a nice view."

He grinned and pulled the shirt over his arms. "Flatterer."

With reality rushing in to interrupt their interlude, nerves began to take hold. She fiddled with the blanket beside her hip and swallowed. "What you said earlier, about the op."

He drew the shirt over his head and tugged it over his torso. "What about it?"

"Was it the truth? You really don't see what happened as my fault?"

His expression filled with understanding. "Honey, of course it wasn't your fault. It's like I said, shit happened. Nobody has a crystal ball, and no one can predict what will go down during a mission. No one's going to blame you for what happened, and you can't either."

"Because I was thinking that he was right."

"Who?"

"My dad. That I'm not cut out for this job. That I'm not good enough."

Warm, gentle hands cradled her face. She looked up into his gorgeous hazel eyes as he spoke in a low voice. "You are good enough. And I believe in you."

His words hit her in her most vulnerable spot. Until that moment she hadn't realized how badly she'd needed to hear them. To know that he had faith in her and her abilities.

She swallowed the sudden lump in her throat and smiled up at him, the sincerity in his voice warming her straight to her soul. "Thank you."

His gaze was both tender and intense. Steady. Seeing every part of her in a way that no one else ever had.

"You're going to find The Jackal. And when you do, we're gonna nail the son of a bitch."

Chapter Fourteen

The words inside the card blurred as her eyes filled with tears and the strains of *Simply the Best* by Tina Turner filled the air. Jaliya angrily wiped her eyes and finished reading the words while the recorded song played.

You're simply the best, it read in bold red letters. Beneath it, her family had all signed it along with little notes saying how much they missed her, and that they couldn't wait for her to come home. Their timing was uncanny, fresh on the heels of the disastrous op last night.

Even her father had put an X and an O under his note, as close to an *I love you* as he ever gave. He wasn't a demonstrative man, and used praise sparingly. He expected them all to just know that he loved them; they shouldn't need him to say the actual words.

But she yearned to hear them nonetheless. Always had, and probably always would.

Closing the card and setting it down on her bunk, she sat up and swung her legs over the edge, looking around her room. It was cold, almost sterile. And it felt emptier than ever after what she and Zaid had done here last night.

He and his team were headed out on another op shortly. She'd helped compile the intel for it this morning, but had asked David that she not be directly involved with the mission. She was too raw, and worried sick about Zaid. David must have seen how upset she was because he'd let her leave at dinner and told her to take the rest of the night off.

Now here she was, alone in her cell of a room, questioning her role here, as well as her capability as an analyst. Hell, as an agent in general.

She glanced at the paperback on the table that Zaid had loaned her. A military thriller. Reading was one of her favorite pastimes but there was no way she could concentrate enough to get anything out of the story. She wanted Zaid, or at least to hear his voice.

Her gaze strayed to her phone, sitting beside the book. It was the middle of the day, but sometimes her mom finished teaching early on Wednesdays.

Needing to hear a familiar voice, she picked it up and called home. After three rings she expected the answering machine to kick in, but then someone picked up.

"Jaliya?"

She automatically tensed at the sound of her father's voice. "Dad? What are you doing home?"

"I'm packing for a conference in Atlanta. I leave first thing in the morning." He paused. "How are you?"

"I'm fine." She tried to sound cheery, but hard to say whether she pulled it off.

"You working hard?"

"Constantly."

"And? How's it going over there?"

She bit her lips as tears threatened, hitting her in a painful rush.

"Hello? You still there?"

"I'm here," she managed in a whisper.

"What's wrong?" he asked sharply.

"Nothing."

"Jaliya. Why are you upset? Tell me."

Even after all the years she'd spent proving her independence, that stern tone had the desired effect. "I'm… It's just been a tough couple of days, that's all."

He was silent a moment. "Are you all right?"

"I'm okay." Mostly. "We…lost some people yesterday. Last night. I saw it happen live."

"I'm sorry. That's terrible."

She nodded, even though he couldn't see her. "It was tough." She bit her lip, bracing for the words she dreaded but knew were coming. *This is why I never wanted you to take this job. You should be here, with a job that isn't dangerous.*

"Is that why you called?"

"Well, I got your card today. Thanks, I needed it."

He sighed. "Your confidence is shaken because of last night. And now you're blaming yourself for what happened."

She swallowed against the sting of more tears. In spite of their differences, he knew her well. "Yes."

"And wondering whether you should be there at all."

Here it comes.

"Well, let me tell you something. That agency is lucky to have you. You're smart and hard-working, and you're loyal. You would never jeopardize people's lives, I know that without question, and therefore I know that you did everything in your power to prevent the tragedy that occurred."

Jaliya listened in stunned silence, hardly able to believe her ears. Was this really her father? Or an imposter that simply sounded like him?

"Whatever happened, it was *not* your fault, and you can't let this setback stand in your way. You're stronger than that. Regroup, take a deep breath and get back in there. Put one foot in front of the other and don't you dare give into doubt."

Her mouth was hanging open now. She had no idea how to respond, but this was the last thing she'd ever expected to hear from her father. Other than the three little words he couldn't utter.

"You've got what—twelve more weeks left in this posting? Finish it off, give it everything you have, and when you come home, you can think about what else you might want to do instead."

Aaaand, there it was. Her real father was back. She closed her mouth, squeezed her eyes shut and prayed for patience.

"There are plenty of other agencies or companies who would fight to have you on their payroll. You could find one that valued you that let you stay closer to home, and then you would have time to have a social life. You might even meet the right kind of man to settle down with."

Oh, God. "Dad. Stop."

"Well, you might. There's more to life than work, Jaliya. Take it from me, the reformed workaholic. You're young, and beautiful and talented. I don't want you to let life pass you by and regret it later. Life is too short for regrets like that."

He was right about the regret part. "I've met someone," she said, mostly to change the subject.

A startled pause answered her. "Is he Muslim?"

She laughed softly at the hope in his voice. "Ah, Dad, I love you."

He grunted. "I'll take that as a no."

No reciprocal "I love you too" from him, of course. "I'm not telling you anything else about him, except that he was a complete surprise." *And I don't know what the hell I'm going to do about him.* "Actually, I think you'd like him. A lot."

Another grunt. "So. You feel better now?"

"Strangely, yes. Thank you." She paused, wistfulness twining inside her. "It's good to hear your voice."

"Good to hear yours. I'm just sorry you're so upset."

"I'll be okay. Like you said, I'm strong."

"Like father, like daughter, eh?"

She smiled, her heart already lighter than it had been five minutes ago. After this call she was going straight back to the war room. She still had a lot to offer her team. And they were going to nail The Jackal. "Yes. Exactly like that."

****

Yes. Finally.

A wide grin stretched across Zaid's face as he shone his high-powered flashlight at the steel door he'd found hidden in a pit dug into the floor of one of the village's houses.

There'd been a brief firefight when they'd entered the village, but the resistance had been small compared to what they'd been bracing for. So far they'd captured several trucks and prisoners, and the search of the village had led to this.

"Check this out," he called over his shoulder.

Prentiss and Colebrook walked over to peer down at him from above. "Now that looks promising," Prentiss said, and got on his radio. "Khan's found something you gotta see," he said to Hamilton.

The team leader and the rest of the guys all entered the tiny house and crowded around the pit as Zaid leaned back to give them a better look. Hamilton whistled. "Awesome."

Yeah, it kinda was. They'd been searching various villages throughout the last couple of weeks with little to show for it. At the pre-mission briefing earlier Jaliya and her team had told them about a hidden tunnel system located in the vicinity.

One of the SEALs appeared in the open doorway behind Zaid's teammates. "You boys need a hand in here?"

"Nope," Hamilton answered without looking at him. "Let your LT know we may have found the tunnel entrance, though." He nodded at Freeman. "Do your thing."

The former SEAL hopped down next to Zaid and took a closer look at the door.

"Don't see any wires," Zaid said. "Probably didn't have time to rig anything before they took off." But some of the drug smugglers might be lying in wait behind the door.

"Yeah, seems like it," Freeman murmured, angling his head as he studied the seam around the door. After taking a good look, he withdrew his sidearm and looked back at the others. "Nothing on the outside."

Hamilton nodded. "You take point. Khan, Colebrook and Prentiss will back you up. The rest of us will cover you from out here."

Colebrook and Prentiss hopped down into the five-foot deep pit and took up their positions, rifles pointed at the door as Freeman reached for the handle. In the silence the metallic squeak of the handle turning seemed loud.

Zaid stood to the left of the door, weight balanced on the balls of his feet, sighting down the barrel of his weapon. Freeman was at his most vulnerable right now, backlit by the early dawn light filtering through the dwelling's open door.

Freeman eased the door open a few inches, his body carefully angled to the side to minimize damage from a possible IED and make himself as small a target as possible should anyone be waiting to shoot from inside. When nothing happened, he eased it open farther with his boot. Zaid peered into the darkness ahead of him with the tac light on the end of his weapon illuminating what appeared to be a tunnel about four feet high and three feet wide.

Moving quietly, Zaid stepped over to Freeman and placed a hand on his teammate's shoulder while Colebrook and Prentiss moved in behind him. A solid hand landed on Zaid's shoulder and squeezed, and Zaid did the same to Freeman's, alerting their point man that everyone was in position and ready to go.

Freeman paused for another moment, then stepped through the doorway. Zaid followed, getting his first good look inside. It appeared as though the tunnel walls had been hacked out by hand with shovels and pickaxes, rather than blasted. More labor intensive, but a hell of a lot quieter, and it made sense that whoever had built it would want to keep as low a noise profile as possible.

It stretched about twenty yards in front of them before curving to the right. Freeman stopped a few yards from it and hugged the wall.

The distant scrambling of feet echoed ahead of them, out of sight. Men, trying to escape.

Zaid would bet they'd been guarding something. Or someone.

His pulse rate kicked up as he followed Freeman around the bend in the tunnel, while Hamilton quietly alerted the SEALs over the radio to apprise them of the situation. Could The Jackal be waiting up ahead?

"Copy that. Stay in your location. We'll take over from there," the SEAL said.

"Roger," Hamilton replied.

Freeman stopped abruptly and Zaid looked past him to zero in on what lay ahead of them. A wave of surprise burst over him. Ahead of them in what appeared to be a surprisingly large room carved out of the rock, was the mother lode.

"Holy hell," Zaid muttered, stepping closer.

Bricks of what had to be hashish sat wrapped in black plastic and stacked floor to ceiling. A few million dollars' worth, at least. There was also a big pile of weapons, including a few RPGs.

"Someone's gonna be pissed that this didn't make it across the border," Colebrook said from behind him.

"Makes me feel all warm inside just to imagine it," Zaid said.

He couldn't wait for Jaliya to find out. Her confidence had been badly shaken by the SF team op the other night. If anything could boost it, this would.

The SEALs joined them several minutes later, glanced at the hidden cache and then carried on down the tunnel to try and capture their prey. Zaid and his teammates took a closer look at what the smugglers had left behind, then catalogued everything before hauling it all out of the tunnel.

When the area was secure an hour later and everyone was accounted for, the mood got even more festive when the SEALs returned with prisoners—one of them on their high value list.

Standing before the pile of dope and weapons, Hamilton grinned at Zaid and held out the sat phone. "You do the honors and call it in. I got a few things to wrap up here anyway."

Zaid took it with a smile and immediately dialed Jaliya's cell number. As far as he knew she wasn't scheduled to be overseeing this op directly, and she deserved to be contacted first.

"Rabani," she answered.

"Hey, it's me."

A startled pause followed. "Zaid?"

God, he loved the sound of her voice. Could still remember the taste of her on his tongue and the bite of her nails in his scalp as he made her come. He couldn't wait to see her again. "Yeah."

"Where are you?"

"At the target village."

"What are you doing, calling me?" She sounded flustered.

"Wanted you to be the first to hear the good news."

"What good news?"

"You were right. We found the tunnels."

"You did?" He could hear the smile in her voice, the joy, and wished like hell he'd been able to see her reaction in person.

"Yep. Along with a big-ass cache of weapons and hash. We even rounded up a few prisoners, including an HVT."

She gasped. "Who?"

"One of The Jackal's lieutenants." He gave the man's name.

"You got him?" She sounded elated. "Did you question him?"

"Tried. He's not talking right now, but the chatter around here indicates that The Jackal was here as of a few hours ago. The SEALs are working on finding his trail right now."

"Oh, that's bloody brilliant," she breathed in her cute British accent.

"Yeah." His girl had done good. "I wanted you to hear it from me."

"Well thank you for that, I appreciate it. So, how are you?"

"I'm great."

"No close calls out there, I hope?"

He smiled. "Nah. I'm safe and sound. We all are."

She let out a relieved breath. "Good. Will you be coming back to Bagram?"

"No. Back to the FOB we launched from, in case we get a lead on The Jackal."

"Ah. Of course."

He was damned pleased to hear the disappointment in her voice. It meant she missed him. Hopefully as much as he missed her. He wanted to spend more time with her, get to know her better and prove this was way more than physical for him. "Absence makes the heart grow fonder."

"Right. They're uh, moving us back to Kabul tomorrow sometime. Not sure when."

Disappointment flooded him. They wouldn't get to see each other, even when his team got back to Bagram. "You'll let me know where?"

"Yes."

Hamilton was motioning for his phone back. "I gotta go," Zaid said, wishing they could have talked longer. Or at least about something more than work. "I'll text you later if I can."

"Okay. And, Zaid?"

"Yeah?"

"Thank you. I'm chuffed that you called me yourself."

Chuffed was good. He was damn proud of her. "You did good, honey. You did *real* good." Hamilton was giving him the steely-eyed stare now, hands on hips. "I'll talk to you soon."

Zaid ended the call and handed the phone to his team leader. As he headed back to where the others were burning the hash, he couldn't wipe the smile off his face.

****

Fahim jumped out of the dilapidated vehicle that had driven him to the main highway through the darkness and immediately crossed to the one waiting for him at the shoulder. He was furious…and scared.

"The shipment's been seized," he said to the new driver as he slammed the passenger door shut. "I need to get back to Kabul as fast as possible."

He ran a hand through his hair and fought to calm his

jangled nerves. That had been way too damn close. He'd barely escaped the village before the Americans had inserted.

If not for the tunnel system, he would have been trapped, and either dead or captured by now. Thankfully he'd received enough warning to make it through the tunnel and out the exit at the end, outside the village walls. He'd made it to the valley on foot, using the terrain to try and screen his movements from any satellites or drones they might have monitoring the area.

Whoever the DEA's informant was, he was linked to someone in Fahim's inner circle. It was the only explanation for how the taskforce had gotten a lock on the shipment's location at some point late last night.

Who was it? Who the hell *was* it? He thought he'd taken care of everyone the DEA had been using for information on him. All of them winding up dead by one method or another should have been a strong enough deterrent to prevent this situation.

Pulling a burner phone from his pocket once he was within range of a cell tower, he called his only remaining lieutenant. "They've seized the shipment and almost got me with it."

A moment of startled silence followed. "Where are you now?"

"On my way back to Kabul." If the military wasn't already following him, he might have a chance to make it back. He pulled in a calming breath before continuing. "We have to find out who their informant is. He's too close, and knows too much."

"I just got off the phone with someone claiming to know who it is. I'm not sure how reliable he is though."

"Follow up on it and report back to me immediately. I want to take action, send a message once we find out who it is." He would show no mercy to whoever had sold him out to the DEA. He paid dearly to ensure the villagers stayed loyal to him and kept his secrets.

"Of course."

"Leave everything else and focus on this. I want to know who it is by tonight."

"Yes, sir."

He ended the call and put the phone away, glancing in the side mirror to see the lightening eastern sky. Another clear, cold day, only a scattering of clouds overhead. Perfect conditions for tracking him with a device.

He thought of his wife and son, imagined them curled up together in Beena's bed. His fingers itched to pull the phone back out so he could call home, but the nights were always hardest and he didn't want to disturb them or rob them of the precious amount of sleep they were able to get.

It took another ninety minutes for them to reach the outskirts of Kabul.

"Take me to my office," he said, reaching into the backseat to withdraw a fresh uniform from a bag left there. After changing, it took just another ten minutes until they reached the building. Since it was barely six in the morning, the heavily secured compound was quiet, with only a few guards on duty.

His assistant wasn't in yet, so he strode straight to his office and opened the door. He stopped short at the sight of his wife sitting in front of his desk. "What are you doing here? Where's Beena?" he croaked out.

Her dark eyes looked bruised underneath, her skin pale and stretched thin over her bones, the weight of exhaustion making her look a decade older. "Where have you been?" she whispered, her expression full of reproach.

His heart thudded against his ribs. "We were conducting an operation." He'd told her that before leaving Kabul last night.

"I called you and called you, but you didn't answer,"

she choked out, and his heart constricted with sheer terror.

"What's happened? Is it Beena?"

The reproach bled out of her gaze, only to be replaced by a haunted look. "He's at the hospital."

His heart seemed to stop beating. *No ...*

"My mother is with him. I...I had to get away, just for a little while." She let out a ragged sigh. "He had a really bad night. The worst night yet. And there was nothing I could do for him except sit and hold his hand while the ambulance rushed him to the hospital—" She pressed a hand to her mouth and squeezed her eyes shut.

Fahim rushed over and went onto one knee before her, grasping her other hand, his fingers locking around her cold skin. "Is he..." He couldn't finish the thought aloud, his heart about to implode.

She shook her head, lowered her hand from her face, but the sheen of tears there sliced at his guts. "He's still with us, thanks be to God. But I fear not for much longer."

He closed his eyes and exhaled in relief. "God is good."

His wife remained in the chair, her posture rigid. "You keep promising me that you've found a solution."

"I *have* found one."

"Then why haven't you done anything yet? What are you *waiting* for?" she cried, the tears finally spilling over.

Fahim reached for her and pulled her into his arms, holding her tight, his cheek pressed to the top of her hijab. He could smell the light floral fragrance of her shampoo as he stroked a hand over her back.

"I'm doing everything I can," he said helplessly. For a man like him, so accustomed to command and control over everything, this was unbearable. Not being able to protect the one person who needed his protection the most. "I've found a surgeon, but locating a donor...could take a while."

She pushed away and wiped at her face angrily. "He

doesn't have a while left, Fahim. It might already be too late."

He blanched and stared at her while blood pulsed in his ears.

She pulled in an unsteady breath and pushed to her feet, leaving him kneeling there on the floor. "I don't know what you've arranged, or with whom. And I don't care. I don't care what you've been up to or how you've raised the money. All I care is that our son gets the chance to be healthy again and live a normal life."

He nodded. "He will get that chance. I swear it."

She looked away, her sadness wrapped around her like a fog. And Fahim would do anything, anything at all, to take away the terrible fear pervading them both, to make their son healthy again.

He pushed to his feet. "You're exhausted. Let me drive you home so you can rest."

She shook her head tightly. "No. I've already left him alone too long."

"He's not alone. And I'll go straight to the hospital to stay with him." When she hesitated, he took her hand and pulled her into another hug, then kissed her forehead. He loved this woman. She was his other half and he couldn't stand to see her hurting like this. "Come with me."

He drove her home personally. They didn't speak, and he could tell from her hollow-eyed stare out the window that she was way past exhaustion.

At their home he took her upstairs and tucked her into bed, pausing to kiss her softly before returning to the vehicle. As soon as he fired up the engine, he pulled out his phone and dialed the number he'd memorized.

"Fahim! Are you calling with good news?"

"My son is dying. I don't know how much longer he has left. We can't wait any longer, we have to act now. Do whatever it is you have to do, I don't care how much it costs. But do it *now*." His voice shook.

"That's going to cost you, *amigo*. Maybe another hundred thousand."

"I don't care."

"Have you got the money?"

"I have another shipment ready to go for tomorrow night." It was foolhardy, practically suicidal after how close it had been last night, but he had no choice. "Once that crosses the border, I'll have enough. In the meantime, I want to get him over there immediately. So that the surgery can happen as soon as a donor becomes available."

"Have you got a plane?"

"I'll get one."

"No need. I can take care of that for you, for an extra cost, of course."

Of course. "Fine, I'll wire you the money today. When?"

"Noon."

He blinked. "Today?"

"You want to wait longer?"

"No."

"Take him and your wife to this airport." He named a private airstrip north of the city. "I'll have a medical team on board. They'll accompany your family here, where they will stay as my personal guests until the surgery can take place."

"Do I have your word that that they will both be protected?"

"Yes. They'll be treated as honored guests while they're here, and will lack for nothing. They'll be safe. I swear it on my mother's life."

The promise carried weight, because it was rumored that the man revered his family, and especially his mother.

It was a huge gamble, to trust the two most precious people on earth to a man with as ruthless a reputation as *El Escorpion*. But with the alternative being watching

Beena die in a Kabul hospital bed, what choice did he have?

"All right. I'll have them at the airport at noon. Text me the amount you want me to wire you."

"Good. And try not to worry. I'll look after them both as if they were my own blood."

His throat tightened. "Thank you."

He ended the call and put the phone away, his mind churning furiously as he turned onto his street and drove to the hospital. His wife would argue at first when he told her the plan. But she would do it, because she loved their son more than anything.

His hands tightened around the steering wheel as he drove through the waking city, the outline of the boxy hospital building coming into view in the distance. He thought of Beena lying in one of its beds, hooked up to tubes and monitors while they fought to keep oxygen flowing through his tiny body.

It couldn't be too late. Not after everything he'd risked to get this far.

Not when he was prepared to sacrifice himself to ensure that his son lived.

Chapter Fifteen

Jaliya knocked on the door to her boss's new office in Kabul before cracking it open and poking her head in. David was at his desk going over some files. "Hey. Can I talk to you for a minute? It's important."

He closed the file. "Sure."

"Not here."

David gave her a puzzled look for a moment but when she gestured for him to follow her, he got up and crossed the room. "Where are we going?"

"If anyone asks, we'll just say we're going to grab some lunch."

He walked with her down to the lobby of the building the DEA had set them up in. But she didn't stop there, choosing instead to exit the building and walk half a block down the street to a tiny park before sitting on the wooden bench there.

"What's going on?" he asked as he sank down next to her.

She didn't care if it seemed like she was being overly paranoid. "I didn't feel comfortable talking about this in there." She nodded back toward the building. "I've long suspected that someone on the inside is interfering with our efforts to find The Jackal, and as of this morning I'm more convinced than ever."

"All right, I'm listening."

"My team has been analyzing all our data and intel for the past two days. We're getting close to identifying who he is."

He frowned at her. "Okay…"

She took a deep breath and pulled a folded piece of paper out of her pocket, showing the pictures of three men. One was the deputy chief of police. One was a suspected lieutenant of The Jackal's.

And one was a military commander linked to the Afghan army. Colonel Shah.

David looked up at her in astonishment. "Are you serious?"

"It has to be one of them. And as of right now, my gut's leaning toward him." She tapped Shah's photo. And she was listening to her gut on this one because the successful seizure last night had bolstered both her confidence and self-esteem. She was feeling good and more determined than ever to nail The Jackal.

"But that doesn't make any sense. It's his men we've been sending out to assist with the various teams. He's been helping coordinate the missions personally—"

"Exactly."

David fell silent, his shocked expression mirroring exactly how she'd felt when she'd finally realized what had been right under her nose all the time. "But his record is impeccable. Beyond reproach. I vetted him personally after the agency did the initial background check prior to bringing him on board, and when we looked at everything again last week due to this leak, he still checked out."

"I know. We think something drastic must have changed in his personal life over the past few months."

David shook his head. "Shit, if it turns out to be him…"

"Yeah." Hence her wanting to talk about this outside of the office.

He ran a hand over his face. "Okay. You're still investigating the other two?"

"Yes."

"So where is the colonel now?"

"Missing."

He looked at her sharply. "Since when?"

"Since yesterday afternoon. No one's seen or heard from him since he left Bagram after the noon briefing. I've got people trying to find him right now." Three of her best analysts, working all their technological wizardry tracking phone signals and satellite feeds.

Her phone rang. She dug it out of her pocket, a jolt of energy running through her when she saw the number.

"Barakat. Where are you?" she asked in Dari. Desperation had apparently made him overcome his aversion to working with a woman. He'd contacted her early that morning with a message saying he had information about The Jackal's whereabouts. They had agreed to meet to discuss it in person but he hadn't shown up. Probably to save his own skin, since she could offer him protection by bringing him to Bagram where he'd be safe.

"They're after me."

She stood, the panic in his voice slicing through her. "Who?"

"The Jackal and his men. They know who I am, and what I've done." He sounded panicked and out of breath, as though he'd been running.

"All right, slow down. Tell me where you are and I'll come get you."

"*No*, they could be following you."

She needed to calm him down. "Barakat, listen to me.

I need you to calm down—"

"No! I'm not dying for you or anyone else. I want out. I'm finished with this."

Think Jaliya, think. "You're not going to die, Barakat. Not if you let me bring you in. I can protect you."

"No you can't," he spat.

"Then why did you call me?"

"Because I don't have anyone else. The elders found out I've been working with your agency and they banished me from the village last night. I think they're the ones who told The Jackal where I am."

Goosebumps broke out over her skin. She pushed Barakat because she was so close to finding the answer, and desperate enough to risk asking. "Do you know who he is? Is it Colonel Shah?"

"I...don't know. But it could be. I heard his name mentioned last night before I was banished."

Jaliya closed her eyes, a rush of adrenaline surging through her veins. *Yes.* "We found evidence against him this morning." But that wasn't important now. "You said you had a location. Tell me where it is at least. Tell me so I can get him and make this all go away. Once he's captured, you'll be safe."

Barakat didn't answer for a long moment. In the silence she made out the sounds of heavy traffic moving in the background. Horns and different kinds of engines. He had to be in Kabul somewhere. Why wouldn't he let her help him?

"He's overseeing a shipment tonight," he said finally. "I heard he's going to smuggle it over the border north of the Khyber Pass."

Her heart beat faster. "When?"

"After midnight."

"Do you know where—"

"I've told you everything I know," he snapped. "Now just leave me alone and don't contact me ever again."

The line went dead.

David was beside her, watching her intently. "It's Shah," she said, only a tiny part of her questioning whether Barakat was telling the truth. The fear in his voice had been all too real, as was his reluctance in telling her. And all their evidence backed it up.

He cursed under his breath. "No one else can know outside of our agency team. It's too risky—we can't afford anyone to leak it. I'm not going to lose Shah now."

Before she could respond, her phone rang again. This time it was one of her analysts. "Tell me you've got something on Shah," she said.

"Got a ping from a security feed at an airstrip north of the city."

Shit. The bastard must have figured out that they were onto him and escaped the city. "Where did he fly to?"

"He didn't."

"What?"

"He dropped a woman and kid off. Loaded them onto a private jet at noon, then drove away."

That didn't make any sense. Shah was unmarried, and had no close relatives that they knew of. "Who were the woman and child?"

"We're working on it."

"Where's the plane heading?"

"Turkey to refuel, then Portugal and on to Mexico."

Mexico? "Where?"

"Veracruz."

She sucked in a sharp breath. My God. The *Venenos*. Shah must be working with them directly somehow. "Who is the plane registered to?"

"A private company based out of London."

"Alert our people in Veracruz. Have them intercept the plane when it lands. I want to know what the woman and kid are doing there."

"Will do."

She hung up and told David the latest. "I need to contact Commander Taggart," she said, dialing his number. He was the only one who could green light a mission based on this intel. "Barakat said there's a shipment going through near the Khyber Pass tonight, and Shah is supposedly going to be there in person."

"Taggart."

Just hearing his voice on the other end of the line made her feel better. She quickly relayed the update and conversation with Barakat and started back toward the office building, her mind whirling.

David was right beside her on a call of his own when she finished with Taggart. "We're meeting him at Bagram in two hours. FAST Bravo is being placed on alert right now," she told him.

He nodded and covered the bottom of his phone with one hand. "Then let's get a move on."

Yes. They were finally going to nail this sonofabitch.

****

In the frigid darkness Zaid gripped his weapon and waited for the command to disembark as they descended toward the LZ. Cold air rushed in through the helo's open starboard side door as they neared the ground. Seconds later the Blackhawk went into a low hover. The door gunner and crew chief verified that the area was clear, then the chief tossed the fast rope out the door.

Everyone knew the mission. They all knew the terrain and the topography through this part of the Spin Ghar Mountains, along with possible hiding spots for enemy fighters and likely ambush sites.

But as he waited for the order to insert, Zaid thought about Jaliya.

He hadn't seen her in a few days but she'd been on his mind constantly. Her smile, the way her eyes sparkled or flashed, and those sweet sounds she'd made as she'd come against his tongue and fingers.

Though he'd sworn to avoid any romantic entanglements while he was over here, she'd gotten to him, and the thought of letting her go now was unbearable on every level. He'd been trying to figure out a way to convince her to take a stab at a long-distance relationship with him, but in all honestly he wasn't sure how it could ever work long-term, with him only coming to Afghanistan once a year for four months.

He had no idea how many more years she was going to serve over here, but she was young and had a long career ahead of her. And when he was here with his team, they were bounced around from place to place, often not staying for more than a few days in one spot.

Sometimes she had business in D.C., though. That was better than nothing, and worth a shot because God knew no other woman he'd met could compare with Jaliya. She was a woman worth fighting for.

Good thing he was a warrior at heart, as well as a lover.

"Radio check," Hamilton said through Zaid's earpiece, pulling him back to the present.

The team checked their equipment and checked in with Taggart back at the TOC at Bagram. Jaliya was there watching. She and her team had been working on intel for this op all day and feeding it to them at the FOB.

He liked knowing she had eyes on him and the others for the duration of the op. He just hoped there wouldn't be a repeat of the disastrous op by the SF team.

Zaid didn't want to die. He wasn't some reckless cowboy who took stupid risks during a mission. He wanted to live a long, full life, and he wanted Jaliya by his side throughout the rest of it.

But if for some reason the worst occurred and his number came up tonight, he didn't want her to see it happen.

Chapter Sixteen

In the back of the helicopter he was riding in, Fahim ended the call and leaned his head back against the wall of the aircraft with a deep sigh. The first truck had made it across the Pakistani border, thanks be to God.

"Sir, eighteen minutes to target," the crew chief told him.

Fahim nodded in acknowledgment but didn't respond verbally, his mind busy reviewing the logistics of the coming op. One major hurdle had been overcome with that truck making it across. But he needed all four to get across if he was going to have a prayer of coming up with the remainder of the money to pay for Beena's surgery. If he had to sell his own soul or die to do it, he'd get the damn money.

He motioned his lieutenant over to review contingency plans. If he should be captured or killed tonight, every last one of his men had been instructed to do whatever was necessary to ensure the drugs made it to their final destination.

The only reason he was overseeing this operation

personally was because the stakes were too high to leave anything to chance. Guilt needled him at what he was about to do, but he ignored it.

It was too late to stop this now. Things had already been set into motion. He was way beyond the point of no return, and second-guessing himself now was pointless.

This final shipment would allow him to escape the region and join his family in Mexico. It would give Beena the chance of living past his sixth birthday. And it was also part of the deal he'd made with *El Escorpion.* Going back on his word would mean his death, and likely that of his innocent wife and child. At least this way, he had a chance of surviving. And if he didn't, his wife would do everything in her power to take care of their son.

He'd waited until Shah had dropped her and Beena off at the airstrip north of Kabul. Then he'd returned to Bagram, sat in on the mission briefing before going dark and making his own arrangements for tonight. Just before boarding the helo he'd received word that his family had arrived safely in Veracruz a few hours ago.

Now he was on high alert, flying through the darkness toward the Spin Ghar Mountains, ready to launch the fight of his life.

The timing of this was critical. The pressure was on him, the eyes and ears of a half dozen international intelligence agencies looking for clues that would lead them to The Jackal. Fahim had to secure this shipment and make it across the border where allies linked to the *Veneno* cartel would smuggle him down to Karachi and fly him to Veracruz.

But first he had to deal with the members of FAST Bravo and the men from his unit who weren't loyal to him. Then he could move the drugs and make his way across the border.

The advantage lay in knowing that no one but the men aboard this aircraft knew what was coming. And that the

Americans thought Shah was The Jackal. That stroke of luck might give Fahim the edge he needed.

He closed his eyes and leaned back against the helo's wall, letting the vibrations calm him, and thought of his family. It gave him strength. And courage. Just a few more hours and he would melt into obscurity in the Mexican desert, far away from all the prying eyes searching for him.

****

Jaliya entered the TOC at Bagram to find Commander Taggart and some of the other key players on the taskforce riveted to the video monitors showing a live feed of the helicopters' progress across Afghan airspace, headed north of the Khyber Pass. Zaid and the rest of FAST Bravo were on one of them, the NIU members on the other.

They had about twenty-five minutes until they reached the insertion point. The most recent intelligence said that The Jackal's latest shipment was being smuggled across the border within the next few hours, in trucks carrying medical supplies.

"How's everything look?" she asked the room in general.

"Everything's on target," Taggart answered without looking at her as he watched the screen, feet planted apart, arms folded across his broad chest.

Her phone vibrated in her pocket. She pulled it out, and when she saw one of her analyst's numbers, she answered. "This is Rabani."

"Your young informant was brought into Joint Craig Hospital ten minutes ago with serious gunshot wounds."

Her lungs seized. "Barakat?"

"Yes. They're getting a trauma team ready right now."

God. "I'm on my way."

"What's wrong?" David asked, putting a hand on her arm.

"Barakat's been shot. They're prepping him for surgery. I have to get there before they put him under." Without waiting for a response she rushed out the door and ran over to the hospital.

By the time she got there and explained who she was, two nurses were already wheeling his bed toward the O.R. at the end of the hall. "Wait!"

They stopped and she flashed her badge at them as she raced over. Panting, she grabbed the rail of the bed and stared down into Barakat's pale, pain-pinched face. He had an oxygen mask over his face and dressings covering his belly, soaked with fresh blood. The sight and smell of it made her stomach pitch.

"Barakat. Who did this to you?" she demanded in Dari.

His dark eyes fluttered open and focused on her blearily. "Hurts," he moaned.

She reached for his hand, wrapped her fingers around his. "I know it does. They're taking you into the operating room. The doctors here are excellent. They'll fix you up." She squeezed his hand. "Who shot you?"

"Jackal's…men," he rasped.

"Ma'am, we need to get him into the operating room now. You'll have to wait until after he's out of recovery."

Jaliya nodded but otherwise ignored the woman, keeping up with them as they wheeled him toward the doors at the end of the hall. "Did you see their faces?"

Barakat shook his head, grimacing.

"Where did it happen?"

He cried out in agony, sweat beading his forehead.

"They found him on the side of the road a few miles from base," one of the nurses said.

She felt badly for him, hated to see him suffering, but there was far too much at stake here to let this go. "Barakat. Were you coming here to find me? Did you need to tell me something?"

He squeezed his eyes shut, managed a slight nod.

Jaliya leaned over him, heart pounding. "Barakat. I know it hurts, but before they take you into the operating room, I need to know what you came to tell me."

His eyes cracked open, and when they focused on her, the fear in his gaze sent a shiver ripping down her spine. "I know…who he is," he said.

The nurses slowed and one of them put a hand on her shoulder. "Okay, ma'am. You'll have to stay here—"

"No, *wait*." She pushed the woman's restraining hand off and bent over to place her free hand on Barakat's scruffy cheek, bringing that pain-glazed gaze back to hers. "It's Shah. Remember? We already talked about it this morning."

"No," he protested, growing agitated. "No. Not…him."

Cold spread through her gut. "What?"

He bared his teeth, the muscles in his throat standing out as he fought the agony.

"Barakat. Are you saying it's not Shah?"

He shook his head. "Help," he begged. "Make it stop."

She clenched his hand tight, desperate to get through to him. "Who is it?"

Endless seconds passed while she awaited his answer.

"Barakat. Tell me who it is. Who is The Jackal?"

He focused on her slowly, his throat moving as he swallowed. "Nasar."

Ice splintered throughout her body. "What?" she whispered.

"Nasar," he repeated, then his face twisted and he bared his teeth as a terrible cry of pain echoed off the walls.

"Let go, *now*," one of the nurses snapped, and shoved Jaliya backward. They pushed through the double doors leading to the operating room.

Shock kept her rooted to the floor for a moment as her mind struggled to compute what Barakat had just said.

General Nasar was The Jackal. And he had coordinated tonight's op with FAST Bravo.

Stricken, she yanked out her phone and dialed Taggart as she spun and ran for the door. It rang and rang in her ear, but he didn't answer.

"Shit," she whispered, hanging up and trying David. "Come on, pick up. Pick *up*."

He didn't.

She swallowed back a scream of frustration and helplessness and ran as fast as she could, trying other numbers, with the same result. By the time she reached the building the TOC was located in she was gasping and light-headed, sweating despite the icy cold air.

She flung the exterior door open, her boots thudding on the linoleum floor as she ran for the second door on the left. Everything was brighter. Louder. Including the thud of her heart in her ears. Zaid was out there, and his team. They didn't know. Didn't realize the danger they faced.

Wrenching the TOC door open, the distinctive sound of gunfire from the live feed hit her and she stopped dead.

Her blood pressure took a nosedive as six pairs of eyes jerked to her. She looked at Taggart, the terrible news she had to deliver frozen on her tongue as he stared at her and shook his head, face grim as he muttered, "All hell's breaking loose down there."

Chapter Seventeen

W hat the fuck was happening?
"Contact, ten o'clock!" Freeman shouted.
Zaid scrambled after Rodriguez over the
rocks and dove behind the cover of a group of boulders
on the hill above the road. "What the hell?"

"You guys see anything?" Rodriguez shouted to Kai
and Prentiss, pinned down a dozen yards or so from them
in a shallow gulley.

"Negative," Prentiss yelled back.

The rest of the team was scattered in two remaining
groups nearby. Cover here was scarce, so they had to
make the best use of what they could find.

Zaid kept his head down and waited for a break in the
firing to steal a peek at what was happening below near
the road. Shit had gone sideways in a matter of seconds.
They'd walked into an ambush moments ago, but he had
no clue who was firing at them, as there hadn't been any
enemy reported in the area. Was there a tunnel system
nearby where the enemy had hidden?

"Fall back," Hamilton ordered, his voice tense.

Oh, shit. They had to be badly outnumbered or outgunned for their team leader to give that order. He snuck a peek through a gap in the boulders, his chin brushing the ground.

"How bad?" Rodriguez asked, sprawled out next to Zaid on his belly with his weapon to his shoulder.

There was enough ambient light for him to make out the shapes of the men moving around by the convoy through his NVGs. More men than they had with them. "Bad." His pulse drummed hard and fast in his throat.

"Khan and Rodriguez, fall back on my command to the north behind the ridge. The rest of us will provide cover fire," Hamilton ordered.

"Roger," Zaid replied, then clamped his jaw tight and maneuvered his weapon into position.

"*Go.*"

Though every one of his instincts told him to stay put, Zaid obeyed his team leader, shoved to his feet, and ran like hell for the ridge above. The volume of fire picked up immediately.

Light from the tracer rounds streaked past him in the darkness, thudding into the rocks and ground, kicking up sprays of dirt.

His lungs strained in the thin air, the muscles in his thighs burning as he pushed himself to run as fast as he could, with Rodriguez pounding over the terrain a few strides behind him. After what seemed like an endless amount of time they reached the ridge and dove over the edge of it.

Panting, Zaid rolled over the far side and crawled back to the lip to peer down at the winding road below so he could find out what the hell was going on. The NIU was retreating in chaos. Several of its members were down, lying strewn across the road and the bottom of the slope.

Then he saw the shooters and his blood ran cold.

"Khan, what do you see from up there?" Hamilton

demanded, still pinned behind cover down the slope with the others.

What the *fuck*? He wasn't even sure what he was looking at. "The NIU. They're shooting at each other— and us." No goddamn wonder they hadn't been able to figure out where the attack was coming from.

"Say again?"

"They're fucking shooting at us!"

"Motherfuckers," Rodriguez muttered, taking aim and firing a few rounds downrange at the men shooting at them from below.

Out of nowhere, Jaliya's face flashed through Zaid's mind. She was probably back at the TOC, watching and seeing all this live via satellite or Hamilton's helmet cam. He thought of his parents back in New Jersey, waiting for his next call or text to tell them he was okay.

This was bullshit. He was *not* dying out here. And neither were any of his guys.

"Maka and Prentiss, you're up next," Hamilton said via comms. "On my command. And…go."

Zaid and Rodriguez opened up on the NIU members firing at them from behind the military trucks as Maka and Prentiss broke from behind cover and raced up the slope. Zaid tagged one guy as he stepped around the back of the last truck. The traitor fell to his knees and keeled over on the road, his weapon still in his hands.

Another target appeared to the left. Zaid aimed and squeezed the trigger just as a round hit the top of the ridge a foot from him. Bits of sand and gravel peppered his right shoulder.

Moments later, Maka and Prentiss made it to the ridge and slid down the far side before scrambling up to join him and Rodriguez.

Freeman and Lockhart darted over the open ground after that, leaving Hamilton, Freeman and Granger still down below.

"You boys got us covered up there?" Hamilton asked, voice tense.

"You know it," Zaid answered, looking for another target. Until they figured out what the fuck was going on and exactly who the enemy was down there, it was a total shit show.

"Okay, on three," Hamilton said. "Two. One. *Go*."

Their three remaining teammates bolted from their concealed position and scattered as they raced up the hill. Zaid and the others opened up on the trucks from behind the relative safety of the ridge. In his peripheral vision he tracked Freeman rushing toward them.

Two thirds of the way up, Freeman fell.

Shit.

"Freeman's down." Zaid's heart slammed against his ribs as the former SEAL struggled to his feet. Had he been hit?

"I'm not hit," Freeman said. "But I'm pinned down and can't move without getting my ass shot off."

Freeman was totally exposed out there, easy pickings for the fucktards firing from behind the trucks. And Hamilton and Granger were too far away to help him.

Zaid was getting him out of there.

"Cover me," he yelled over the gunfire, and darted behind the others to the left, angling for the closest concealed position to Freeman.

He could hear someone else moving behind him but didn't stop to look back. Granger and Hamilton made it to the ridge and jumped over the edge to safety. Zaid kept running, paused only a moment when he reached the spot he'd chosen, and risked a look down the slope with his weapon up, ready to fire. Freeman had found a medium-sized boulder to crouch behind, but he was taking heavy fire.

"You guys ready?" Zaid asked his teammates, loading a fresh mag into his rifle. They were all poised behind the lip of the ridge, weapons aimed downrange.

"Roger that," Maka replied without looking up from his M4. At the far right of their line, Hamilton was on the radio, hopefully requesting air support.

Zaid looked back down at Freeman, who hadn't moved, still returning suppressive fire from his spot. Now the NIU survivors were racing up the slope toward FAST Bravo's position. But how the hell were they supposed to tell friend from foe?

"What a fucking nightmare," he muttered under his breath.

Freeman was still holding on.

"Let's do this."

Zaid glanced behind him to find Prentiss crouched there. He nodded. "Cap?" he asked Hamilton.

"Ready. Freeman, Khan and Prentiss are coming to you. Get ready. Rest of you, concentrate your fire on those trucks," their team leader said.

"Copy," Freeman answered, the foreign note of stress in his voice sending a surge of adrenaline through Zaid's body.

He pulled in a deep breath and let it out slowly, his muscles tensing, weight poised on the balls of his feet. *Now.*

He charged over the lip of the ridge, firing at the targets moving below on the road while his teammates opened up with suppressive fire. Prentiss was right behind him.

"Move, Freeman," Zaid ordered, rushing to his teammate as he fired, the retreating NIU members coming up the slope adding to the confusion.

Freeman bolted from behind cover and hauled ass up the slope. The moment he reached them, Zaid and Prentiss began their retreat, firing as they moved. Rounds whizzed around them, the tracers streaking past in the darkness. Zaid's heart pounded against his sternum as he raced back to the safety of the ridge and jumped over the lip.

Panting, he closed his eyes for a moment and said a prayer of thanks before looking over at Hamilton, who was still on the radio but watching the situation below with a sharp eye. Using hand motions, the team leader ordered them to move east, staying behind the ridge. All nine of them got up and moved single file toward a rise that would give them a good vantage point so they could see what was happening below.

"Gunship should be on station within the next six minutes," Hamilton reported as they ran in a crouch to their new position. "Khan, see if you can find out what the hell's going on from those guys," he said, meaning the NIU members racing for the safety of the ridge.

Zaid didn't know what kind of aircraft Hamilton had requested, and he didn't care so long as it showed up in a hurry to clear off those traitorous assholes below. He searched the faces of the NIU members scrambling up the hill.

He recognized one as the man slid over the edge of the ridge and ran toward the guy, weapon up. "Drop your weapon!" he yelled in Dari.

The man whirled, his eyes wide, and quickly lowered his weapon before holding his hands up.

"Why are you shooting at us?"

"Not us! Them!" He waved an arm toward the chaos unfolding below them. "Our own members opened fire on us before turning on you."

"Where's General Nasar?" He was supposed to be here directing his men. Had he been hit?

"I have not seen him," the man panted.

This was so fucked up. FAST Bravo had worked with this same NIU unit for three consecutive deployments now, and FAST Alpha longer than that. And Nasar couldn't just have disappeared into thin air. Zaid had seen the guy getting onto another Blackhawk back at base.

"How many attacked you?"

"At least half of our force."

Half their own force had turned on the other? "Why?" Why the fuck would they do this? Were they hoping to capture the shipment themselves, then get it across the border and sell it to make a profit?

"I don't know! I swear I don't know what's—" The man broke off and hunched over, his expression twisting as he dragged his hands down his face with a choked sound.

Zaid reported his findings to Hamilton as he hurried back to his own team. Until they knew who they could trust on the NIU, that unit was on their own.

Hamilton was on the radio again. "Copy that." He cursed and grabbed for his weapon. "You're not gonna fucking believe this," he said, and Zaid's stomach dropped. Every man on the team was watching Hamilton now. "It's Nasar. He's The Jackal."

Zaid reeled at the announcement. But it made so much sense all of a sudden.

Nasar had been at all the briefings. He had the training and knowhow to pull something like this off. He knew the mission inside and out. How many men would be here, the timing, everything.

Rage built inside Zaid, a hot pressure expanding beneath his ribs. That *fucker*. That fucker had set them all up to die here so he could get his dope across the border.

The sound of approaching aircraft filled the air. Zaid glanced to his left just as the two Apaches appeared out of nowhere, rising into view from where they'd been hidden behind a hill in the distance.

A roar of approval rang out from the team. Zaid rolled to his belly and put the stock of his weapon to his shoulder, peering over the edge of the ridge as the attack helicopters unleashed a stream of withering fire on the enemy from their 30 mm cannons.

The world below them exploded in a blast of light and sound. Then a 70 mm rocket hit the center truck and detonated. The blast wave ripped through the air and ground, thudding against Zaid's eardrums and compressing his chest. When he opened his eyes to look down, all three trucks were nothing more than twisted hunks of burning metal.

Bye bye poppy juice, and whatever the hell else had been in there.

Grim satisfaction tore through Zaid. He kept searching for a target, but the only men moving down there now were on fire as they crawled away from the wreckage.

"Let's move out," Hamilton ordered. "Blackhawks are coming in to extract us at exfil site delta. Everybody up."

As one they turned north and started down the back side of the ridge. Zaid had only taken a few steps when gunfire suddenly erupted from the right. "Contact!" He dropped to one knee and took aim at the new threat.

The outlines of at least a dozen men appeared on a slight rise to the east. Two of them held something on their shoulders. No sooner had Zaid focused on them than two RPGs screamed over their heads, streaking toward the Apaches.

"Shit…" Zaid held his breath as the pilots took emergency evasive maneuvers and launched their chaff and flare countermeasures.

Blinding streaks of light split the dark sky, followed by two brilliant white fireballs and deafening booms as the RPGs exploded short of their targets. But one of the gunships was trailing smoke now. It dropped, then righted itself and turned to the west, limping away and losing altitude as it flew.

"Fall back! Move!"

At Hamilton's sharp order Zaid pushed to his feet once more and ran after his teammates, heading north. Scattered shots rang out from the enemy force approaching from the east, but they were still too far away to do any damage.

Now it was a race. Zaid and his teammates were running low on ammo. They had to make it to the exfil site before the enemy got to them. The Apache could clear their tail no problem, but only if it remained on station until Zaid and the others made it to the Blackhawks.

A whooshing sound brought his head up. Through his NVGs he caught the streak of another RPG that had been unleashed.

"Get down!" he yelled, and dove to the ground.

A heartbeat later the terrain in front of them exploded in a hail of rock and dirt, shooting a small geyser of debris into the air. Then a telltale rumble started up.

"God dammit," Zaid breathed, and scrambled to his knees as the ridge they were descending seemed to crumble beneath their feet.

Rock and earth gave way in a mini landslide set off by the explosion. He had no footing. His boots slid over the ground helplessly, unable to find purchase. He held a death grip on his weapon as his feet went out from under him.

Down he went, tumbling once, twice over the loose earth. A grunt of pain escaped him as he bounced on a rock, the sharp edge digging into his left shoulder with bruising force, but at least his helmet was still on.

Somehow he found his footing again and managed to stand up. A strong hand shot out and grabbed hold of the back of his uniform, yanking him to safety. Zaid crashed face first into a wide chest, bounced off, and fell to his knees. Panting, disoriented, he looked up into Maka's taut face.

"You good, brah?" his teammate asked.

"Yeah," Zaid managed, climbing to his feet once more. He was sore and banged up a little and his NVGs had snapped off somewhere, but otherwise good.

"Assholes got what was coming to them," Maka spat, and spun to follow the others.

Zaid glanced over his shoulder to check the eastern horizon. His eyes barely picked out the silhouettes of bodies littering the ground from the enemy position. He didn't know if they were all dead or not, but wasn't waiting around here to find out.

"We're on our own, boys. Both Apaches are returning to base." Hamilton kept them moving at a fast clip. "Let's get a move on."

"Okay, Cap," Zaid managed.

FAST Bravo hurried across the open terrain, heading for the incoming Blackhawks. But two hundred yards from their destination, they came to a sudden stop when another line of figures appeared on the top of a small rise in the distance.

Zaid's stomach sank as he took in the number of enemy blocking their way, too far away for him to make out any faces or other details. His team was outnumbered at least two to one, they had limited ammo, and their fire support had just returned to base.

"Freaking hell," Freeman snapped ahead of him. "It's Nasar."

Chapter Eighteen

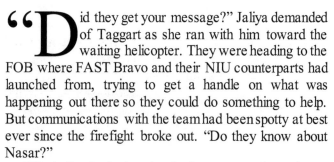

"**D**id they get your message?" Jaliya demanded of Taggart as she ran with him toward the waiting helicopter. They were heading to the FOB where FAST Bravo and their NIU counterparts had launched from, trying to get a handle on what was happening out there so they could do something to help. But communications with the team had been spotty at best ever since the firefight broke out. "Do they know about Nasar?"

"Yeah. But both Apaches had to return to base due to damage. My guys are out there on their own, and they're low on ammo. And we need to get them the hell out of there *now*," he growled.

Her insides clenched into a hard knot of fear. "How far away is their exfil point?"

"Half a mile. But in that terrain and with an enemy force blocking their way, it might as well be fifty."

Helplessness tightened her throat. *Please God, let them make it out of there. Let Zaid be safe.*

She glanced over her shoulder. David was a few strides

behind her, along with furious Afghan army officials who were bent on capturing Nasar and punishing him for his treachery. Jaliya wanted to see the bastard locked away too, but even more than that she just wanted Zaid and his teammates to make it back unharmed to the FOB.

Taggart was on his radio again, trying to coordinate more air support for them. He shot her a hard look as they neared the waiting Blackhawk. "How did we miss this?" he demanded.

She felt sick to her stomach. The answer had been there, right in front of their faces the entire time. "He was smarter than all of us." She swallowed past the restriction in her throat, thinking of Zaid trapped out there in the mountains. "How long until we get to the FOB?"

"Thirty minutes at least after takeoff. In the meantime, you listen to every word those guys say," he said, gesturing to the Afghan army officials, "and tell me anything that might be useful."

The only reason he was letting her come along at all was for her translating skills. "Of course."

Hold on, Zaid. Help is on the way.

She needed to see him for herself as soon as possible, and that meant being at the FOB when they landed instead of waiting back here at Bagram for word.

****

From his position on the ridge, Fahim stared down at the members of FAST Bravo with utter loathing. The RPG detonation had slowed them down, but all nine of them were still alive.

His heart had seized up when the circling Apaches had unleashed a stream of fire that obliterated half of his surviving men and all three remaining trucks. He'd watched, helpless, as everything he'd worked for, everything he needed, went up in smoke. With only one of the trucks having made it safely across the border some hours ago, it was likely he'd just lost his only chance of getting the remainder of the money necessary to secure Beena a new heart.

He'd just failed his son. And now Beena would die because of it.

Rage and anguish poured through him. He refused to accept that outcome. Would never accept it.

His heart pounded out of control as he stood there, madly trying to come up with a plan that would allow him to escape. His dirty secret was out. Every intelligence agency operating in the country would be hunting him now, and likely on the Pakistani side as well.

"Sir, what are your orders?" one of his men asked beside him.

He had only twenty or so of his trusted troops left. All the others were either dead or on the run. The ones remaining were loyal to him to a point, but with their promised money for their services smoldering on the road in the valley below, they could turn on or abandon him at any moment. Right now they needed him because they were depending on him to get them to safety.

If he was going to escape, he had to do it now. Dying wouldn't help his son—he needed to get away and regroup. Find somewhere to hole up and evade the masses of agencies hunting him, and find another way to come up with the remainder of the money he owed *El Escorpion*. Perhaps he could get across the border into Tajikistan and hide there.

Out here there was only one place that was safe for him now.

"To the cave. Hurry!" he ordered, then spun around and took off running. The ancient tunnel complex entrance was three-quarters of a kilometer away. It would give him concealment, maybe even a chance to lose FAST Bravo and buy enough time to organize a new extraction site deeper in the mountains.

Out of the corner of his eye he glimpsed several groups of his men veer away from him, running in the opposite direction. He didn't bother shooting or trying to stop them. It was actually better if some deserted now; a smaller group was easier to escape with, and he had to conserve his ammo.

He leaped over a cluster of boulders and slid down the far side of the ridge, ignoring the shouted command to stop behind him. The soles of his boots thudded against the earth as he jumped and hit the bottom of the rise.

He grunted at the force of the impact, pitched forward and caught himself on his hands and knees. He knew this terrain well. Knew exactly what route he could take to the cave that would provide maximum concealment. His pilot would be on station somewhere nearby but out of sight. If he could put enough distance between him and FAST Bravo, he could stop to set up an extraction.

He didn't pause to check how many men were still with him, because he didn't care. At a spire of granite that marked the edge of an ancient trail, Fahim turned left and ran up the steep slope, following the old switchbacks worn into the hillside by countless feet and goats' hooves.

Risking a glance behind him, he noticed that only a handful of his men were following now. Shots rang out behind him in the distance, FAST Bravo keeping up the chase.

Fahim tore up the remainder of the hill as fast as he could, then made a sharp right into a gulley and followed it to a craggy outcropping of rock that marked the entrance to the tunnels. He kept pushing his body harder, the thin, cold mountain air sawing in and out of his lungs as he calculated which tunnel to take.

The second one led to a narrow mountain trail. It would be hard for anyone to follow him once he reached it. He darted inside the opening, hunching to avoid the low ceilings, and squeezed his way into the narrow rock tunnel.

Rock debris littered the ground, but he soon lost the ability to see as blackness squeezed out the tiny amount of light coming through the entrance. There was no going back, so he pushed onward, using his hands to feel his way along because he couldn't risk using a flashlight and give away his position.

Muffled voices from the entrance sent an icy cold splinter of fear through him. He moved as fast as he could through the darkness, ignoring the bruises and cuts he sustained from the rough rock walls he scraped against, slipping over the loose rock on the ground.

The tunnel seemed to go on forever, twisting and snaking its way through the mountain. It narrowed even further ahead, and for a moment he feared he was trapped in this subterranean warren. Then it widened once more, and a few minutes later the air turned cool and crisp. The exit was somewhere close by, just out of sight.

Behind him, something scuffed along the tunnel, the eerie echo of footsteps disturbing the loose rock on the ground sending a shiver up his spine. Then the tunnel behind him lit up with the faint glow of a distant flashlight beam.

Whoever it was had the advantage of sight, and was getting closer with each second.

Fahim pushed himself to go faster, turned left with the tunnel, then it began to rise toward the surface. Moments later he glimpsed a slight brightening ahead in the darkness. The dry, dusty scent of the tunnel gave way to fresh, cold air. Freedom lay just ahead.

Almost there.

All he had to do was make it through to the other side, contact his pilot, and get to the new rendezvous point. He drew his sidearm, ready to fire at anyone waiting for him on the other side. His heart slammed harder against his ribs, hope giving him an added rush of speed as he burst free of the confining rock walls and out into the open.

Only to find himself on the sheer edge of a cliff that plunged hundreds of feet into the darkness below.

He gasped and instinctively flattened his back against the cool, jagged rock that had protected him up until a moment ago and now threatened to send him to his death. He'd forgotten how sheer the cliff edge was.

Frantic to escape, he darted a glance left then right, searching for a place to run to. But the trail here was dangerously narrow and he could barely make out the shape of the terrain in the darkness. One wrong step and he would plunge into the yawning abyss below.

He had no choice except to go forward, however. He couldn't stay here another moment.

With grim determination he turned left and started up the trail, setting one hand against the side of the mountain and leaning his weight into it. Wind gusted around him, tugging at his uniform with cold fingers, as if trying to pluck him into the gorge below.

His boots slipped on some loose shale. Terror ripped through him as he slid precariously toward the edge of the trail. He dropped his pistol and gripped at a piece of rock jutting out from the wall of granite and clung, straining with all his might to pull his body upright. Just as he gained his footing once more, movement from behind him made his heart seem to stop beating.

"Stop and put your hands up!"

At the sharp, Dari command he whipped his head around to look behind him, his heart thudding in his ears. Squinting in the darkness, he focused on the man standing at the tunnel exit.

A FAST Bravo member.

Khan.

The man stood there alone, his weapon pointed dead center mass at Fahim's chest, poised and ready to fire.

Fahim's fingers twitched, itching to snatch his pistol from the ground. The tactical vest he wore might save him from a body shot, but not from a bullet to the head. Khan was an expert shooter, and well within range to make the shot an easy one.

As the spurt of panic faded, steely determination took its place. Slowly, he turned to face Khan, the hair on his nape standing on end. *You will not take me.*

Everything crystalized in his mind. It had all come down to this moment. Fahim had fought too hard to have everything taken away from him. He would kill this damned American, escape, and live to see his family again.

****

Zaid struggled to get his breathing under control after the steep climb through the last bit of the tunnel and held his ground as he faced off with The Jackal. General fucking Nasar, a man they'd trusted and had now betrayed them, putting their lives in peril.

He didn't dare break his concentration even to contact his teammates to alert them that he'd found Nasar. They were all busy checking out the other tunnels, except Granger, who was only a minute or so behind Zaid.

Nasar stood there on the ledge for a few heartbeats, staring at him from thirty yards away. Frozen. His hand hovered near the ground where a fallen pistol lay.

Zaid aimed dead center at Nasar's chest, his finger on the trigger. Dammit, it was hard to see without his NVGs, but he could clearly make out Nasar's outline.

Go ahead, asshole. Give me the excuse I need to put a bullet between your eyes.

His grip was solid on his weapon, his prey trapped on the precipice above the sheer cliff that dropped away on one side. The wind gusted around him, rising up from the canyon below. Taking Nasar out would be easy from this distance, but that's not what the agency wanted. They wanted to bring him in alive so they could grill him about every last smuggling operation he had ever been involved with, and everyone who had worked with him.

The bastard still hadn't complied with Zaid's first order. "Put your hands *up*," he shouted, still using Dari, his voice ringing off the wall of granite beside him.

Nasar didn't budge. Zaid took a step toward him, conscious of the sheer drop-off to his right. The bastard knew they wanted to take him in alive. Did he really think they wouldn't shoot him if necessary?

He kept careful watch of Nasar's hands and took another menacing step forward. Nasar edged backward. "*Stop*," Zaid commanded, his patience at an end. "One more step and I pull the trigger."

No sooner had the words left his mouth than he heard rushed footsteps behind him at the mouth of the cave. "Whoa, shit!"

Zaid whipped around in time to see Granger spot the cliff too late and hit the brakes, his boots sliding over the gravel. Zaid's heart lurched as his teammate skidded toward the edge of the cliff.

Forgetting Nasar, he wheeled around, slinging his weapon across his back. The blast of a gunshot rang out behind him as he took a few running strides and launched himself at Granger. More shots cracked through the darkness in rapid succession, ricocheting off the rock next to him.

Zaid hit Granger in the side in a flying tackle, stopping his momentum toward the cliff's edge. Both of them grunted as they hit the ground, Zaid on top, and skidded into the wall of rock with a bone-jarring thud.

"Fuck," Granger breathed, scrambling up as Zaid rolled off him.

Zaid had barely gotten to his hands and knees when

three more rounds peppered the rock beside his head.

Nasar, trying to pick them off with his pistol.

Son of a...

"I got him," Granger said, settling on one knee as he took aim, his NVGs in place.

Zaid reached back for his own weapon and swiveled to face Nasar, who appeared to be edging his way up the goat trail, his pistol in hand.

Nuh-uh.

"Tag him," Zaid growled.

Granger fired. A roar of pain split the air. Nasar fell to one knee and braced himself against the mountain to keep from pitching over the edge.

"Drop your *weapon*!" Zaid yelled, beyond pissed off.

"He lost it," Granger said from behind him.

Zaid set his jaw as he stared hard at Nasar. *You're mine, asshole.* "Stay where you are," he commanded, and began creeping his way forward once more.

Granger hit Nasar with the high-powered beam from his tactical flashlight, lighting him up like he was in a spotlight. Nasar turned his head away and threw up a hand to shield his eyes. Blood dripped from it.

Hope that hurts, you son of a bitch.

"Where'd you hit him?" Zaid asked, transitioning into medic mode. Whatever hole Granger had put in him, Zaid would have to plug before they transported him out of here and back to base.

"Lower leg," Granger answered, staring down the barrel of his weapon at Nasar.

Too bad it wasn't his ass.

Zaid slung his rifle across his back and drew his sidearm before picking his way toward their target, now bleeding and trapped on the cliff's edge. "Come this way," he ordered gruffly. Man, he wanted to plow his fist into Nasar's face when he reached the bastard.

Granger was moving in behind him, staying close to

provide backup if necessary, the brilliant beam from his flashlight cutting through the darkness like a laser. Nasar didn't move, still crouched against the rock, just stared back at them with utter loathing as his blood pooled into the dirt.

Zaid set his jaw. They were going to have to go grab Nasar and drag him back to the cave. The idea of a wrestling match on such a narrow ledge didn't thrill him, even with Granger here to back him up. He'd rather put another bullet in Nasar in a more vital place and haul his unconscious ass back to the cave to await the others.

"Target acquired," Granger said behind him over the comms, alerting the others, and gave their position.

"Copy that. Moving to you now, ETA whenever the fuck we get out of this tunnel," Hamilton replied through Zaid's earpiece.

Even though Nasar was wounded and unmoving, Zaid approached him with the utmost caution. The guy had been trained by U.S. SOF guys and knew all the same dirty tricks Zaid did. Zaid wasn't taking any risks up here.

"Put your hands behind your back," he bit out, pistol trained on his quarry. He was still using Dari because it felt more personal that way. This was between him and Nasar.

Nasar glared up at him for a moment longer, then let go of his wounded leg and slowly moved his hands behind him.

Zaid reached into a pouch on his vest for a pair of flex cuffs. "Stay right there. You move so much as an inch, and I'll put more holes in you."

Even while squinting in the intense beam of the flashlight, Nasar's expression managed to convey utter loathing and defiance. But Zaid didn't care, his attention riveted to Nasar's hands and body. The prisoner reluctantly brought both hands behind his back and waited there, but the tension in his body set off all kinds of warning bells in Zaid's head.

He edged closer to Nasar, closer, until only a few feet separated them. Granger was right behind him, now using the tac light on the end of his weapon instead of the flashlight. Zaid angled his body toward the wall of rock and crouched down in front of Nasar.

"Turn around and give me your hands," he ground out, his entire body wound tight and ready to spring if Nasar tried anything.

The man shot him one more lethal glare before turning slightly, his hands resting at the base of his spine. Zaid shifted his weight and roughly grabbed hold of the prisoner's wrists. He had the cuffs on in seconds, and pulled tight.

A measure of relief hit him. He holstered his pistol and sat back on his haunches to grab his dressing kit, prepared to bind Nasar's wound.

"Zaid, look out!" Granger said.

He jerked his head up in time to glimpse two men emerging from a gap in the rocks above them, weapons up.

Fuck.

His hand flashed down for the sidearm in his holster. He drew it lightning fast and raised it just as Granger fired at the figures above them.

Too late.

Nasar lunged and knocked him over as gunfire ripped apart the silence, hurtling them both toward the cliff's edge. Zaid bit back a curse and wrenched his body to the left, toward the safety of the rock. Nasar let out a feral snarl and tried to lash out with a boot, but Zaid blocked it and slammed a fist into the side of Nasar's face. Pain shot through his hand as the bastard's head snapped back and hit the rock wall.

Shaky and breathing hard, Zaid rolled to his knees and grabbed Nasar, who appeared to be at least stunned, if not unconscious, then secured his feet as well. Granger was still ahead, keeping watch on the rocks above, and finally the rest of the team emerged from the tunnel.

"Holy shit," Hamilton breathed, backing away from the sheer drop off.

"I got Nasar," Zaid called over his shoulder. "Gimme a hand."

It took them eighteen minutes to haul Nasar's dead weight back through the tunnel, to the LZ where Hamilton had called in the Blackhawks to pick them up. Some of the friendly NIU guys were there as well, many of them wounded.

"He dead?" the team leader asked.

Zaid set two fingers beneath the angle of Nasar's jaw, felt the steady beat of his pulse. "Nah. But he's gonna have one hell of a headache," he said with satisfaction.

Zaid was never so glad to see a helo in his life when the two Blackhawks appeared in the midnight blue sky and flew toward them. As soon as they touched down, a mad rush of the survivors ensued.

Two men from one of the helos ran toward them, likely PJs to assist with the wounded. He hoisted Nasar over his shoulder and headed for the helo, handing him off to Maka before climbing aboard the second bird. Two of his teammates each loaded a dead NIU member on board.

As soon as everyone was inside, the pilots took off. They climbed skyward and turned to the west, ready to fly back to the FOB. Zaid couldn't wait to get there, finish up work for the night, and call Jaliya. He needed to tell her he was okay, and he needed to hear her voice.

A spray of bullets peppered the right side of the helo.

"God *dammit*," he bit out, hitting the deck with everyone else. The door gunner opened up on whoever was shooting at them below.

More rounds strafed along the aircraft's metal skin, punching through it and sending bits of insulation raining down on them. The pilots veered sharply to the left and climbed. Then Zaid smelled it. Fuel. Even though the fuel cells and lines were self-sealing, they were leaking fuel and at risk of exploding should anything ignite it.

"You gotta be fucking *kidding* me," Colebrook snarled, bracing himself as the bird pitched hard left and dropped.

Zaid couldn't answer because his heart was stuck in his windpipe. They'd survived the ambush and Nasar, only to die in a helicopter crash?

The crew chief shouted at them, his voice carrying over the noise of the laboring engines. "Hang on tight, boys."

Zaid closed his eyes and reached out blindly for something to anchor himself with. His hand met skin, and immediately strong fingers locked around his. He opened his eyes to see Prentiss gripping his hand, his expression grimmer than Zaid had ever seen it.

Zaid held on tight and shut his eyes again as the helo bucked and dropped sharply, summoning a picture of Jaliya's face. She was smiling at him, her expression soft.

More bullets thudded into the aircraft. Screams of agony filled the cabin.

Trapped in the wounded bird with nowhere to hide, Zaid's only comfort was that at least Jaliya wouldn't see them crash into the mountain below.

Chapter Nineteen

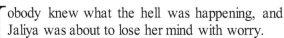

Nobody knew what the hell was happening, and Jaliya was about to lose her mind with worry.

Her palms sweated inside her gloves as she stared across the helo at Taggart while he desperately tried to make contact with FAST Bravo and the Afghan army officials tried to reach what was left of the NIU force on the ground. She'd passed on anything that might be of use to Taggart, but there was little he could do for his men at the moment. And she'd received word ten minutes ago that Barakat had died on the operating table, taking any remaining insider intel with him.

The blood roared in her ears along with the thump of the Blackhawk's powerful rotors, muted by her headset. She was fighting to hold it together, her heart throbbing so hard it hurt. Her stomach was a massive knot of fear.

Zaid and his team were out there somewhere in the darkness, miles from the helo's position, fighting for their lives. The last report they'd had from the team said that they'd chased Nasar through some kind of tunnel complex and managed to corner him, but then an unknown number of rogue NIU members had attacked as they were taking off in the helo. They'd taken serious small arms fire and the helo was badly damaged.

There were casualties, but she didn't know who or even from which unit, let alone how bad the injuries were. Taggart had tried to get more details from the team but they'd lost radio contact along with the feed from Hamilton's helmet cam a few minutes ago, as the team was boarding one of the choppers.

All Jaliya knew was that a combat search and rescue team were en route to FAST Bravo's position right now, might even have arrived on scene already. The not knowing was killing her. The *waiting* was killing her.

She wanted to go straight to Zaid's location, but the closest she was allowed to get was the FOB. Another gunship had been deployed to their position to help clear off any remaining enemy force converging on the area, but it might already be too late.

She bit her lip and fought back the acidic sting of tears at the thought of Zaid being shot. She couldn't lose him. And she wished with everything in her that she hadn't turned away from the opportunity to have him when she'd had the chance.

Stupid. You are so stupid, and now he might be gone forever. She pressed her lips together and swallowed past the horrible restriction in her throat, the regret and fear all but suffocating her.

Across from her, Taggart suddenly straightened and adjusted the laptop screen, his gaze riveted to whatever was happening. After a few minutes he toggled the switch on his headset and spoke to her. "Live feed from the satellite shows a handful of remaining enemy scattering to the west." He angled the laptop so she could see the infrared footage herself.

She scanned the scene, took in the dots moving around—and the ones that weren't moving. There was no way for her to tell friend from foe. And there was no way for her to tell if Zaid was one of the motionless figures. "What about the casualties on board the helos?"

"CSAR was at the LZ, but they took heavy fire after takeoff. That's all I know." He went back to staring at the laptop.

Jaliya closed her eyes and prayed silently as the minutes ticked by, her throat so tight it felt like she was being strangled. *He can't be gone. He just can't.*

After what seemed like an eternity the pitch of the Blackhawk's engines changed and they began to descend. The FOB appeared below them, a tiny blip of light in a sea of black. They dipped lower and went into a hover as they approached the base.

Finally the pilots landed inside the perimeter and began shut down procedures. Jaliya took off her headset, unbuckled her belt and followed Taggart out into the open.

Another team was waiting for them and rushed them inside the medium-sized cinderblock building into a room that acted as the TOC. A flurry of confusion followed, with the Afghan military officials crowding around, arguing amongst themselves, pointing fingers and shouting at one another.

"Jesus Christ," Taggart growled. "Find out what they know about my team," he said to her. "I need to keep trying to make contact with them."

Without wasting a moment, Jaliya elbowed her way through the knot of arguing men and shouted to get their attention. "*Stop!*" They were so surprised that everyone stopped and stared at her and she didn't dare give them the chance to begin arguing again. "What do you know about the American team?"

"This man's traitors attacked them," one colonel sneered.

The accused man's cheeks went red. "My men are not

traitors, but yours are!"

"*Enough*," she yelled, thrusting a warning finger at both of them. She was ready to punch someone, and didn't care if it got her ass fired. "Tell us what you know about the Americans." They'd worry about the attackers later.

The colonel shot a venomous glare at his counterpart and crossed his arms over his chest. "I heard they captured Nasar."

What? She whipped around to find Taggart. The instant she made eye contact he stood from where he'd been working to establish comms with the team. "They got Nasar." She turned back to the colonel. "And? Are any of them wounded?"

The man shrugged. "I don't know. All I know is that half our men turned on their brothers tonight, and I want every one of them hunted down like the traitorous dogs they are."

More arguing broke out, and this time she didn't bother trying to keep the peace. She hurried over to Taggart, who had a headset on and was being briefed by the FOB team who had been monitoring the situation. She caught the basics: the CSAR team was on its way to the FOB with the critically wounded.

Another helo was bringing in FAST Bravo…and two KIA.

Jaliya's heart lurched as she stared at Taggart, who was trying to reach the second helo's crew to get an update. But before he could, the soldier manning the radar pointed out the two Blackhawks. "They'll be arriving in a few minutes," he said.

Face grim, Taggart tossed aside his headset and headed for the door with Jaliya right behind him.

Together they stood out in the cold with the wind whipping at their clothing, and watched the eastern sky, not saying a word. Jaliya kept praying silently, begging for Zaid to be okay.

After an agonizing wait, she heard the faint thump of distant rotor blades. She craned her neck back to look toward the mountains rising into the midnight-blue sky. A black speck appeared, streaking toward them through the scattered clouds. Moments later, a second one appeared.

A crew began to gather around with fire extinguishers and medical kits to await the damaged aircraft and human payloads.

Her heart pounded as the helos drew nearer. One of them carried Zaid, whether he was alive or…

No. She refused to even think it.

The first Blackhawk circled the base before finally coming in to land inside the secure perimeter. One of the ground crews rushed into action, converging on it with fire extinguishers at the ready. In the bright perimeter lighting she could see bullet holes pock-marking its side.

Taggart started toward it but Jaliya held back, a sudden streak of terror weakening her legs and freezing her in place. If Zaid was dead, she couldn't bear to find out.

The helo's side door slid open and men began jumping out. She strained to see them as they emerged, one by one.

Two men climbed out carrying a stretcher. Jaliya watched Taggart. The commander approached them and said something. Their answer had him striding back toward her. There was no way he would have left that spot if any of his team members had been aboard, so Jaliya turned her attention to the second Blackhawk.

It circled high overhead. She peered up at it, hope constricting her ribcage. Her heart slammed so hard it felt bruised as she waited for Taggart to get within earshot. "What did they say?" she shouted over the noise of the engines.

"Two KIA. They don't know who."

She closed her eyes. Fuck. *Fuck*.

Her eyes snapped open when the second bird came in to land. She stood there with her heart in her throat, holding her breath as it touched the ground. Even from where she stood she smelled smoke and jet fuel. It looked like the entire tail section was riddled with bullet holes that streaked up the length of the helo's right side.

The ground crew moved into action as the crew shut down the engines.

Then the bullet-riddled door slid open. Jaliya stayed where she was as Taggart jogged over to meet his guys.

A man with dark skin jumped out first. Freeman. Then Colebrook and Rodriguez. Hamilton appeared next with Maka. Together the two of them reached back into the helo's hold and dragged out someone with his arms secured behind his back.

Rage and shock blasted through her when they came near enough for her to recognize Nasar's face. But just as quickly her gaze shot back to the helo. She didn't even care that they'd captured The Jackal. She only cared about what had happened to Zaid.

Lockhart hopped out. Then Granger.

A queasy sensation twisted through her gut when an eighth member of the nine-man team appeared in the opening. His back was to her as he struggled with something, and when he stood and turned around, she realized it wasn't Zaid.

Prentiss. He was carrying something large and black draped over one shoulder.

A body bag.

Oh God, no!

Agony engulfed her. Her legs went out from under her like someone had severed her tendons with a knife. Her knees hit the ground with a hard thud but she barely felt the pain, the agony tearing through her chest eclipsing everything else.

She couldn't hear anything, couldn't feel anything, could only stare at that hideous black bag draped over Prentiss's shoulder.

Zaid. Zaid Khan, the man she loved.

He was *gone*. She and the other taskforce members had sent him to his death. Because that bastard Nasar had fooled everybody.

Cold wetness filmed her cheeks, and she realized she was crying. Someone was crouched down next to her, trying to talk to her. She couldn't even bring herself to look at him, much less try to listen to what he was saying, too overcome with grief and horror while she stared at the body bag that carried the man she loved.

A strong hand landed on her shoulder. "*Jaliya*."

Gutted, she wrenched away from the touch, unable to take her eyes off Prentiss and that bag. He was only a dozen yards from her now. Her heart was shattered, lying in a million broken pieces at the bottom of her chest cavity, and nothing would ever put them back together again. She'd done this. She'd killed him.

An eerie, high-pitched sound came out of her, a thin wail of grief torn from the depths of her soul and carried on the icy wind that couldn't touch the cold inside her. She clapped her hands over her mouth, her entire body shaking as Prentiss drew near. She couldn't take this. Was terrified of the grief crashing down upon her.

Another man was next to her now. He and the first one grabbed hold of her arms, lifted her to her feet. She stood but wasn't aware of doing so, her entire body numb. Her teeth were chattering, the pain of loss so sharp she wanted to scream.

"Hey! Jaliya, *look* at me." Taggart.

She shook her head, unaffected by his sharp tone. She didn't want to look at anyone but Zaid. She needed to see him, to see with her own eyes that he was really gone.

As Prentiss drew near she was vaguely aware of someone else emerging from inside the helo.

"Jaliya, for Christ's sake, look at me." Taggart stepped in front of her and grabbed her face in his hands, jolting her out of her shock. His dark blond brows were drawn together in a fierce frown as he glared down at her. "Zaid is alive."

She jerked. "W-what?"

Seeming relieved that she had given even that tiny response, he relaxed and gave her a half-smile. "He's okay. Look." He let her go and turned aside for her to see.

Her shocked gaze landed on a man climbing out of the battle-damaged helo carrying another body bag. For a moment she was sure her mind and eyes were playing a trick on her. That she was hallucinating and had imagined the past five seconds.

Zaid. Walking toward her.

Oh my God...

"*Zaid*!" It tore from her in a desperate scream as she bolted toward him, her legs like jelly.

His head snapped up and he stopped, an expression of pure relief crossing his handsome face in the perimeter lights. Her face crumpled as she ran for him, the tears streaming down her face preventing her from seeing anything else. Someone else rushed over and took the body bag from him and then he was running toward her.

Jaliya flung herself into his arms and locked hers around his ribs, holding on with all the strength she had in her body as she buried her face in his throat and cried. Zaid crushed her tight to his chest, his arms like iron bands as they locked her to him.

You're alive. You're alive...

It was the only thought running through her head as she clung to him and cried her heart out, releasing all the grief and fear and guilt that had been choking her.

Gradually, the endearing sound of his voice penetrated the haze in her brain. "I'm okay, honey. I'm okay."

She couldn't stop crying, or shaking. "I th-thought..."

"I see that," he said with a soft chuckle that hit her square in the heart. "What did they tell you?"

She shook her head, fought to get control. It wasn't like her to cry like this, let alone in public, but she'd fallen to pieces and didn't know how to get herself together. "Just t-two…KIA," she managed in between hitching breaths.

"Oh, baby, you had a real bad scare, huh?" he soothed, his mouth next to her ear.

She nodded, not trusting her voice. Not willing to let go, half afraid that he would disappear if she did.

Zaid held her for a minute longer, smoothing a hand up and down her back while keeping one arm locked around her waist. "It was close, but I'm fine. See? Right here holding you."

In answer she burrowed in closer and he let out a low groan/chuckle as he gathered her tight once more. "So you really do care, huh?" he murmured.

He was teasing her to try and get her to stop crying but his words shredded her swollen, battered heart.

Pulling her wet face from his chest, she looked up into his eyes. Gold and green flecks glittered back at her in the lights coming from behind her. "I love you."

His eyes flared hot, an expression of absolute joy crossing his face before he dragged her back into his arms and buried his face in her hair. "Love you too, sweetheart."

A hot, sweet pain sliced through her at the endearment, the tender intimacy in his voice as he said the words she'd dreamed of hearing. "Should have told you before," she muttered, her shoulders hitching.

"Nah. Way more romantic this way."

A watery laugh bubbled out of her. "Stuff of dreams, right here."

"They'll make a movie about us someday. Star-crossed, black sheep Muslims finding love in a war zone. It'll be epic. Probably win an Oscar for best movie."

That made her chuckle. Her legs didn't feel so weak

anymore, and she was no longer a frozen block of ice inside. Warmth was flooding her system, bringing with it a heavy wave of exhaustion and relief. It felt like she was floating, and Zaid was the only thing anchoring her to the ground.

She let out a shaky sigh and relaxed against him, savoring the thump of his heartbeat beneath her cheek. "I love you. Can't believe I almost lost you before I worked up the nerve to tell you."

"You can make it up to me later." He tipped her head back with one hand and ran an assessing gaze over her face, gently wiping at her tears. Then he smiled and her heart rolled over in her chest. "Come on. Let's get out of the cold."

She nodded, leaned into him as he wrapped an arm around her shoulders and guided her back to the main building. Now that the torrent of emotion was behind her, she cringed inside as Taggart and the others all stopped what they were doing to stare at her and Zaid when they walked in.

She stiffened but Zaid kept his arm firmly around her, and she had to admit she liked the proprietary gesture, the feeling that he was claiming her in front of the others. Not that there was any doubt in anyone's mind how she felt about him, after that display outside.

Taggart seemed to fight a grin before he brought the team's attention back to him. Her boss, however, had a different reaction.

David walked straight over and stopped in front of them with his hands on his hips, wearing an annoyed expression. "If you're done here, we have to get Nasar back to Bagram."

Her whole face heated up. "Yes, of course." She pulled away from Zaid, glanced up into his face and gave a tiny smile before following David into a back room. Feeling awkward, she cleared her throat. "I'm sorry. I thought he was in that first body bag."

He shot her an irritated look and kept walking. "Just do your job, okay? We've been working for months to find this sonofabitch, and there's no time for an emotional crisis right now."

Ouch. But she supposed she deserved that after the scene she'd just made. "Yes, sir."

In a tiny holding cell in the back room, Nasar was bound hand and foot and had a hood over his head. Jaliya wanted to punch him.

"We'll take him back to base and interrogate him there. I want everyone there. Set it up," David told her.

Jaliya immediately pulled out her phone and began making calls to alert the team. This was going to be a long night and she was already beyond exhausted. That crying jag had taken the stuffing out of her.

Another helo arrived with more prisoners, from the rogue NIU agents who had attacked the others. It was going to be a hell of a mess trying to figure out who was dirty or not. Crews were still out there retrieving the dead and wounded.

Forty minutes later, Jaliya headed outside with David, Nasar and the two armed soldiers tasked with guarding him. One of the Blackhawks already had its rotors turning, ready to fly them back to Bagram.

She glanced around, searching for FAST Bravo, but didn't see any sign of them. They'd probably been called out to assist with the cleanup effort, or had been taken to a meeting somewhere.

With a heavy heart she climbed aboard the chopper and took her seat. The crew took off with the right side door still open. As the crew chief moved to close it, Jaliya spotted a lone figure standing below them.

Zaid.

He raised a hand in farewell even though she was certain he couldn't see her, and pain sliced through her.

She loved him, but she couldn't have him yet, and God only knew if or when they'd see each other again. It was why she'd fought so hard not to give into her feelings for him; she'd known this moment would come, whether now or in a few weeks.

But he'd said he loved her, so she was going to fight for her man.

****

Exhausted and lucky to be alive after the harrowing, fucked-up night they'd had, Reid Prentiss walked out of the main building at the FOB to find Zaid standing alone, staring up at the dark sky. Watching the Blackhawk carrying Jaliya and Nasar back to Bagram.

Reid felt bad for the guy. Jaliya's reaction when she'd seen him carrying the body bag earlier, and then the way she'd run to Zaid when she'd realized he was alive had touched even Reid's cold, jaded heart. He'd known something was going on between the two of them, but he'd never guessed it was anything that serious. Clearly she and Zaid had formed a stronger attachment than anyone had realized. He hoped it worked out for them.

Reid walked up next to him and stood there while the Blackhawk disappeared into the darkness. "You okay?" he asked without looking at Zaid, feeling the need to ask.

"Yeah. You?"

He grunted. "I want to hear my little girl's voice." Wanted it so bad his chest felt tight. That had been way too fucking close tonight. If he'd been killed, would Autumn know how much she meant to him? How much he loved her?

It sliced him up inside to even wonder about that, or to think that she might forget him in time. As soon as he got back to their barracks, he was calling her. He didn't care what time it was back in D.C., or whether he woke up his ex to do it. He just needed to hear Autumn's voice and tell her he loved her.

"I bet you do." Zaid was quiet a moment. "How the hell am I gonna make this work, though? We'll be back in D.C. in a few weeks."

Beats me. Relationships were fucking hard enough without adding in a geographical separation of that magnitude. But, maybe that was the key. Only seeing each other for a few months a year. Could be the secret to making it work long-term. "I suck at relationships, so I'm not really the guy to ask."

Zaid huffed out a laugh. "Right. Forgot."

He felt the need to say something comforting. "Talk to Rodriguez. Or Colebrook or Granger. They seem to have it figured out."

"Yeah. Maybe I will." Zaid looked at him. "We ready for the next meeting?"

He nodded. "In about five minutes."

Zaid turned and started for the building, then stopped. "Crap. Left my gear in the helo."

"I'll grab it. You go take five." He strode around the far side of the building where the Blackhawk crew was still inspecting their damaged aircraft. The tail section looked like Swiss cheese, and the right side of the fuselage didn't look much better. It still amazed him that his team had made it back here in one piece.

He climbed inside the open door to grab Zaid's gear. When he emerged, the crew chief was by the tail section, talking to one of the pilots, whose body told him was a woman. Reid nodded at them and started to turn for the building, but stopped when the pilot pulled her helmet off to reveal honey-blond hair twisted into a knot at the base of her neck.

He stared in astonishment at the pretty female pilot he recognized, trying to remember her name. Something Russian or Polish that ended in "ski". He'd seen her around Bagram a few times, and at a couple of the briefings. Was she army? DEA?

She gave him a tired smile and nodded back. "How's your team?" she asked.

He unstuck his tongue from the roof of his mouth and found his voice. "We're all fine, thanks to you. Your bird sure took one hell of a beating out there."

She gazed at the Blackhawk with a fond expression. "She did. But she still got us home."

"No, *you* got us home." It freaking amazed him that anyone could have flown back with a bird that badly damaged. "That was some damn fine flying."

The smile she flashed him hit him square in the chest, taking him off guard along with the flare of interest he felt. The first time he'd experienced it in…well, forever. "Just doing my job. And I've got a great crew. Have a good night."

"You too." He walked back into the building and joined his teammates for the next meeting. But even as his commander got down to business, Reid couldn't get that gorgeous smile out of his head.

Chapter Twenty

I'm back at base now, Zaid's text read. *Got time to talk?*

Jaliya would *make* the time. It had been eight days since she'd last seen him. She needed to hear his voice, have the conversation she'd been dreading. Ironically he and the rest of FAST Bravo were all back at Bagram now, and she was here in Kabul. But with their crazy schedules over the past week, they'd only been able to talk over the phone a handful of times.

You have to let him go, her conscience told her.

She ruthlessly dismissed the thought. There had to be a workable solution to resolve the geographical obstacle between them.

She'd wracked her brain for the past eight days, and the only thing she had to show for it was the continued determination to fight for her man. With her career up in the air now and Zaid based out of D.C., how were they supposed to make anything work long-term? She could apply for a position there, or maybe even with another agency where she could utilize her skill set and experience, but that didn't mean she'd get the posting.

It might be far kinder to both of them to say goodbye…except that wasn't an option for her. The man held her heart in the palm of his hand.

She strode to her hotel room window and sank into a chair as she dialed Zaid, gazing out at the snow-capped mountains in the distance as the dial tone droned in her ear. She was still reeling from everything that had happened over the past twelve hours.

When the agency decided on something, they moved fast. With Nasar rotting in a max security cell at an undisclosed black CIA facility in Eastern Europe and the DEA making good progress in uncovering his vast network, the most critical job was done.

"Hey," Zaid answered, a smile in his low, sexy voice.

She couldn't help but smile back, even though her heart was heavy. She missed him so much it hurt. "Did I catch you at a bad time?"

"No, this is perfect, actually."

Sounds of a scuffle and shouting erupted in the background. She frowned. "What's going on?"

"Nothing. Maka's getting the beating he deserves for shooting Hamilton in the head with a Nerf dart, and the other guys are jumping in to get their revenge for the same."

Um… "Okay…"

"It's damn entertaining, I gotta say, but as much as I love watching this, I'd rather hear your voice. Gimme a sec." The background noise receded and a moment later all was quiet. "There we go. So, how're things?"

"Good." She took a deep breath and just said it. "Well, not really. I'm leaving."

"Leaving?" He sounded shocked.

She sighed. "The agency's decided that I'm too widely known here after the past few weeks, and with a bounty on my head it's too high risk for me to stay on in Kabul or anywhere else in Afghanistan. Or in South Asia, for that matter. Basically, they're kicking me out of the region for my own good."

"Shit, I'm sorry."

She shrugged, even though it hurt like hell to know she wouldn't see him for a long time. "Nothing I can do. I already pled my case, but at least the agency values me and my work enough to find me another placement somewhere." She'd request D.C. and beg if need be.

"Where will you go?"

"London, for the time being. At least until they decide what to do with me."

"Can you request a placement?"

"Yes, but my language skills and cultural knowledge are my big ticket items, and if I'm not using them on a consistent basis, I'm not much use to them."

"You could put those to good use in D.C."

The note of hope in his voice touched her, and so did knowing that they were on the same wavelength. "You would want me to transfer there?"

"Are you kidding? More than anything."

She raised an eyebrow. "Even more than sleeping with me?"

"No, you're right. I'd like it second best."

He was so damn cute. How was she supposed to leave without seeing him? "Hmm. Maybe I'll think about it," she teased. This had to work. They had to wind up together.

"You should. That way I'd be able to spend quality time with you. Date you properly."

"Date me?" She laughed again. The idea was absurd after everything else that had happened between them to this point.

"Yeah, you know—dinners and walks on the beach, movies. We'll take getaway trips together and stay up all night to watch the sun come up."

"It sounds so…normal." And romantic. "You sure that's what you want?"

"If I told you what I really wanted, it might scare you away."

Scare her away? "Well now I'm all kinds of intrigued. What is it you really want? Aside from getting me into bed."

"When do you leave?"

The abrupt change in topic wiped the smile from her face. "My flight's in just over four hours. So I wanted to talk to you before I left for the airport."

"Shit, I gotta go."

She blinked, a crushing weight of disappointment and sadness pressing down on her chest at his abrupt announcement. "What? Now?"

"Right now. I'll text you later, okay?" He sounded like he was in one hell of a rush. Maybe Taggart had called them in about something.

"Okay." There was so much she still needed to say, but she couldn't now. "I…be careful. I miss you." *And I love you.*

"Miss you too, sweetheart. Bye."

He was gone before she could reply.

She lowered the phone to her lap and stared at it for a long moment, feeling utterly dejected and more alone than she ever had in her life. In a few hours she'd be on her way to the U.K. where she'd try to pick up the pieces and form a new life for herself.

Alone. All while nursing an aching heart.

The thought hurt so much she couldn't bear it, so she got up and went straight to the shower, where she stood under the hot spray until the water began to go cold. Once she was dressed and had her hair blow-dried, she headed for the long dresser on the other side of the room to begin packing. After tucking away the last of her sweaters, she lugged her bursting suitcase off the bed and rolled it next to the door where the rest of her things waited.

With nothing left to do but wait, she stretched out on the bed and called her parents to update them, but she was too down to talk long. As soon as she hung up with them, reality set in, making her throat close up and her heart feel like it was splitting in two.

Her phone chimed with a text. From Zaid. She jolted into a sitting position to read it.

You there?

Yes, she responded.

Open your door. I sent you something.

What, flowers maybe? A card delivered by the front desk?

She got up and crossed to the door, not even bothering to check through the peephole before opening it. A gasp tore from her when she saw Zaid striding down the hallway toward her, dressed in his utilities. That trademark grin of his lit up his face and he broke into a jog, not stopping until he grabbed her up in his arms and lifted her from the floor as he walked them back inside her room.

"What are you doing here?" she cried, precariously close to tears as she locked her arms around his back and buried her face in his neck.

"Pleaded my case to Taggart, called in a few favors and hopped a last-minute transport flight here." He set her down and took her face in his hands. "Didn't seriously think I'd let you leave without seeing you, did you?"

She smiled so wide it hurt her cheeks. "You just want to get me into bed."

He shook his head. "Ah, ye of little faith. But hell yes, I do."

And with that he bent to sweep her up into his arms and carry her toward the bed.

ZAID'S PULSE POUNDED out of control as he pulled the covers back and laid Jaliya down on the soft, white sheets. With her gorgeous thick, dark hair spreading across the pillow in waves, she gazed up at him with such love and longing on her face he thought his heart might explode. He'd panicked when she'd told him the agency was flying her out in a matter of hours, and was so damn thankful he had been able to be here with her.

She slid a hand around the back of his head and pulled his lips down to hers. He speared his hands into her hair, gripped tight as he plundered her mouth, taking possession the same way he wanted to take her body. She made a sound of longing in the back of her throat and arched into him, the softness of her breasts crushed against the plane of his chest, her pelvis cradling his painfully hard erection.

He rocked against her, needing so much more but not wanting to rush things. He remembered what she'd said about her first time, that she hadn't enjoyed it. Whatever happened, he didn't want her to feel the same way about this, or worse, regret it later. He never wanted her to regret him. Ever.

They tugged at each other's clothing until he was naked and she was in nothing but a black bra and panties. His breathing was erratic as he slipped them off her, revealing her to him in all her naked glory. A low growl came out of him at the sight of her full, round breasts and the tight, brown nipples begging for his mouth, the neatly-trimmed triangle of dark hair between her thighs.

She ran her hands over his chest and shoulders, her eyes heavy-lidded as she stroked him, her right hand slipping down his abdomen to curl around the hot, rigid length of his cock. He hissed out a breath and closed his eyes a moment, unable to keep from pushing into her grip just to feel that electric friction along his sensitive flesh.

Pleasure rocketed up his spine, his heart surging so

hard he was dizzy. He grabbed her hand and pulled it from him, then locked his fingers around her slender wrists and raised them over her head.

"Lie still and let me touch you," he said in a rough whisper. He wanted to make her blind with pleasure before pushing into her. Needed to make sure she enjoyed this to the fullest so that she'd crave him, think about him constantly while they were apart.

Because he was determined to make this work between them somehow.

Those dark, mysterious eyes stared up at him, full of heat and a trust that made his heart squeeze. Her breasts rose and fell with her rapid breaths, drawing his gaze. With a silent groan he cupped her in his hands, savored their soft warmth before lowering his mouth to one straining peak and dragging his tongue across it.

"Ah!" she cried out, grabbing hold of his head as she arched her back, asking for more.

He gave it, pulling her nipple into his mouth and sucking while his fingers played with the other. She smelled so fucking good, soap and light perfume and pure, hot woman. More perfect than he'd even imagined.

Jaliya twisted beneath him, pushing her hips up to rub against his throbbing cock. He groaned and switched to the other nipple, teasing and stroking until she was panting and moving restlessly.

Easing his body to the side, he kept sucking as he eased his free hand down her ribs, over the indent of her waist to the rise of her hip. He stroked the rounded curve, squeezed it before gliding down the length of her leg and back up the inside.

When he brushed against the heated folds between her thighs she whimpered and he bit back a groan at how slick she was. He caressed the tender flesh gently, petting and stroking before dipping a finger down to slide inside her.

Her breathing hitched. Zaid looked up the length of her

body to find her staring at him, eyes glazed with arousal, her teeth sunk into her bottom lip. Watching her face, he eased his finger out and slid up to circle the swollen bud of her clit peeking through her flushed folds. Her thighs quivered at the gentle touch.

"Zaid, please. Want you inside me," she rasped out.

He made a negative sound and kept doing exactly what he was doing. He wanted her on the verge of coming before he pushed into her. When he made her come this time, it would be with him inside her.

She whimpered as he rubbed her clit. Releasing her nipple, Zaid kissed his way down her body until he could replace his finger with his tongue. He slid two fingers inside her, curving them as he dragged them back and forth over her sweet spot, and settled his mouth over her clit.

"Oh, Zaid…" she moaned, her fingers digging into his head, the muscles in her thighs twitching as her belly drew taut.

She tasted so sweet, so hot, and he couldn't get enough. Loved pleasuring her this way, hearing the throaty, ragged sounds she made as he pushed her toward release.

"Zaid. *Zaid.*"

God, he loved the sound of his name on her lips.

He eased up the pressure on her clit, teasing her with flutters and strokes of his tongue while he reached for his pants strewn over the side of the bed. He fished a condom from a pocket and slid it on, his entire body pulsing with the need to claim her.

She half sat up and reached for him as he stretched out on top of her, her arms and legs locking around him. Zaid braced his weight on his forearms and slid his hands into her hair, holding her head still while they stared into each other's eyes. With one hand he reached down to position himself, then set his thumb against her clit and rubbed as he eased his hips forward, burying the head of his cock into her heat.

She gave a soft, choked cry and closed her eyes, the expression of sensual agony on her face all but destroying him. He was breathing hard, all his muscles twitching, his body straining with the effort to hold back when all he wanted to do was plunge as deep and fast as he could.

Jaliya moved with him, meeting each rock of his hips, her little whimpers of need flaying his control like lashes of a whip. He'd wanted to take her the first time face-to-face, but now he wanted something else.

Withdrawing from her slick heat, he shushed her cry of protest with a deep, hungry kiss before urging her to turn over onto her hands and knees. She tossed her hair over one shoulder and looked back at him, and he almost lost it at the raw hunger in those dark chocolate eyes, the luscious curve of her hips and ass on display for him.

With a low growl of need he gripped her left hip and eased his cock into her from behind. She hummed in approval and tipped her head back, an expression of ecstasy on her face. Holding onto the last vestiges of his control, Zaid slipped an arm around her waist to cup her mound, and drew his fingers through her slickness before rubbing circles around her clit.

"Oh, God," she moaned, and rocked backward into him, impaling herself on the length of his cock. "Zaid," she whimpered.

"You feel so good." He kissed the side of her neck, nipped the sensitive spot where it curved into her shoulder. "Rub your clit against my hand," he murmured, his mouth at her ear.

She did, and a shudder ripped through her. He thrust forward and stayed there, kept his fingers steady against her clit so that each rocking motion of her hips drove him back and forth over her sweet spot and rubbed the swollen bundle of nerves beneath his fingers.

Jaliya gasped, her inner muscles clenching around him. Zaid groaned and bit at her shoulder again, soothing the slight sting with his tongue. She was so close, he could feel it in every trembling line of her body.

"Love you," he whispered. "Love you so damn much."

She whimpered, driving back onto his cock harder, faster. He gritted his teeth and held on, reached his free hand up to cup her breast and roll the nipple while she pleasured herself with his cock and fingers.

A wild moan burst free from her lips as she clenched around him, her orgasm exploding through her.

Yes.

Zaid buried his face in the curve of her neck in triumph and held on, waited until she'd slowed and grabbed his hand to still it between her thighs before letting go of his control. He thrust deep and hard, rushing headlong to the release he'd been fighting from the moment he'd first entered her.

With his arms wrapped tight around her waist and ribs he drove deep one last time and let the wave obliterate him. He was dimly aware of his shout echoing around them as the pleasure slammed through his body, leaving him gasping and weak.

On a low groan he eased them both down until she was lying flat on her stomach, his weight sprawled across her back and his head resting beside hers on the pillow. He didn't know how long they stayed that way, but finally his heart rate returned to normal and he was able to summon the strength to raise his head.

He kissed her nape, the silken curve of her cheek before bending down to cover her lips with his. She made a murmuring sound and returned the kiss, slow and soft and tender.

Finally he eased out of her and struggled to his hands and knees. "Be right back," he murmured, kissing the top of her head before heading to the bathroom to deal with the condom.

When he came back she was curled on her side beneath the covers, her dark eyes roving over the length of his naked body as he climbed in and pulled her straight into his arms. He groaned when she snuggled up against him like a sleepy kitten, her cheek nestled on his bare chest.

He'd checked the nightstand clock on his way back from the bathroom. They still had over an hour until she had to leave for the airport. Maybe more, if he could convince her to stay a little longer.

"I always dreamed it would be like that with the right person," she murmured, gently running her fingertips over his chest.

He couldn't help but smile. "No regrets, I hope?" Because he sure as hell didn't regret one moment of this.

"None."

That made him happier than she'd ever know.

"So, I have news," she said softly.

"Yeah? What about?"

"Nasar. He finally broke this morning and told us why he'd done it."

"And?" Not that there was any reason on earth good enough to justify his actions, and the cost.

"His young son. He suffers from a progressive heart condition that is fatal in over ninety percent of cases. Nasar was working with the *Veneno* cartel because *El Escorpion* promised to get the boy a heart transplant if Nasar could get enough shipments through to pay for it."

Zaid stilled in shock. "Whoa. So that's who flew to Veracruz that day. Nasar's wife and son."

"Yes. I don't condone what he did, but…I understand why he did it."

Yeah, Zaid wasn't seeing the situation in plain black and white now either. "And did his son get the surgery?"

"No one knows. But Nasar will never see him or his wife again, regardless."

A heavy price to pay, but he'd cost many men's lives.

Jaliya was quiet for a long moment before speaking again. "What did you mean earlier, when you said you'd scare me if you told me what you really wanted."

He stroked a hand down her spine, savoring the silken softness of her skin. "Sure you wanna know?"

"Yes."

Okay then. "I want it all." Simple.

She tipped her head back to look at him and raised her eyebrows. "All?"

He gave a slow nod. "Everything."

"As in…" She let the sentence trail off, as if not wanting to make a fool of herself by making assumptions in case she was way off. As though he couldn't be saying what she thought he was.

But he sure as hell was saying it. "Yeah. That."

Her eyes widened. "What, marry me?"

He nodded. "That'll make it easier for you to get posted to D.C."

She laughed again. "You can't marry me just to get me a posting in D.C."

He hugged her close. She might not want to admit it to him right now, but he knew damn well her conscience would be pricking at her even now for sleeping with him without a ring on her finger at least. "I can if I've found the woman I want to spend the rest of my life with."

A startled smile curved her lips. "You really mean that?"

"Every damn word. You're mine, Jaliya. I'm not letting you go." Not today, not *any* day.

She bit her lip and tucked her face into his neck, pressing as close to him as she could get. "That was really beautiful," she said in a choked whisper.

A low, primal growl came from the back of his throat and he tightened his arms around her. Even though he would put her on that plane in a couple hours, the distance wouldn't change anything. She was still his. Forever. And he wanted the whole world to know it. "So you'll make an honest man out of me, then?"

She drew her head back to meet his eyes. Hers shone with a glimmer of tears, but the smile she gave him told him they were happy ones. "Zaid. Have you really thought this through? Are you sure? We've only known each other a few months."

"Longer than that, counting the time we spent getting to know each other online."

Her lips twitched. "Well, *sort* of getting to know each other."

He kissed the tip of her nose. "I'm sure, and I know everything about you that matters. We have similar backgrounds and values. We like each other as people. We understand and respect each other. We *fit*. Do you know how incredibly rare that is?" He'd had a lot of time to think it over the past week, and coming face to face with the Grim Reaper sure had a way of putting things into perspective. He wanted to make Jaliya his wife.

"I do."

"Okay, then. What do *you* want?"

"I…" She looked away, seemed almost shy as she answered. "I would love to marry you."

Ah, sweetheart. He closed his eyes, pressed his cheek to the top of her head. "No take backs. You said that loud and clear."

With a soft laugh she tipped her head back to kiss him. "I wouldn't ever take it back."

"Are you worried about what your family will think?"

"No. They don't get to decide who I marry."

His heart swelled. He loved her so damn much. "When do you want to do this?"

She frowned. "I don't know."

"You know the best thing about being a black sheep?"

She shook her head, a smile tugging at her sexy mouth.

"What?"

"They do whatever the hell they want. So let's elope."

Her eyes widened again. "Elope?"

"As soon as I'm done with this deployment, I'll meet you in London and we'll elope."

"Hmmm, I think I like the sound of that." She traced a fingertip over his chin, tickling his beard. "You gonna shave this thing off for the ceremony?"

"If you say yes, I'll shave any damn part of me you want."

Her soft laugh twined around his heart and squeezed tight. "Then yes. Let's run away and elope."

Hell yeah. Zaid buried his hand in her hair and took her mouth in a hungry kiss.

EPILOGUE

Jaliya eased the hotel room door open and crept inside to set the tray down on the dresser. Closing the door quietly behind her, she tiptoed over to the bed and stood admiring the sight of the man in it.

Her husband of less than eighteen hours was sprawled out on his stomach in a puddle of early spring sunshine streaming through the window. The crisp white sheets lay low across his hips, exposing the long, muscular line of his back and the length of his powerful arms where he'd tucked them up beneath the pillow.

His dark hair was longer now than it had been the last time she'd seen him a few weeks ago in Kabul, and as promised his beard was gone, exposing the hard, strong line of his jaw. Her heart fluttered at the mere sight of him, and even though she wore his ring and remembered every heartfelt word he'd said to her during their vows, it was still hard to believe he was really hers. A small part of her felt guilty about not including their families, but eloping had been a lot less hassle and it suited their independent natures.

Things had moved fast between them, but there was no part of her that questioned her decision to marry him, and she had no regrets. He was loyal and strong and steadfast, and she was so damn proud to be his wife.

The weeks without him while she'd waited for him to finish up his deployment had dragged by, even though she'd been swamped and in the midst of applying for a transfer to D.C. She'd buried herself in work to keep busy, helping to unravel the network Nasar had created, including arresting Colonel Shah.

Nasar was still in the CIA facility awaiting trial, but word had trickled through the grapevine that his young son had received a transplant in Mexico and was doing well. David had told her Nasar had broken down and sobbed like a baby when he heard the news. Jaliya was glad he'd been informed about his little boy, and no matter what the courts decided when he finally went to trial, the harshest sentence of all would be to live the rest of his life without ever seeing him again. She was sure Nasar thought it was worth it, though.

Zaid's breathing was deep and even, each rise and fall of his ribs shifting the muscles in his back.

And he's all mine.

Setting one hip on the plush mattress, she woke him by gently running her fingers through his hair, adding pressure as she moved to his nape before dragging them down the length of his spine in the way she'd learned he loved. Zaid let out a sleepy, sexy rumble in response and opened his eyes.

The slow smile he gave her as he turned onto his side sent a wave of arousal through her. If frenzied sex with Zaid had been good back in that Kabul hotel room, lazy, sensual sex here where they had hours of uninterrupted privacy was unbelievable.

They'd already made love twice since the ceremony out in the gardens of this gorgeous hotel, and she was eager to do it again—but she didn't want to spend their entire first day as husband and wife holed up in their room. Besides, the anticipation would only make it better later on when they finally made it back here.

"There's my sexy bride," he murmured, reaching for her hand and bringing it to his lips for a lingering kiss that made her heart beat faster.

"Here I am," she whispered, bending to kiss him softly before sitting up again. It was the middle of the afternoon and she was itching to go out and explore the Cotswolds with him. It had been years since she'd been here with her family on summer vacation, and she'd been dying to come back. "I went down and got us some tea. Well, scones and biscuits and tea, plus coffee for you." She wrinkled her nose. Vile stuff.

"You're an angel," he said, reclining on one elbow. "What time is it?"

"It's nearly four."

His eyes flew wide as he jerked upright. "What?"

At his panicked expression, she blinked. "Three forty-two, to be precise. Why, what's the matter?"

"No," he breathed, and jumped off the bed like it was made of hot coals, shooting past her to the bathroom.

"Zaid, what's wrong?" she called, trailing after him, totally confused. "We don't have reservations or anything."

"I made us an appointment."

Huh? She frowned. "An appointment for what?"

"You'll see. Just give me five minutes to shower. Go put a dress on and do your hair."

The order made her scowl. "What? Why?"

"Trust me. You'll thank me later."

"Yeah, I'm not so sure about that," she muttered, annoyed, but did as he said. She'd planned for them to wander around the village of Upper Slaughter and then Bourton-on-the-Water for a leisurely dinner and a romantic stroll afterward. The weather was still chilly, but it was crazy gorgeous here, and not packed with tourists at this time of year.

By the time he came out of the bathroom a few minutes later and changed into a dress shirt and slacks, she was ready too. "Where are we going?" she demanded as he took her hand and towed her toward the door.

"Patience," he chided, pausing to check his hair in the mirror.

He *never* did that. Was he nervous or something? Where was he taking her?

She'd half made up her mind that she was going to hate whatever he had planned when they reached the lobby. "I wanted to take you to a couple of my favorite villages," she protested.

"Yeah, sure, in a bit. Hey, what's that over there?" he asked, pointing.

She followed his finger toward the front doors of the posh hotel and gasped, both hands flying up to her mouth at the sight of her parents and sisters smiling at her. "Oh my God," she cried, and ran over.

Four pairs of arms engulfed her amidst the familiar and delighted ring of her family's laughter. Jaliya hugged them all, gobsmacked by the sight of them. "What are you all doing here?" she demanded, stepping back to wipe her cheeks.

Her father smiled down at her, his short beard impeccably trimmed as always, and nodded over her shoulder. "We got an invitation from him."

Jaliya turned to stare at Zaid. "I don't believe it. How did you…"

Smiling, he crossed over to wrap an arm around her shoulders. "Even though you told me otherwise, I was pretty sure it bothered you on some level not to have your family here for this. So I asked them to fly here and meet us the day after the deed was done. Hope that's okay," he added in a whisper.

She shook her head at him. "Just when I thought I couldn't love you more," she said, her voice catching on the last word. He was so sweet to her.

His arm tightened, his eyes gleaming with mischief. "Even though I wear the pants in this relationship?"

She leaned her head back to narrow her eyes at him in mock warning. "Watch it, mister."

"Don't make her cry," one of her sisters laughed, and stepped in front of Zaid. "Hi. I'm Shayda. Nice to meet you finally."

Zaid shook her hand. "Likewise."

Jaliya's heart was full to overflowing as she introduced him to the others, ending with her father. She held her breath as she watched them shake hands, aware of the way her father was scrutinizing Zaid. But then he gave a warm smile and clapped Zaid on the shoulder once. "Welcome to the family, son."

"Thank you, sir."

Oh, damn, now she really was going to cry.

Her other sister pressed a tissue into her hand. "Here."

"I'm not crying," she insisted.

"Sure you're not."

"So," her father said, turning to the rest of them. "I understand we're all going to dinner together in Bourton?"

"I can't wait, it's been years since I've been back here," her mother exclaimed, sidling up to Zaid to slide an arm around his waist and resting her head on his shoulder. "You both look so happy."

Jaliya smiled through her tears up at Zaid as he laced his fingers through hers. "I'm so happy."

Her mother and sisters chatted with Zaid as they walked toward the road that led to the village of Upper Slaughter, and her father lingered behind to speak to her alone. Jaliya braced herself for a lecture or at least a few sharp-edged questions.

"You always did like bucking tradition and going your own way," he began in a wry tone.

She didn't argue, because it was true.

"Does he go to mosque regularly?"

"Daaaad," she groaned. "I already told you all this. He's like me." She'd told him over the phone. Her preferred method of communication with him when they had to talk about something contentious. Which was pretty often, throughout their history.

He grunted and kept walking, staying a handful of strides behind the others. "You know I don't approve of the way you went about this."

"I know." He would rather have met Zaid in person first, grant his permission and then wait for the religious ceremony performed by an imam. She and Zaid hadn't wanted any of that.

"But I can't say I disapprove of your choice."

Jaliya glanced up at him in surprise. "You mean that?"

He smiled. "I do. I like him. And it's obvious you both love each other dearly."

"We do."

Another nod, and he shifted his gaze to the others. "Then I'm happy for you. And I'm proud of you."

"You are?" she whispered.

He nodded, frowning at her. "We might not see eye to eye on a lot of things, Jaliya, but I love you, and all I've ever wanted is for you to be happy. And I believe you'll be happy with Zaid. He's as strong as you are."

The *I love you* did it, piercing her heart like a razor-sharp blade. They were the words she'd longed to hear her whole life, and he'd just casually thrown them into the middle of the two most loving sentences he'd ever said to her.

She started to cry. Right there in the middle of the beautiful village path in the early spring sunshine, she stopped and covered her face with her hands as the tears began to flow. All her life she'd secretly longed for her father's approval, and when she'd least expected to receive it, he went and did this.

Her father gave a gruff laugh and curled an arm around her, patting her back awkwardly. "Are you so surprised?" he asked.

Nodding, she fought to get a grip on herself. Couldn't. "Jaliya?"

She hurriedly wiped her face and put on a shaky smile for Zaid, who was hurrying toward her, his face full of concern. "I'm okay."

"You sure?" he drew her to him, casting a suspicious look at her father, who raised his hands in a gesture of surrender.

"I gave my blessing, that's all. I promise. I wish you both a lifetime of happiness together." Tossing her a final grin, he strode over to Jaliya's mother and sisters, who were all watching them.

Overwhelmed, Jaliya leaned into her husband's embrace and watched her father walk back to her family, so full of joy she thought she might burst. It was too much. "I never dreamed I'd hear those words from him, let alone to my face."

"So it's okay that I invited them here? I went back and forth about it a couple of times, then decided to go for it."

She leaned back to look into his eyes, her love for him filling her entire body with warmth. "It's perfect. The most perfect wedding gift I could ever imagine."

He smiled and kissed her tenderly on the lips, a heated promise of what awaited her when they got back to their room later. "Good, because there's one more gift coming, as my parents are flying in tomorrow." He grinned down at her, raised his eyebrows. "Surprise."

Laughing, she leaned her head on his solid shoulder, wrapped an arm around his waist. "I can't wait to meet them."

Zaid slid an arm across her shoulders and kissed the top of her head. Together they followed her family down the winding path lined with cherry trees full of fluffy pink blossoms, ready to spend a magical evening celebrating the first night of their lives together with the people she loved—and the people who loved her—the most.

—The End—

Thank you for reading STAND FAST. I really hope you enjoyed it and that you'll consider leaving a review at one of your favorite online retailers. It's a great way to help other readers discover new books.

If you liked STAND FAST and would like to read more, turn the page for a list of my other books. And if you don't want to miss any future releases, please feel free to join my newsletter:

http://kayleacross.com/v2/newsletter/

Complete Booklist

ROMANTIC SUSPENSE

DEA FAST Series
Falling Fast
Fast Kill
Stand Fast

Colebrook Siblings Trilogy
Brody's Vow
Wyatt's Stand
Easton's Claim

Hostage Rescue Team Series
Marked
Targeted
Hunted
Disavowed
Avenged
Exposed
Seized
Wanted
Betrayed
Reclaimed

Titanium Security Series
Ignited
Singed
Burned
Extinguished
Rekindled
Blindsided: A Titanium Christmas novella

Bagram Special Ops Series

Deadly Descent
Tactical Strike
Lethal Pursuit
Danger Close
Collateral Damage
Never Surrender (a MacKenzie Family novella)

Suspense Series
Out of Her League
Cover of Darkness
No Turning Back
Relentless
Absolution

PARANORMAL ROMANCE
Empowered Series
Darkest Caress

HISTORICAL ROMANCE
The Vacant Chair

EROTIC ROMANCE (writing as *Callie Croix*)
Deacon's Touch
Dillon's Claim
No Holds Barred
Touch Me
Let Me In
Covert Seduction

About the Author

NY Times and USA Today Bestselling author Kaylea
Cross writes edge-of-your-seat military romantic
suspense. Her work has won many awards and has been
nominated for both the Daphne du Maurier and the
National Readers' Choice Awards. A Registered Massage
Therapist by trade, Kaylea is also an avid gardener, artist,
Civil War buff, Special Ops aficionado, belly dance
enthusiast and former nationally-carded softball pitcher.
She lives in Vancouver, BC with her husband and family.

You can visit Kaylea at www.kayleacross.com. If you
would like to be notified of future releases, please join her
newsletter: http://kayleacross.com/v2/newsletter/

Made in the USA
Columbia, SC
20 December 2017